A SPECIAL
RAMSEY
CAMPBELL
EDITION

Ramsey Campbell is the greatest inheritor of a tradition that reaches back through H.P. Lovecraft and M.R. James to Mary Shelley's *Frankenstein* and the early Gothic writers. These special, collectable hardcover editions celebrate Campbell's 60 years in publication. They feature the dark, masterful work of the painter Henry Fuseli, a friend of Mary Wollstonecraft, to invoke early literary investigations into the supernatural.

THE INCUBATIONS

RAMSEY CAMPBELL
THE NEW NOVEL

Also Including an Afterword
& Bonus Short Story

FLAME TREE PUBLISHING

6 Melbray Mews, Fulham,
London SW6 3NS, United Kingdom
www.flametreepublishing.com

First published and copyright © 2024
Flame Tree Publishing Ltd
Text copyright © 2024 Ramsey Campbell
Bonus story 'Second Sight' © 1987 Ramsey Campbell,
originally published in *Masques II*, edited by J.N. Williamson.

Publisher's Note:
This is a work of fiction. Names, characters, places, and incidents are a product
of the author's imagination. Locales and public names are sometimes used for
atmospheric purposes. Any resemblance to actual people, living or dead, or to
businesses, companies, events, institutions, or locales is completely coincidental.

The cover is created by Flame Tree Studio, featuring a detail of:
Henry Fuseli, *The Nightmare*, 1781, oil on canvas. Detroit Institute of Arts,
Founders Society Purchase with funds from Mr. and Mrs. Bert L. Smokler
and Mr. and Mrs. Lawrence A. Fleischman, 55.5.A.

HB ISBN: 978-1-78758-929-2
US PB ISBN: 978-1-78758-930-8
UK PB ISBN: 978-1-78758-931-5
ebook ISBN: 978-1-78758-932-2

A copy of the CIP data for this book is available from
the British Library and the Library of Congress.

3 5 7 9 8 6 4 2

Printed in China

THE
INCUBATIONS

RAMSEY CAMPBELL
THE NEW NOVEL

Also Including an Afterword
& Bonus Short Story

A SPECIAL
RAMSEY
CAMPBELL
EDITION

FLAME TREE
PUBLISHING

for Summer (썸머), with love –
from far away and long ago

CONTENTS

THE INCUBATIONS

CONTENTS

CHAPTER ONE

As Leo turned along **Bridge Street** the dashboard resonated with a clank. It was only the phone, announcing a message from Hanna in Alphafen. In her profile her delicate features resembled an elegant portrait embossed on a souvenir locket. He halted outside a low-browed shaggy cottage to read what she'd said. *Busy in our shop*, she wanted him to know, *many walkers in the mountains*, and he typed a brief response: *Just putting a pupil in for her test.* As the message sped across the ocean he drove to the Fenton house.

Lucy Fenton and her father were waiting outside The Cottages, though Leo wasn't late. Ronnie was resting one large calloused hand on the roof of Lucy's yellow Citroen. His broad face looked inflamed by scrubbing off some of the plaster dust that had reddened his eyes and appeared to have paled his unkempt ruddy hair. He pointed at the slogan on the Fiesta as Leo climbed out – PASS WITH PARKER. "She will, won't she," he made it plain he wasn't asking.

Leo gave Lucy the answer. "I wouldn't have booked your test if I wasn't sure you would."

"You show them you're a Fenton, girl." Her father dealt the Citroen's roof a paternal pat close to a thump. "Just so she can drive herself to uni," he said. "I've got enough jobs on as it is."

Their home consisted of a pair of cottages Ronnie Fenton had run together despite neighbourly objections, dismissed by his friends on the council. A signboard stood above the glossy privet hedge, declaring FENTONS FIX YOUR PROPERTIES. Lucy didn't speak until she'd climbed into the Citroen. Her face seemed determined to avoid looking like her father's, even if abstinence hadn't lessened its width much. With a broad but unsure smile she said "Try not to mind my dad. He's like that with us as well."

"If it doesn't bother you there's no reason it should bother me."

"I won't let it." She waved to her father, who was loitering beside the hedge. "Don't watch me," she mouthed and barely said. "I'm going to be fine."

Fenton turned away, startling a butterfly out of the privet. It fluttered at the car and sailed over the windscreen to disappear above the roof. "Start the car whenever you're ready," Leo said, "and move out when it's safe."

The engine caught first time, and Lucy set about performing caution. She didn't just consult the mirrors but leaned towards them to peer, stretching her neck. She raised the indicator lever with visible deliberation, as though operating an altogether weightier device. As she inched the car with exaggerated care into the roadway Leo said "We're going over the bridge."

A tributary of the Ribble separated Settlesham Old Town, where the Fentons lived, from Settlesham Fields, a grid of flat-faced fifties houses built to replace makeshift dwellings hastily erected for munitions workers during the Second World War. Driving examiners favoured the area, and Leo had made sure he knew it well. Beyond the bridge he said "We'll turn left at the next junction."

Pasture Road led into Meadow Lane, names that felt like bids to recapture a buried landscape. Lucy mimed her scrutiny and the wielding of the lever before she made the turn. Halfway along and with no sign of traffic, Leo slapped the dashboard to require an emergency stop. His pupil tramped on the brake at once. "Was that all right?" she said.

"Entirely. You'll make your family proud."

"So long as I can read the number plate when I have to. I never said, but I'm a bit dyslexic."

"I used to dream I was." At once Leo saw this hardly helped. "Nobody would know you were," he said. "Let's go right next, next right, I mean."

Her emphatic preparations for the turn reminded him she planned to study drama. He waited until they passed a parking space on

Woodland Drive. "Now reverse in here," he said, and she set about backing so gradually he found her pace close to hypnotic. It had begun to lull him when he lurched forward to thump the dashboard and made to grab the handbrake. "Stop," he gasped.

Lucy trod so hard on the brake the engine stalled. "Will that be in the test?" she said, then stared at his hand hovering beside the lever. "What did I do wrong?"

"Didn't you see them?"

"What was I meant to see?"

"Whoever was stepping out behind us."

She peered at the mirror and twisted around. "Where are they, then?"

Having glanced back, Leo craned out of the window. Apart from the occasional tree standing for the suppressed landscape, the pavement was deserted. As a cloud masked the sun, the shadows of the trees burst their outlines and flooded the road, and he could only assume he'd glimpsed some movement of the kind. "I'm sorry," he said. "I honestly thought someone was there."

"The examiner won't do anything like that, will they?"

"I'm sure they won't. Now listen, you were doing fine. Just finish parking in your own time and we'll be on our way."

Once she'd lined the car up parallel to the kerb he sent her left along Orchard Avenue, past saplings refusing to fruit. When she slowed for a car laboriously backing into a space the passenger held up a hand that suggested an admonition more than an acknowledgment. He wasn't gesturing at Lucy, Leo realised as he recognised Fred Latimer. Although Leo's father had taught Latimer to drive, the similarity of the slogan that crowned his Fiesta – LEARN WITH LATIMER – wasn't meant as any kind of tribute. As Lucy coasted alongside he instructed his pupil to lower her window. "Going for a test?" he called.

This wasn't directed at Lucy either. His mouth shaped loose amusement while he tapped the side of his expansive nose as though to send a tutors' secret sign, presumably designed to convey satisfaction with the lesson he was giving. "On our way," Leo said.

"Good luck then, love. Hope he's taught you everything you need to know."

Leo succeeded in keeping quiet until Latimer's car was behind them. "Don't let him bother you," he urged. "That was aimed at me."

"Why would he do that?"

"Just fishing for business and not too particular how."

"My parents said he was good, but my friends said you were. You are for me."

"So long as you're getting your money's worth."

"My dad is and I've told him."

Leo's bid to outdistance embarrassment hadn't worked too well. "Take the next left," he said. "We'll go back across the river."

The second bridge sent them along the edge of Settlesham Old Town. Since examiners avoided the narrow winding lanes that barely allowed vehicles to pass each other, Leo kept the car clear of them. Once it reached the broader streets that the Victorian arrival of the railway had produced he said "Next left. One more manoeuvre and then you can use your navigator."

The examiner would ask her to, and Leo felt oddly relieved to delegate control. Had Latimer managed to put him on edge? So long as Lucy wasn't, and she'd given him no reason to feel anxious on her behalf. She completed her elaborate routine and turned along a wide suburban street where just a few cars were parked. Once she'd passed a lengthy gap between two cars Leo said "Pull over on the right and then reverse."

She aligned the car precisely with the pavement and focused on the windscreen mirror as she inched the car backwards, and Leo felt compelled to use the side mirror. It framed the nearest vehicle behind them and its driver intent on his phone. Was he too preoccupied to notice his car wasn't secured? It had started to crawl towards Lucy's, and now it was gathering speed. "Stop," Leo blurted and hit the horn.

"I was," Lucy protested. "I saw him."

"Sorry. Just making sure." At least the unchecked car had halted, but he twisted in his seat to send the other driver a grimace. "Reverse another few feet and we'll be off," he said.

The slam of a car door made him glance in the wing mirror, which showed him a large man growing swiftly larger. He knocked so hard on Leo's window his knuckles flared pink, and lowered his resolutely hairless mottled head like a bull about to splinter the glass. "What's your problem?"

"I was letting you know your car was on the move."

"Move my arse. You want to get your eyes fixed."

"This lady saw it too."

"You want to watch out, girl. He's got you seeing things. What's he making out you saw?"

Not too far from an apology Lucy said "I did see you creeping."

"Watch who you're calling a creep," the man said and planted a resonant hand on the roof to adopt a more threatening stoop.

"Would you mind going away now?" Leo said. "You're disturbing my pupil when she's preparing for a test."

"Christ, we don't want any more like you on the road." The man glanced at his phone and brandished it at Leo. "Look what you've fucking done," he said. "Now I've got no signal."

"I don't think that's anybody's fault. It isn't ours, at any rate."

"Better not have fucked up my bank transfer."

He poked his face so close to the window that a ragged greyish oval blossomed in front of his mouth. Apparently satisfied that his antagonists felt menaced, he tramped back to his car, jabbing the phone with a violently impatient finger. Leo would have welcomed the departure more if it hadn't left him indefinably nervous. "Will you be all right, Lucy?" he hoped aloud.

"I already am. I don't let men like him get to me."

"Let's be on our way, then."

He wasn't concerned just to leave the irate driver behind. He was growing anxious to let her phone take over. He directed her into Railway Avenue and then Brook Lane, beside which an elongated grassy cleft traced the route of the vanished watercourse. "Pull over when you can," he said and once she had "Ask your phone to guide you to the test centre."

Lucy showed the phone her face and then peered closer. Having lifted the phone almost to the roof and higher outside the window, she complained "There's no coverage."

"Use mine if you like," Leo said, since he had a different provider. He activated his phone, reviving Hanna's tiny face, which made him think he'd solved the problem until he saw the four bars at the top of the screen were emptily pallid. "Mine's gone too," he wished he didn't have to say.

"Never mind, I like you telling me what to do."

"So long as you don't mind the examiner doing it, or maybe you'll have coverage by then."

"I'd really rather have a human being. I wasn't saying only you."

He tried to quell any awkwardness by gauging the distance to the next junction. "In three hundred yards turn left," he said.

Lucy's laugh as she moved off seemed to be awaiting confirmation. "What did you just say?"

"In three hundred yards, well, less than that now—"

"I thought you said three humbled yards."

"More like three mumbled yards, was it?" He was reaching for another of her laughs but felt he'd failed to justify even its predecessor. "I'll see I'm clearer," he said.

"Do you think the examiner will be saying how far?"

"I don't suppose so now you mention it. I'll just tell you which way to go."

"You can say the street names if you know them. That'd be a help."

He'd directed so many pupils through the town that the layout was fixed in his brain. "Next left at Bullock Street," he said.

Lucy sounded as if she'd decided to complete her laugh. Had she misheard him somehow? She preceded the turn with her usual flamboyant routine while Leo trained his mind on the way ahead.

Halfway down the sedate suburban street he said "Turn right into Guggisberg Road."

She giggled at Guggisberg, which he supposed was understandable. On the other hand, he wouldn't have expected her to laugh at Capper Place, and she seemed to have to force a hint of mirth at Gorringe Road. He'd sent her along Festing Street when she said "You don't have to keep doing it, Leo."

"Sorry, what am I doing?"

"Having fun with all the names. I appreciate you trying to make it easier for me, but I don't want to start laughing if they bring me back this way. It might get me failed."

"Why, what did you think you heard me say?"

"I didn't just think. You said Feasting Sleep, which isn't even much of a joke."

Leo opened his mouth to protest, and then it stayed mutely ajar, because he seemed to recall saying what she claimed he'd said. "I won't do it any more," he promised and took care to enunciate "Turn right at Maude Hill."

He was almost certain he'd said that, not Made Ill. At least Lucy didn't laugh, but pursed her lips so hard they clenched her face. "Maude," he pronounced even more deliberately, "Hill."

"I heard you the first time."

What was the next crossroad called? His mental map of Settlesham felt in danger of imploding with the pressure of his concentration. Bulfin Terrace, that was the name he could see ahead. He rehearsed it under his breath one syllable at a time, only to fear he wouldn't be giving Lucy enough notice of the turn. "Next left at," he said, "Bulfinch Terror."

For an instant he imagined the bird that swooped across the junction somehow validated his mutation of the name. "I asked you not to do that any more," Lucy said.

"Sorry. Bull," he said or thought he did. "Fin. Ter. Race."

"Don't do it like that either. Just tell me where to turn."

He couldn't resist pronouncing the name of the next street in his head, or trying to: not Spin Dream but Spring Green, which he was glad he didn't have to articulate aloud. "Tape the necks right," he surely didn't say instead.

Lucy jerked her head towards the mirrors and slapped the indicator lever on the way to making the turn. As she drove past the golf course and the Countryside Experience nature trail Leo heard a click like a switch being set in his skull – the impact of a club against a ball. "Nest left," he declared, which put him in mind of the bird at the junction.

Lucy's preparations were more forthright still – violent nods at the mirrors, a punch at the lever – and he feared she was close to losing control. "Sorry," he pleaded. "You know what I meant to say."

"I'll have to, won't I. Only if it's how you think you need to get me ready for the test, you really don't."

He had no time to deny it when he needed all his mind to compose the words he ought to speak. He mustn't say "Turn awry" but was afraid he had, and "Leave tear" as well. It didn't help that he felt compelled to read every street sign, to ward off his misreadings. More Street was Moor Street, of course, and Part Crow was actually Park Brow, while Oaf Grave could only be Oak Grove. The names distracted him from noticing he'd diverted Lucy out of Settlesham New Town into the old streets. "Soggy," he said as he struggled not to. "I've broad arse out of our way."

Lucy stamped on the brake, halting the car with a screech so harsh it could have been lending nerves a voice. "Don't do that on your test," Leo said with all the calm he could manufacture, "or you'll fail."

She twisted to face him, plucking at her seat belt. "Is that what you want? You've got me feeling I will."

"Of course I don't want that for you. I—"

"Then why do you keep messing up your words? What are you trying to do to me?"

"I'm not trying. I mean, I'm trying not."

"See, you can talk properly when you want to. Was all that supposed to be about my dyslexia? It wasn't much of a joke."

"It wasn't meant to be any of that. It was like my problem I told you about, the one I used to dream."

"Today isn't supposed to be about you, is it? My dad's paying to get me off their hands, and I want to stop depending on them. All I need is confidence."

"You deserve to have plenty. You certainly should for your test. Forget what I said before. It was my fault you had to brake, and we'll call it an emergency stop. You wouldn't be marked down for that, I promise."

Regaining control of his words was restoring his confidence too, and he was about to resume guiding her when a car appeared at the far end of the road. He knew the sign it sported like a coxcomb didn't say DREAM WILL LAST ME, but those were the words he read. Though the man beside the driver looked as though he'd been crowned with his name above the windscreen, this failed to help Leo decipher the sign, which refused to regain its appearance as it advanced on him. "Can you find your way to the centre now?" he tried not to seem to plead.

Surely he hadn't said placenta, but Lucy's frown didn't welcome whatever she'd heard. "No," she said and snatched her phone from the dashboard, only to let it drop back. "You'll have to direct me," she said. "Still no use."

Leo tried his own mobile, but it was as unresponsive as Hanna's miniature face. He saw Latimer bearing down on him, readying another remark. "Let's shit the road," he said too fast to falter. "Next turd left."

Lucy sent the car into a headlong lurch and stalled at once. "That's all," she said and twisted the key until the engine gave a shrill snarl. "I've had enough. I'm going home."

"You mustn't let me put you off." His language seemed to have settled down again, but he didn't trust it any more. "Just try to hear what I want you to hear," he pleaded.

"I have and I've finished." Loud enough that Latimer and his pupil turned to stare at her as they cruised alongside, Lucy said "I want to go home."

"Then I'm really sorry. I don't know what else to say."

"So don't say anything." As Leo failed to keep his lips shut Lucy warned him "Anything at all."

She drove so fast and confidently through Settlesham Old Town that he was tempted to urge her to make for the test, but whenever he started to speak she shook her head, a violent gesture akin to a nervous spasm. He was able to read every street sign all the way to Bridge Street. She swung the car in front of his and parked with a vicious rasp of the handbrake, then stared at him until he retreated to the pavement. As she climbed out her mother hurried down the path so fast her eagerness appeared to quiver her pudgy surprised face. "Have you passed already?" she cried. "That was quick."

"I haven't, no. I never went."

"Lucy, why ever not?"

Lucy jabbed a hand at Leo, which seemed to be her answer until she said "He was making fun of my dyslexia."

Her father had emerged from the conflated cottages just in time to hear. "He was what," he yelled and marched down the path so furiously that Leo heard the clatter of a dislodged paving slab. Fenton had almost reached the gate, preceded by his fists, when Lucy stepped in front of him, stretching her arms wide. "Leave him, dad," she said. "I have."

Fenton raised his fists, but only to brandish them at Leo. "What have you been doing to our girl?"

"I don't know what hatstand," Leo heard himself respond. "Some pig is wrong."

"A pig is right." Fenton lurched at the gate, but Lucy's mother helped her restrain him. "Better get your head seen to," he shouted. "Be glad you've got women to save you. Get away from here and don't come back. We'll be putting the word round about you."

He made another ferocious bid to reach the gate, but the women had captured his arms and were murmuring to him. As Leo drove away, having controlled the trembling of his hands to an extent, he saw the women ushering Fenton towards their house. "I don't know what happened. Something went wrong," he found he could pronounce, too late. It fell short of reassuring him, and so did reading all the street names on his way back to Settlesham New Town, because he had no idea how he could judge whether he'd left the nightmare behind.

CHAPTER TWO

"Prescient."

The newsagent raised her flimsy gilded glasses on their minutely beaded lanyard to scrutinise Leo's face. "I beg your pardon?"

"England's green and prescient land." He pointed at the headline on the Sunday newspaper. "That's what it says."

"If you say so."

"The paper does," he insisted and read the rest of the headline. "Cannabis farming moves to the countryside. They're saying people are getting ready in case it goes legal."

"Not in my lifetime, I hope. They can keep it out of Settlesham." She let the glasses loll askew between her demurely contained breasts as if she didn't care to read the report, but kept her gaze on him. "So why are you so interested?" she said.

"I was just checking it said that." He wasn't anxious to explain further, even to himself. "I'll be taking it," he said.

"The paper, I hope."

He found coins to plant on a tabloid snapshot of three drugged musicians, lending each of them a queenly profile. Five minutes' stroll through the standardised suburban streets brought him to Moss Row. Like all its neighbours for at least a mile around, his house was half a boxy pale-faced pair beneath a steep red roof. As he opened the plump white plastic front door the house greeted him with shrill beeps, which he quelled by typing the year that had ended the last world war.

His grandfather had let the house grow defiantly dilapidated at the end of his life. Leo's parents had presented it to Leo, and Ronnie Fenton had renovated it, rendering it as anonymous as the exterior. Leo had added some personality – jazz albums on the corner shelves flanking the television and the sound system, the kitchen redolence of Asian spices his mother's father had abhorred as invasively foreign, the accumulating Century Classics in the dining-room bookcases. 1942 had just presented him with Camus, but he was busy three years earlier with *The Grapes of Wrath*. The house was gathering a sense of Ellen's presence from the items she'd scattered through the rooms: an English version of a recent Spanish novel poking out a magpie's piebald feather for a bookmark on the armchair opposite his, an electric toothbrush charging in the bathroom, a skimpy nightdress keeping her place on the bed. He was reading the paper to prove he could while he waited for her to come over from her apartment – another Fenton renovation in the Old Town – when his phone gave a peremptory clank.

The message was from Ellen: *Waiting at your parents*. Both its look and its significance disconcerted him. She would never normally omit the apostrophe, and although she passed their house on her way to his, she usually collected him. *Five minutes*, he responded and left the newspaper to sprawl asunder on his chair. Less than five minutes at the pace he felt impelled to keep up took him to the house on Mead Lane, where two of the PASS WITH PARKER triplets were parked. It made a bid to snag a little of the past with its oak front door that contained a dinky stained-glass window. The bell Leo rang tolled like a minimised church, summoning his father. "Leo," his father said as though he was pondering the prospect. "We've been hearing from Ronnie Fenton."

His contemplative blinks were as deliberate as ever, and his wide straight lips hinted at a smile they wanted to find reason for, but his habitual calm – the sense he conveyed of considering a situation in case this gave it time to resolve itself – seemed a little strained, unusually resolute. "What's he been saying?" Leo felt expected to ask.

"He wants all his money back."

Before Leo could respond his mother flustered out of the front room. She was a head shorter than his father and small enough to hide behind him, all of which appeared to compress nervous energy she had to hold in check. "Give him a chance to sit down at least, Brian," she urged.

Leo's father joined her at a speed that suggested his bulky frame was further weighted by his large shaggy head. As Leo followed them into the front room Ellen said "Come and sit with me, Leo."

She was perched on a third of the white leather sofa. For company she had a section of a Sunday newspaper, the rest of which was divided between the armchairs, twin offspring of the couch. Had everyone been seeking distraction? As ever, Ellen's wide-eyed capacious face looked eager for some cause to grow quizzical if not skeptical – to disbelieve what she'd been hearing about Leo, perhaps. "How long have you been here?" he said.

"Just a few minutes. Beverley saw me passing."

"Have you been talking about me?"

"We thought we had to, old chap," his father said.

"Don't stand there like that," Ellen said and held out a slim ringless hand. "I'm certain we can deal with it, whatever you have to tell us."

"That's why we're all here," his mother said.

Her innate optimism had surfaced, as it was perpetually eager to do. Leo sat beside Ellen, leaving the portion of the newspaper between them. "So let's talk," he said to nobody specific.

"Tell us what happened with Lucy Fenton," his mother said.

"It's the first time we've ever lost a pupil," said his father.

"I know it is. I wish it weren't." This felt too close to being tricked by his own words. "I made her nervous," Leo said. "I did everything I could to put her at her ease, but it only made things worse. I'm sorry we lost her, but I'm sure I'm over whatever went wrong. I'll cover our losses, of course."

"They could add up to more than you think," his father said, "if Ronnie starts mouthing off."

"You haven't told me what he said yet."

"Some of it I'd hope he wouldn't say in front of these two. The gist was you'd been mocking Lucy's disability."

"I said I couldn't believe you'd do anything like that," Ellen assured him.

"None of us could," his mother said.

He felt relentlessly scrutinised, in his absence as well. "I started mixing my words up and she got the idea I was imitating her. She'd mentioned she was dyslexic and it must have set me off somehow."

"It doesn't sound like much," Ellen evidently didn't want to say. "You've never seemed that vulnerable."

"Maybe her dad made me nervous. He was going on about how important it was for her to pass her test. And then we came across Fred Latimer on the road and he wished her good luck, but you could tell he was trying to bring us down, and maybe he did."

"Leo, now you're starting to sound paranoid. Does he usually behave that way?"

"Never," his mother said, and then "Not since he was at school. He did wake up from a bad dream once and we couldn't understand him."

"Not Leo," Ellen said with a sally at a laugh. "Mr Latimer."

"We just stay polite," Leo's father said, "if we come across each other."

Leo was growing desperate to grasp an explanation everyone seemed eager to drag out of his reach. "And we had a row with a driver who let his car move while she was reversing."

"You're saying all these things made you start talking the way you did," his mother said, "that time you woke us up."

"What else does anybody think could be responsible?"

His father cleared his throat so vigorously he might have been dislodging an idea. "Did anything happen while you were visiting your friend abroad?"

"Such as what?"

"Were you having to speak foreign? Do you think that could have muddled up your language?"

"They all spoke English. I felt a bit guilty, to tell you the truth."

With what Leo took for dogged hope his father said "Did you try speaking German?"

"They wouldn't let me. They said they wanted me to feel at home."

"Well, now you are," his mother said as if everything had been resolved.

"Will you be ready for pupils tomorrow?" his father said.

"I can't see why I wouldn't be."

"Do you think you should make sure?" his mother said. "Lunch can wait. I was thinking we could take one of the cars for a run so you can practise if you need to."

"Why don't you start by driving," his father said, "and that ought to give you your confidence back."

"I said I would," Leo reminded them, only to realise he'd told nobody but Hanna that he was planning to go for a drive. "I mean, I promised myself."

"You'll have lunch to look forward to," his mother said. "I've put corn in. I know you both like corn."

He couldn't look at Ellen. They always enthused over his mother's cuisine, however haphazard it proved to be. He'd learned early that any hint of criticism or even insufficient praise could shake her faith in herself, and not just in the kitchen. She seemed bent on involving corn anywhere she could: mince and corn fritters, gammon and plums with corn, cod in an insecure carapace of corn, spicy corn that purported to be Mexican.... As he and Ellen left the house ahead of his parents, he took the chance to raise a different issue. "Have you warned your folks the parking people may be up to no good with their car?"

"There's not much they can do while they're at the villa, and I don't want to spoil their holiday."

"Maybe just tell them to check it when they come back."

"I'll message them when they're flying home."

His father released the locks of the car and handed him the keys, a gesture that felt like trusting he'd come of age. Leo strapped himself in while his father took the tutor's place beside him and the women sat in the back. Sitting in the pupil's seat brought him close to pantomiming preparations as Lucy Fenton had, but he only needed to remind himself he could drive so that he could teach. "Is everybody comfortable?" he felt required to ask.

"So long as you are," his mother said.

When he checked for traffic in the mirror he found her and Ellen watching him. Of course they were simply wishing him well, not that there was any call for it, and at least the wish would be more sincere than Fred Latimer's offer of luck. His father was clasping his hands in his lap, which oughtn't to suggest he was praying inside his head, and staring through the windscreen. This needn't mean he would rather not watch Leo; no doubt he was anxious not to distract him or inhibit him. Since the road behind the car was clear, Leo twitched the indictor lever up, only to grasp that he'd neglected to start the engine. He pressed the clutch pedal against the floor and turned the key as gently as his nerves would let him, then remembered just in time to reconsult the mirror. The women were more intent on his behaviour than ever, but surely his father hadn't started to grip his hands together. All that mattered was that the road was still empty of traffic, and Leo quelled the nervous tic of the indicator as he eased the Fiesta away from the kerb. "We're off," his mother apparently thought someone should be told.

She'd made it sound like a family outing, and he did his best to feel in charge. Had he left the handbrake not quite off? The car felt sluggish, and he lurched sideways so vigorously to free the lever that the seat belt bruised his chest. The lever was already supine. "Take it steady, old chap," his father murmured.

This made Leo feel altogether too observed. He trod hard on the clutch to ensure the gears didn't clash as he changed them, but had to glance at the pedal to establish he'd pressed it all the way down. Why couldn't he have judged this without looking? When he sent the car forward at a speed meant to counteract the sense of retardation, somebody drew in a sharp breath like a disapproving sniff. Did they think the uncollared dog that had started pacing the car was about to run into the road? It slumped on the pavement, its obese whitish sides heaving in a way Leo might have taken for evidence of mirth, to train its pink-eyed gaze on him as he turned a corner. "I'd like to know whose that was," he said. "Someone needs to take more care."

This didn't appear to mean much to his passengers. He might have explained if the steering hadn't begun to trouble him. Was it looser than it ought to be? He could have fancied the wheel had softened and grown flimsy in his grasp. It reminded him of the toy steering wheel he'd played with as a child – reminded him how powerless the device attached to the back of the driver's seat had been. His nerves must be inflicting the sensations on him, and he had to control them. If he was forced to concentrate on driving, shouldn't this restore his confidence? He'd reached the edge of Settlesham Old Town, and turned along the narrowest street he could find.

Cars were parked at intervals along the left side, halving the roadway. It felt like a sketch of an obstacle course. He was watching to be certain no vehicle pulled out unannounced when he saw a car on its way to confronting him. It was a head taller than the Fiesta and half again as broad, all of which made him glad to let it pass. He trod on the accelerator, surely not too forcefully, to speed the car into the next space beside the kerb.

At once he was assailed by several high sounds – an angry screech of brakes, at least two voices crying his name in chorus – as his father stamped on the pedal in front of the instructor's seat. He seized the wheel and twisted it so hard it bruised Leo's fingers. As the Fiesta swerved into the space, barely missing the nearest parked car, the oncoming driver sent his window down and thrust out his empurpled face, which a moustache and its twin infant siblings of eyebrows helped to bristle. "Who are you trying to kill, you damned lunatic?" he shouted. "You shouldn't be let anywhere near a road."

His car took up his roar, and Leo's father didn't speak until it faded. "What did you think you were doing, Leo? Didn't you see him?"

"Of course I did. I just didn't realise he was that close." Leo stared ahead, only to discover he had no idea how long the street was. Even the parked cars didn't let him judge the distance to the next junction, which meant he would be unable to gauge how close any vehicle came. "I can't do this," he said. "I need help."

"We can give you some, Leo," his mother cried. "That's why Brian's there."

"Not that kind of help. You heard what that fellow just called me. Fenton said something of the kind as well. I'm starting to agree with them."

"I might know of someone you could see," Ellen said. "She helped one of my colleagues who used to be scared of flying."

"A therapist, you mean?" Leo's father clearly hoped.

"A bit more than that."

"Whatever I need is fine." Leo released his seat belt and felt as if a greater burden had been lifted from him. "I can't drive any more now," he said, "and I don't know when I'll be able to. I won't be any use at tuition either. I'm sorry to let you both down."

Everyone watched him climb out and pace around the car, passing his father on the way to swapping seats. Nobody appeared to want to be the first to speak, but as he took the place his father had vacated, his mother broke the silence. "Never mind," she said, "maybe you'll feel different once you've had some lunch," and for a moment the hysteria Leo was struggling to contain came near to making itself heard as a wild helpless laugh.

CHAPTER THREE

To judge by the multitude of plaques the sun above the Georgian roofs lent a brassy glitter, Rodney Street swarmed with medical folk. Dr Chattopadhyay's practice occupied the ground floor of a house in the midst of a terrace opposite a churchyard distinguished by a monumental pyramid like an occult symbol twice as tall as Leo. On either side of the immaculate white doorstep a basement caged by railings peered beneath a lintel over the edge of the pavement, too thinly to reveal its secrets. Leo had scarcely left a fingerprint on the polished bellpush when a discreet grille beside the stack of gilded names cleared its throat with the rattle of a microphone. "Dr Chattopadhyay's office."

"Leo Parker. I've an appointment with the doctor."

The door responded with a terse demure buzz, inviting him into a long white hall that led between a pair of glossy potted palms to a staircase beneath an arch that borrowed its outline from the spread glass fan over the front entrance. The genteel vista seemed to embody a past too enduring to have succumbed to the blitz that had once demolished streets less than half a mile away. As Leo eased the door shut, another opened halfway down the hall, letting out a slim youngish man in a suit as pale as the corridor. "Doctor oughtn't to be long," he said.

Leo followed him into a wide high-ceilinged room a quieter blue than the sky beyond the tall windows. The receptionist's desk overlooked a trio of armchairs, each attended by a low table laden with art books. Leo leafed through several, all of which offered images so abstract he could have taken them for a psychological test, though they made him fancy he was searching catalogues to match the tint of the room. Soon he heard a door open across the hall. "I'll look forward to seeing you next month," a woman said and accompanied the visitor to the street, then returned to look into the room. "Mr Parker? Do please join me whenever you're ready."

She was small and plump and wore a sari amber as a sunset. Her round unemphatically alert face looked calm enough to donate at least half that quality without loss. She led the unhurried way into her consulting room, which was painted the same therapeutic blue as its twin opposite. Her chair stood in front of her desk, presumably to render her chummier. It faced a straight chair and a deep capacious armchair and, as if the function of the room had to be acknowledged at least that much, the inevitable couch. "Please sit wherever you're most comfortable," Anita Chattopadhyay said. "Everything here is your choice."

Leo told himself this was a means of putting patients at ease, not a test of any kind. As he settled in the armchair the psychiatrist sat in front of her desk. "Please call me Anita if it helps," she said, "and what name would you like?"

"The one I've got will do." This didn't sound like much if any of a joke. "Leo is fine," he said.

"Leo, then. Just remind me why we're here."

"To fix me, I hope."

"We'll do our very best. Tell me whatever you want me to hear."

"Something's made me so I can't drive."

"How important is that to you?"

"Pretty crucial. It's what I teach."

"Can you describe your difficulties to me?"

"I've lost my skills all of a sudden. I started talking rubbish to one of our pupils when I was meant to be getting her ready for her test, and then I couldn't stop. So I tried just driving the next day, and I can't even do that any more. I couldn't tell how far away a car was, and I nearly had a crash."

"Do you think one problem may have led to the other?"

"I think it's all part of the same thing, and maybe I've figured out what caused it."

"That would be quick." As Leo wondered whether she felt he was usurping her job, she said "Anything that helps us help you. What's your conclusion?"

"My parents run the driving school I'm part of, but they made me learn with someone else."

"Do you know why?"

"So they wouldn't favour me when that wouldn't help me learn, they said. So I had to go with another school we had in Settlesham."

"Why do you feel this might give you problems now?"

"It did back then. It wasn't just another school, it was their rival. He did everything he could to put me off, at least that's how it seemed to me."

"And how did you feel about that?"

"I used to have nightmares about the next lesson. I only passed my test because I'd been watching how my parents drove, and I wasn't going to let him get the better of me. Not just me, them as well."

"Did you tell them how you felt?"

"I wasn't going to let him get to them even that much."

"But how did you feel about their having sent you to him?"

"A bit peeved, if I'm honest."

"You must be if we're to make any progress, Leo."

"I thought we were." When her expectant gaze didn't falter he said "All right, more than a bit."

"Yet you didn't tell your parents."

"I'd have felt I was letting him score a point, so I never said."

"Sometimes only confrontation can resolve these issues." This didn't lead him to expect her to add "But I wonder if you've identified the real cause of the problem. My instinct is that might be buried deeper."

"I'd forgotten about it till I was on my way here. Doesn't that mean I'd suppressed it and so it could work on my mind?"

"How easy was it to remember when you did?"

"Just as easy as telling you about it was. It all came back at once."

"And would you say it was painful to remember?"

"Not after all this time. I understand why my parents did what they did, and I know they wouldn't have if I'd let them see how it was affecting me."

"Can you recall if it felt as bad as the problems you're having now?"

"Nothing ever has that I can remember. Nothing except the nightmares I told you about."

"Your driving issues feel like those and nothing else that comes to mind."

"That's what I said," Leo declared, and then his conviction wavered. There was a memory he'd never admitted to anyone, and the prospect of describing it to the psychiatrist felt like a promise of release. "Come to think, that's not quite true," he said. "I must have felt like that on the worst day I ever had."

CHAPTER FOUR

"Get down, quick," Billy Wallace urged. "Here comes another bomb." The boys ducked just before the missile struck with a massive thump. The end of the terrace in Settlesham Fields collapsed with an extensive rumble that disintegrated into a shrill lingering clatter of bricks. A mass of dust blundered across the road, clogging Leo's nostrils, and he tried to snort the harsh dry stench away as he retreated towards the solitary surviving terrace. "Better not get dust on us," he said.

Billy's answer might have been the jet of dusty sputum he contributed to the road. His pale chubby face was strewn with freckles like spots of the red of his hair, scattered by an inaccurate painter. He wrinkled his plump lips and broad nose in disgust, though not at his own behaviour. "Afraid your mam will tell you off?"

"I'm not afraid of anything, only we don't want anybody thinking we've been in the factories when they said not to at school."

"They can't tell us what to do when we aren't there."

"They're allowed. It's not fair."

A final thump of the wrecking ball interrupted their complaints. The demolition team was razing the last streets of the suburbs to make way for new houses. The compacted single-storey terraces had been hastily erected to accommodate munitions workers in the forties; no wonder they resembled barracks. Leo could have fancied the bombing of the factories had lain dormant to spread like a blight through the suburb almost half a century later. As the colossal ponderous pendulum swung to a standstill while the latest cloud of dust subsided, revealing jagged desolation where someone used to live, the driver climbed down from his cab to join his workmates. As they made for Settlesham Old Town he turned to shout "You kids stay away from our machinery."

One of his colleagues doffed his yellow helmet like a mockery of politeness and cupped it in front of him as though inviting a donation. "Stay off our site as well."

"You don't own the street," Billy muttered.

In a bid to equal his rebelliousness Leo said "You don't own us."

Several hundred yards of road framed just by grassland led from the edge of Settlesham Fields across a bridge into the Old Town, where the Tithe Barn pub overlooked the river. The men trooped into the beer garden, and one marched to the riverside fence to encircle his mouth with his hands. "We said get off our site," he shouted. "Get right away."

"Let's go into town," Leo said. "Maybe they'll let us try some games in Computer Shooter."

"I'm banned." With some pride Billy said "I had a fight with some kid and his dad that wanted a go on the one I was on."

"We can see where else there is."

"There's nowhere. There's just crap. I want to see the factories. You can just look at the outsides if you're going to be a wimp."

Leo launched a punch his friend deftly dodged. "I'm not a wimp and don't tell anyone I am," he said and stalked along the road in a bid to live up to his declaration.

The houseless streets resembled a plan of themselves and smelled as he thought a desert would. The main road stretched for half a mile to the boundary where the houses used to end. The emptiness beneath the low white sunless February sky left Leo feeling acutely conspicuous, but would he genuinely mind if someone intervened? You didn't have to be a wimp to want to stay safe.

The blitz had left more fragments standing than the demolition team had. Most of the munitions factory was still outlined by its remains. The remnants – isolated jagged stacks of bricks, uneven lengths of wall, doorless entrances to desolation, the occasional upright window frame bereft of the glass a bomb or a vandal had smashed – showed that the buildings had been widely spaced, presumably for safety. The cracked roads strewn with rubble put Leo in mind of holidays in Turkey with his parents, who liked to spend hours wandering around sites that appeared to have nothing to offer beyond bits of stone left behind by ancient structures. At least the present ruins were closer to modern, less unrecognisable. He was admiring a mass of girders so entangled they resembled a giant's attempt to tie a metal knot when Billy tramped past him. "What are you hanging round for?" Billy demanded. "There's where we want to go."

Leo wasn't sure he did. Ahead at the edge of Settlesham Fields a building seemed to have survived the air raids mostly intact. It looked like a declaration of defiance, not against just the enemy but adults and their prohibitions in general. He could only follow his friend, feeling Billy wasn't much of one despite lending Leo all the computer games his parents bought him. Since he couldn't see a door, perhaps there would be no way in.

The elongated block was taller than he thought a single storey had any reason for, and decorated with extensive cracks in the red brick. Its several hundred yards of frontage contained dozens of windows, all of which were boarded up. Billy scowled at the lack of an entrance and stumped around the corner. "Sorted," he said.

There was a door in the end of the block. No doubt it had been secured when the windows were covered, but someone had wrenched it wide open. Billy stepped through the doorway and poked his head around the ragged frame as Leo glanced back to see Settlesham Fields was deserted all the way to the river. "Stay out," Billy said, "if you're going to be a little wimp."

Leo thought Billy might be striving to incite him because he didn't want to venture in by himself, but if the name was provocative, the adjective was unbearable. "I said don't call me that," he retorted and followed Billy in.

The building consisted of a single room stretching into a distance that looked blanched with remoteness and dust in the air. Along the wall that faced the open countryside beyond Settlesham, the boards nailed over a number of windows had been dislodged, admitting the chill pallid February light. A central aisle separated several hundred pairs of lengthy tables bare of anything except debris, each attended by twin benches encrusted with rubbish. Dozens of rusty perpendicular girders supported their horizontal relatives under the roof. Here and there an upright girder had been wrenched loose, leaning out of a patch of pulverised concrete to point through a gap in the roof at the sky. None of this impressed Billy much. "Let's see if they left any bullets," he said, "or whatever stuff they made."

Leo didn't think the workers would have, but he set about searching the tables and the gloomy floor, finding only rubble. How unsafe might this mean the place was? He didn't like the cracked walls or the holey roof or the huge snapped bolts that lay near the no longer vertical girders. "I don't think there's any," he tried saying.

"Won't find any if you're scared to look," Billy scoffed and fell into a triumphant crouch to grope under a table. "See, I got one."

He straightened up to examine his gleaming prize, only to fling it away in a rage. It was an anonymous sliver of metal, which struck an upright girder with a clang, dislodging a sprinkle of rust. "Spose you think that's funny," he said like a warning.

"I wasn't laughing."

"Better hadn't, neither."

At first Leo felt relieved when they reached the far end of the enormous room, having searched all the tables and under them too. Occasional dull glints had caught his eye, but every find proved to be rubbish, which he shied out of the nearest uncovered window to demonstrate his aim. Billy lobbed his prizes at the girders, which failed to temper his fury but aggravated Leo's nervousness. Now the useless hunt was done they ought to leave, and Leo made for the exit the dusty dusk outlined in the back wall, only to discover the door was nailed shut from outside. Bruising his shoulder against it failed to shift it, and it persisted in resisting when Billy joined in. Leo felt steeped in gritty sweat by the time they gave up. He took a breath that parched his mouth with the taste of shattered bricks, and was about to head for the distant entrance when Billy said "I'll have you a race."

At any rate this seemed to promise speed. Leo didn't even mind much that Billy did without a countdown and broke into a sprint at once. Coughing halted Billy halfway down the room. "I," he spluttered before a cough interrupted him, "won."

"No you didn't." Leo managed to overtake him before his own coughs caught up with him. "I did," he said when he could.

Billy spat and spat again between a pair of benches, eventually ridding himself of coughs as well. "Let's do a different one," he said and vaulted onto a bench. "Bet you can't do this."

"Could if I wanted to."

"Can't do this." Billy leapt across the gap between the benches to land on the next one, bumping his shins against the edge of the table. "Didn't hurt," he vowed and grabbed a knee to lever himself onto the table. "Let's race like that."

Leo thought he saw the table shiver. "You can if you want. I'm not."

"Then you're a wimp."

"Don't care what you call me. I'm still not," Leo said and set off down the room.

"Watch this then, wimp. See what I can do." As Leo glanced back no less reluctantly than resentfully, the other boy leapt from the table across the gap to land on the further bench. He wobbled before grabbing the next table to steady himself. "You can't do that," he challenged.

"Wouldn't want to. If you keep doing it," Leo said and realised how much like a parent he sounded, "you'll fall."

"No I won't, cos I'm not a wimp."

Leo turned his back on this, and was several benches distant when Billy called "Now look. Watch."

Leo twisted around, but only to say he wouldn't watch any more. He had no chance to speak. Billy sprang across the gap between another pair of benches, colliding with a table. Leo saw it tremble, but his friend was too busy wincing to notice. With a grimace he jumped onto the table from the bench, then dashed along the table, an action that looked like a run at another jump. Leo never knew what he had in mind, because the result was a vicious snap of wood. One of the legs closest to the outer wall gave way, and the table collapsed.

Its tilting hurled Billy against the nearest girder, which was leaning towards the wall full of boarded windows, and unsupported except by a mass of splintered concrete. The impact sounded like the tolling of a huge dull bell, muffling a cry of outraged anguish. Leo saw the girder tremble with a metallic creak that seemed to reverberate through the floor towards him. He felt as if his denial of what he was having to watch had slowed the spectacle down to the pace of his agonised thoughts. The concrete wasn't really heaving up as the column tilted further, he fought to think; the girder wasn't really toppling towards the wall. Then he saw and heard it smash the bricks, widening a crack that gaped with a stony crunch as it raced upwards to let a horizontal girder sag out of the wall. What was Billy doing? Didn't he realise he was in danger? He was lying on his back in the midst of an explosion of concrete the fallen column had strewn around its base. He looked stunned if not unconscious. "Get out of the way," Leo cried and stumbled towards him. Billy didn't move, and Leo barely had when he heard a clangour of bolts snapping apart across the room as the overhead beam sailed down like an axe aimed at a chopping block.

Leo didn't merely squeeze his eyes shut, he clapped his hands over them, digging his nails into his forehead. He might have done better to cover his ears so as to keep out a sound that reminded him of a butcher's slab. He felt hearing a scream might be more than he could cope with, but when none came he forced his eyes wide, just in time to see Billy perform a last protesting twitch of all his limbs. The end of the metal beam had rammed deep into his head, leaving no room for a face.

Leo threw up several times on his way to the exit, even after he felt sure he had nothing left to give. He was almost too preoccupied with vomiting to stay afraid of being buried by a collapse of the roof. As soon as he staggered out of the building he began to cry for help. He reeled around the corner to see Settlesham Fields was still empty of life. No, the demolition team was returning across the bridge. "Help," he shouted and floundered down the ruined street. He was aching to ask them a question that felt like a defence against the appalled guilt growing in him – guilt at failing to stop Billy, at not having found them a different activity, at having watched without dragging his friend to safety.... "Why didn't you knock that place down as well?"

CHAPTER FIVE

"What can anybody tell me about Alphafen?"

Mr Turvey passed a hand over his scalp as though the gesture might restore his hair and raised his eyebrows high, inviting an answer they were making space for. From his desk in the middle of the classroom Leo met the English teacher's gaze with a blankness meant to fend the question off. The gaze if not the question lingered on him until Paddy Bloore jerked up a hand excessively padded with flesh. "Yes, Mr Bloore," the teacher said.

Paddy heaved his bulk to its feet and crouched forward as if his rotund stomach needed propping on the desk. "They got some kid killed in Settlesham."

"Do straighten yourself up, Mr Bloore. We aren't about to run a race." Once Paddy had complied with ponderous deliberation Mr Turvey said "Which rumour are you citing?"

"We bombed them for starting the war, then some spy told Hitler we'd made the bombs here and he bombed us to get his own back."

"Thank you for the summation. Do sit now." Although Paddy appeared eager to continue, the teacher sank a hand through the chalky air to hush him. "There is some truth in what Mr Bloore says," Mr Turvey said. "The munitions do seem to have been manufactured locally, and a spy may indeed have tipped Mr Hitler off."

"He didn't usually target places like that though, did he, sir?" Gareth Bentley said.

"Well spotted, Mr Bentley. Perhaps he sought to discover the location as a propaganda exercise, to show we couldn't conceal information from him. Or perhaps Mr Churchill's ruse infuriated him so much he was careless of putting his spies at risk."

"What ruse was that, sir?"

"Alphafen appears to have been a favourite spot of Mr Hitler's, an aspect of an Alpine view he valued. Since it had no strategic significance, Mr Churchill had no reason to send in the bombers except to undermine his adversary's confidence. Mind you, some say the same of Dresden." The teacher made a visor of his hand to search for a response. "You'll be aware of Dresden," he urged.

By now Leo felt safe to speak. "Tell us, sir."

"It was a city Mr Churchill bombed towards the end of the war. Thousands of civilians were killed, and some irreplaceable art was destroyed. Scores by Albinoni, and who can say what else." He shaded his eyes again, only to narrow them as though the burden of his hand if not the sight that met them had weighed the lids down. "Some of you will know the name," he said not too far from a prayer.

Leo took another risk. "He wrote music, didn't he?"

"Deftly deduced, Mr Parker. Can you hum his famous melody?" When Leo shook his abruptly dull head, the teacher's disappointment veered elsewhere. "Nearly all the score was lost," he said, "but enough remained for a musicologist to reconstruct. Otherwise we would never have heard this."

Leo clenched a good deal of himself as soon as Mr Turvey began to sing. "La la, la la, la la-ah…" Adding to the embarrassment he sensed he shared with all his classmates was the sight of the teacher's eyes growing moist at the wistful melody if not the thought of its loss, and Paddy's interruption came as a relief. "What's that got to do with us?" he complained and sounded close to omitting "Sir."

"Reconstruction, Mr Bloore. Restoration. Those should be our goals." He was addressing the class now. "I take it you all know we are twinned with Alphafen," he said, "but who knows why?"

"Because we're meant to be friends now, sir?"

"Indeed, Mr Bentley. To help ensure we've put an end to war with Europe. So Coventry is twinned with Dresden, for example. I imagine you all know how it feels to make up with a friend you fell out with, and historically Germany have been our friends."

"They still got that kid killed," Paddy Bloore objected. "My dad says we shouldn't forget him."

"I'm certain nobody proposes to do that, Mr Bloore."

The teacher wasn't looking at Leo, which only convinced him he was on Mr Turvey's mind. No doubt the whole town knew about him, a thought that assailed him with the sight of Billy Wallace twitching like an insect with its crushed head impaled by a stick. He was struggling to quell the memory when Mr Turvey said "Do remember the ordinary townsfolk of Alphafen were bombed too. I would hope neither group still bears a grudge, which brings me to your homework."

Joining in the ritual chorus of groans released Leo from the memory that had seized his mind. "Do restrain yourselves until you've heard what is required," Mr Turvey said. "Since it is fifty years since both towns were targeted, it has been agreed that the occasion should be marked by an exchange of friendship. I have here a list of children your age in Alphafen. Please choose a correspondent each."

"Have we got to write to them?"

"That was rather the idea." Mr Turvey appeared to have wearied of adding Paddy's last name. "Your letters will be handed in as weekly homework," he said, "and I shall forward them to the appropriate recipient."

"What happens if our dad says we shouldn't write?"

Mr Turvey hoisted his eyebrows while he searched this for authenticity. "He would need to discuss a dispensation with the school. I hope the rest of you will occupy yourselves with selecting your opposite number."

When the page inscribed in Mr Turvey's extravagantly looping script reached Leo he saw it was entitled Pals for Alps. No doubt the teacher had rearranged the syllable as one of his weighty jokes that seemed to hold themselves aloof from inviting a laugh. There weren't many girls on the list, and Leo wrote his name beside the solitary unselected female, Hanna Weber. Corresponding with a German boy would have felt too close to substituting him for Billy. When he passed the sheet to Paddy it drew the same unwelcoming stare he did. "Mr

Bloore," the teacher said, "kindly add yourself until any issue that requires resolution is resolved."

The bell ended the school afternoon as the list finished circulating. "Gentlemen, I should like at least a page in your best handwriting by tomorrow," Mr Turvey said. "Introduce yourself to your new friend and supply some details of your life. Mr Parker, if you would linger for a moment."

Several boys glanced back at Leo as they left the classroom, visibly wondering what his offence had been as much as he did. "Pray close the door after you, Mr Barton," the teacher called. "Mr Parker, may I enquire whether you feel comfortable with the situation?"

"What one, sir?"

"Which, I believe you mean." In the same tone of gentle reproof Mr Turvey said "Are you at all of Mr Bloore's mind?"

"I don't think so, sir."

"He has not infected you with his demurral or roused any of your own."

Comprehension seemed to be receding ever further out of reach. "Which are those, sir?"

"Vengeful feelings, we may call them. Regrettable but understandable in your case more than his."

"About Billy, do you mean, sir?"

The teacher tilted his head as though to guide a thought into its proper place. "Billy being…"

"My friend who was killed." This proved so difficult to articulate that Leo nearly neglected to add "Sir."

"You may dispense with the formalities if it will help you talk about the tragedy."

"We shouldn't have gone in the factory. We weren't supposed to."

"You were just a junior behaving as I fear they often do. Look to leaving all you can behind now that you've moved up a school. Seek the man within yourself."

Leo tried to feel consoled but felt bound to point out "It's only been a year, sir."

"A substantial period at your age. You'll see many of them before they grow shorter." For a moment the teacher seemed overwhelmed by the wistfulness that had glistened in his eyes while he'd sung his tune, and then he blinked them neutral. "Maturity brings responsibility," he said, "which I believe you are displaying now. Was the adventure your idea?"

"No, his, but I didn't need to let him make me go."

"We have all done things we would give much to take back. I fear regret comes with being human." The emotion glimmered in his eyes before he said "Would your friend have ventured in unaccompanied?"

"I think, yes, sir."

"Then you can hardly be to blame. Did Mr Bloore's persistence trouble you unduly?"

"He brought things back."

"I trust our discussion has armed you against any further comments of the kind. You will appreciate who else should not be held responsible for the loss of your friend."

"Who's that, sir?"

"Miss Weber in Alphafen. Born many years after the bombing that brought such a tragic aftermath. We cannot change the past, but we can make reparation. You and all your classmates may call yourselves ambassadors." His gaze strayed to the Pals for Alps list and grew briefly uncertain. "Let us hope it may be all," he said. "I trust our conversation has afforded you some solace."

Leo's response consisted largely of awkwardness, but so had the rest of them. "Yes, thank you, sir."

He expected the schoolyard to be deserted, but a succession of hollow thumps announced that Paddy Bloore and a bunch of his cronies were playing a rudimentary version of football. After school they commonly pursued pupils from Settlesham Girls next door, to pester more than woo them, and Leo suspected Paddy had loitered to accost him. "What did Topsy want?" Paddy said to everybody in the yard. "Was he after a bit of a grope?"

"He never touched me. I don't think he touches anyone." As this provoked various demonstrations of mirth along with skepticism, Leo said "He wants us to be ambassadors. I don't mind being one."

"Then you'll be a traitor."

"Mr Turvey doesn't think so."

"Don't care what queer old Topsy thinks. You sure he didn't stick his finger up you?" When Leo headed for the gate without speaking Paddy shouted after him. "I know what I'd like to send them. Some of their bombs that didn't go off. Never too late to get even, my dad says," he declared at increasing volume, until it felt as though an insubstantial pursuer was following Leo along the road. "I'm going to make things right," he said, too low for any of the boys to hear. "That's what I've got to do."

CHAPTER SIX

"So your schoolmaster** made you see you weren't responsible," Anita Chattopadhyay said.

"Yes, but now I think I was."

"When did you reach that conclusion?"

"Just now, while I was telling you what happened. I think Billy wouldn't have behaved like that if he hadn't had an audience. That's why he wanted me to go in there with him, and if I hadn't he might still be alive. Do you think that's behind my problem?"

"What are you thinking is behind?"

"Feeling guilty after all and how I wasn't letting myself realise. Isn't it usually stuff that's suppressed that causes the kind of problems you deal with?"

"Perhaps more than usually." She laid her gentle searching gaze on Leo's face. "Tell me what you were afraid of," she said.

"That the roof would fall on me before I could get out, or something would. That's the most afraid I've ever felt till this business started with the car."

"And how did you feel once you'd escaped?"

"Scared to tell anyone what I'd done when we'd been told not to. Afraid to let my parents know most of all. They reacted how you might expect, angry with me and trying not to show they were relieved it wasn't me who'd died. I wasn't allowed out of the house for weeks except to go to school, and they drove me there and picked me up even though I used to walk. It was supposed to be a punishment, but half of that was how concerned I made them."

"How did you feel about being driven?"

"How any boy would at that age, I'd think. Embarrassed, and I couldn't even persuade them to drop me where nobody would see."

"Eventually all that came to an end, of course."

"Something else did too. For a while I was afraid of seeing Billy. Not just remembering what had happened to him, that took a long time to go away, but actually seeing him come back."

"Did you ever think you did?"

"Never. Sometimes I thought I heard not him but how he'd died. One of our cars developed a creak that sounded like a noise just before the girder fell on him. My parents got it fixed, but they never knew how I felt till they did."

"How did you feel?"

"Panicked. Couldn't speak because I was afraid to say what I was remembering. Desperate to swallow because my mouth was so dry. Like I was trapped by the seat belt, but I knew I mustn't take it off."

"Is that how the condition you're asking me to help you with makes you feel?"

"Not really." With a sense of having resisted an explanation Leo amended this to "Not much."

"Then how would you say the experiences you've described led to that condition?"

"I was hoping you'd tell me."

"I should say they don't. I doubt they're at the root of it, at any rate. Please don't regard any of our session as a failure. The first ones are very often like this. They're just a stage on the way to reaching deeper."

"Are you saying we've finished?"

"Just for today." She turned her wristwatch towards him, requiring him to peer at the tiny dial, on which a silvery filament was picking off the seconds. "Let me say I think we've made a good start," she said, "and I look forward to making more progress next week."

"I was stupid to think you could fix me today, wasn't I?"

"You're by no means a stupid person, Leo, and that's my professional diagnosis. There's no reason why you should have been familiar with the procedure." A thought or caution made her pause. "Or have you undergone treatment before?"

"Never. My parents mustn't have thought I needed it. I'd say Mr Turvey gave me any therapy I did need."

"Tell yourself we're on the way to identifying your problem." As she stood up Anita Chattopadhyay said "You might consider taking how you learned to drive up with your parents if you feel you should."

Leo felt as if she'd set him homework. Surely he could do it if it helped. When she shut the front door behind him he did his best to take the sunlight as a promise, however vague. At the end of Rodney Street he turned downhill on Leece Street, which led to St Luke's Church, left roofless in remembrance of the blitz. Just now it reminded him too much of the ruined factory in Settlesham, although that had been demolished decades ago. He was hurrying past the church when he heard a boy's voice hurtling towards him. "You don't own the street," it said and then "Sorted."

Leo swung around to see a cyclist hooded like a cobra bearing down on him. No doubt he was on his way to deliver drugs. The gibe had been aimed at a pedestrian who'd objected to his riding on the pavement, and his last word was to his phone. He sped past Leo and across the next road as a sketchy figure flared red to halt walkers in their tracks, and Leo strove to feel the cyclist had taken any threat with him. Surely the session with Anita Chattopadhyay had at least begun to bring Leo's nightmares to an end. As he headed for the train home he turned his mind to the last few weeks, where he could think of little that should trouble him.

CHAPTER SEVEN

E llen was waiting outside the council offices where she worked. The long grey two-storey concrete block faced the red-brick edifice of Settlesham Town Hall like a youngster giving the past a blank look. Above the pedimented entrance topped by a massive tympanum, the town-hall clock brandished an eternal ten to two. As Ellen climbed into the Pass With Parker car she said "It just came to me it looks as if I'm still your pupil."

"If you hadn't been we might never have met."

"I was only reminiscing." She gave him a kiss, though just on the cheek. "Do you know what's due this month?" she said.

"Some anniversary of ours?"

"Not another one of those just yet. I was looking in the archives. It'll soon be the day the town was twinned, and that's the same day of the month the place in Germany was bombed." As the car coasted through Settlesham New Town she said "Do you think it's why your pen pal has invited you? The twinning, I mean, not the bombs. If they were the reason I'd wonder why."

"The same for either, I should think. International relations." Leo thought it best to add "The kind our teacher was trying to promote."

"Ours was too." Ellen released her seat belt, which fled into its slot as Leo yanked the handbrake. "All the girls in my class had a correspondent," she said, "but I don't know anyone but you that's kept it up till now."

"I'll tell you one who didn't." Leo followed her up the terse path to his house, where she unlocked the door and switched off the alarm. "He's a councillor now," he said. "Paddy Bloore."

"I've been subjected a few times. I'd like to teach him to say please. Thank you would be a bonus." Ellen sniffed the air and then inhaled. "Chilli," she declared.

"I hope I've made it hot enough for you." In the kitchen Leo roused the heat beneath the casserole and turned it high. "Taste," he eventually said.

Ellen gave it a stir like a Christmas wish and tried a dainty mouthful from the wooden spoon. "That's how we like it," she said. "What were you saying about the councillor?"

"His father wouldn't let him make friends with the enemy, or anyway that was his excuse. Only after he brought in a note letting him off the assignment, he wrote to the person he'd marked on the list, some rant about how the revenge wasn't over. He didn't know the boy's address, so he just sent it to him in Alphafen."

"How did the school deal with that?"

"They didn't much." Leo impaled the cork of a bottle of merlot and levered it out with an emphatic pop. "His father was a governor," he said. "They made Paddy write a letter of apology, but that was pretty well it. I don't think he ever heard back. We could tell our teacher wasn't happy, but there wasn't a lot he could do except let Paddy know what he thought of him."

"Let's hope they've forgotten about him over there by now."

"They will have, surely." He filled two glasses and dealt Ellen's a clink in search of a reason to celebrate. "I wouldn't have been asked over otherwise," he said.

"A lot of us were, weren't we? The girl I used to write to asked me, but my parents thought I was too young to travel by myself. I don't think anybody ever went, so you'll be making up for everyone." Almost casually enough to sound indifferent Ellen added "What did your invitation say?"

"Take a look," Leo said and passed her his phone. "Read as much as you like."

Ellen scrolled through Hanna's messages as if she was eager to leave them behind, only to linger over the most recent. Leo couldn't judge how much she relished asking "Is her English a bit shaky?"

"I wouldn't have said so. What are you looking at?"

"You will meet the alps."

"Did she write that? I didn't notice." When Ellen held up the phone in the manner of a minor triumph Leo said "She can sound like a translation sometimes, or else it's the usual curse."

"Which one is that?"

"Predictive text, and she meant to write see."

Ellen was as silent as the phone she handed back to him. "Have you thought any more about moving in?" Leo took the chance to ask.

"I'm still thinking."

"If you sell the flat you should have plenty left once you pay off the mortgage."

"It's not just about the money, Leo. Not even mostly."

"I should hope not. I mean, I know." He took her hand, which responded with a squeeze so gentle it felt like a reference to itself. "I'm only trying to give you more reasons if you need them," he said.

"I don't. I just need time," Ellen said and released his hand. "Shall we wait and see how you feel about the situation when you come back from your visit?"

"I can tell you now, I'll feel exactly the same."

"Then let's see how I do." Ellen blinked a hint of apology into her eyes. "I do quite like a bit of independence," she said.

"You'll always have as much as you like. Just say if I ever make you feel you haven't."

As he waited for a pan of rice to finish simmering Ellen said "Be careful flying."

"How am I meant to do that?"

"Ignore me. I'm only being fanciful." She negated her advice by saying "I haven't told you what else I found out, or maybe you know about the mayor and the rest of them."

"Why, what have they been up to?"

"Not the current bunch, the mayor who went to sign the agreement in Alphafen, and some councillors went to the ceremony with him. None of them came back."

Leo lifted down a pair of dishes from the wall rack with a hollow bony clatter. "What happened to them?"

"The plane ended up in the sea and everyone on board was drowned."

"Well, it was nearly eighty years ago. Flying's a lot safer now. Do we know what went wrong?"

"The pilot called for help but nobody got there in time."

"I meant with the plane," Leo said and ladled a glistening swarm of rice into a dish.

"Nobody's certain. The pilot said one thing they never managed to figure out."

"What was that?"

"It's got in," Ellen said, and for an instant Leo felt as if a gelid past had seized him by the neck.

CHAPTER EIGHT

y the time the baggage carousel grew deserted apart from a pair
of skis that kept returning like a dogged invitation, Leo's only
reassurance was a cluster of his fellow passengers still waiting
for their luggage on the far side of the elongated U. When the skis
reappeared yet again they were leading a clutter of suitcases. For a
dismaying moment Leo couldn't see his, and then he located it in the
midst of the tipsy clump. As they lumbered towards him the bags lost one
another's support, and his was among those that toppled on their faces.
He stooped to separate it from the jumble, only to uncover a German
name and address on the baggage tag. "Nine," its owner shouted across
the carousel. "Minor."

Knowing how the words were spelled in German, Leo might have
expected them to rhyme. He could only watch the curtained entrance to
the sluggish belt in the hope of conjuring his suitcase forth. He saw the
dangling plastic strips perform a prefatory flutter, but nothing emerged.
The owner of the case he'd tried to claim scarcely needed to bend his
stumpy trunk to retrieve his property, while his neighbours at the belt
bowed in obeisance to their bags. They departed one by one with a
thunder of trundling, and Leo was staring at the paralysed plastic strips
when he saw what the last passengers had hidden from him. Someone,
presumably the owner of the identical case, had removed Leo's from the
belt and laid it flat beyond the carousel.

Leo muttered all the German vulgarisms he knew as he ran to grab
the suitcase, which accompanied him with a grumpy bumbling rumble
all the way to the arrivals hall. He was relieved to see a line of people
awaiting passengers on the far side of a barrier composed of tape on
poles – at least, he felt reassured until he saw all of them were men. He

tramped past the barrier and halted the case to take out his phone. He'd brought up Hanna Weber's icon from his contacts list when he caught sight of a young woman making for the nearest exit. Although the sign on the clipboard she carried was partly obscured, he could read LEO FOR ALP. "Hanna," he called, and louder "Hanna Weber."

Several people glanced or gazed at him, but she wasn't among them. Even when he shouted her full name again she didn't look around at once, and turned so slowly he concluded she had no idea where his voice had come from. As she located him her face stayed blank for some seconds before blossoming into a smile. "Leo," she said or at any rate mouthed, and showed him the placard. LEO PARKER FOR ALPHAFEN, it said.

As he pocketed the phone she paced over to him. Her approach seemed to render her features more delicate than they looked in her icon: eyes of the brightest blue, long thin nose with a humorously upturned tip, slim pale pink lips, all framed by a soft helmet of glossy black hair. A ruddy highlight Leo thought she'd applied to her unblemished porcelain skin proved to be a fading blush. She took both his hands without speaking and kissed him on each cheek. "Leo Parker," she said.

Her long-fingered hands were so cold he had to restrain an impulse to massage them. "Hanna Weber," he felt prompted to respond. "Great to meet after all these years."

She scrutinised his face before releasing him. "You are here."

"Had you given me up? It was just my case. It went absent without leave for a while."

"I could not give you up now."

"I hope that's your choice, not a duty."

She accorded this a smile too fleeting for interpretation, little more than a twitch of the lips, and he could only think first encounters made her awkward – this one, at any rate. Her language was more formal than her messages, and seemed close to ritualistic. As they emerged into muted afternoon sunlight she said "I am in my car."

A pair of towering black vans almost concealed a rounded viridian Volkswagen in the airport car park. Overhead a plane apparently

composed of mist was merging with a cloud. As Leo climbed into the
car, having laid his case on the back seat at Hanna's bidding, the vans
closed a premature twilight around him. Hanna seized her safety belt as
soon as she was seated. "Secure yourself," she said.

"I'm the last person you should tell."

"You are." Since this resembled agreement, he didn't expect her to
add "Why do you say so?"

"It comes with my job. It's where everything starts."

"Yes, you have that job. I was saying because we go fast."

"I'm sorry, have I made us late for something?"

"It will wait," Hanna said and backed the car out from between the
vans at speed.

Leo felt it wise not to distract her until they left the car park. As she
swung the Volkswagen onto a road for the moment clear of traffic he
said "I was asking because you said we need to go fast."

"We do here."

"There isn't some event we oughtn't to be late for."

"I do not want you to be." Presumably this was why the car doubled
its speed. "We must be there," she said. "Alphafen."

"I've really come for you."

"I know it." She seemed about to say more, but the blare of a horn
as a lorry veered around the car left silence in its wake. She didn't speak
again until they were surrounded by miles of meadows, beyond which
the horizon grew gloomily mountainous under a lowering sun. "Will I
pass your examination?" she said.

"You have." The abruptness of the question took him aback. "Full
marks from me," he said.

"Then it will not be different where you are."

"I shouldn't think so," Leo said but had to ask "What are we
talking about?"

"The driving."

"I'm sure you'd get through."

"That is good." With what he fancied was wistfulness Hanna said
"But I do not think I shall ever visit."

"You'll be welcome if you ever decide to."

"You should be careful what you welcome." Before Leo could interpret this she said "What did you think I asked?"

"What I thought," Leo said and risked adding "Of you."

"You are kind. I think the way you say it is you are too kind."

"I wasn't being that then. It's just good to meet at last."

"We had to."

There was surely no reason why this should seem at all apologetic, and he could only suppose the long largely monotonous day had exhausted him more than he'd realised. "Do I measure up?" he felt driven to ask.

"Nobody will measure you. There is no need."

Leo thought it best to laugh. "No, I mean am I what you hoped for."

"You must be." As if she realised she was stumbling over usage Hanna said "You are."

He thought he understood why she sounded regretful. "I know we could have got together years ago."

"Yes, there have been those years."

"You know I would have liked to come, but my parents stopped me."

"They have had the years as well. They will have enjoyed them together with you."

The conversation had begun to feel as though it was taking place in a dream. "You'll have had yours," Leo heard himself respond.

"My years."

"Your parents."

"Those beside."

Any meaning she intended him to grasp had withdrawn out of his reach. The road kept guiding the car towards the sun, which looked to have abandoned its descent, reddening with the effort to sink. The recurrent spectacle of its paralysis and the incessant murmur of wheels on the road combined to entice Leo towards sleep. Soon the journey consisted of somnolent glimpses reminiscent of dreams: villages composed of houses that seemed to be turning into bouquets of flowers, churches reaching to spear the suffused sun with pointed domes, sudden mountains draped with cloud or demonstrating how the masses of white plush appeared to have spilled down the sheer slopes and frozen. The sight of them prompted him to mumble "Have we reached the Alps?"

Hanna glanced at him as though to establish how aware he was. "They come to us."

He supposed so in a vague way, and subsided into slumber. He had no idea how long he slept before Hanna spoke again. Before he could retrieve an impression that she'd kept murmuring to him he heard her say "You should wake and see."

He blinked his sticky eyes wide to find himself on the outskirts of a town. Its white houses had retained the sunset – no, the multitude of lanterns they sprouted were tinting them with gold. Painted decorations effloresced around many of the windows, while others sported sprays of flowers for beards. Wide overflowing plant-pots stood on balconies, above which greenery drooped from extravagantly prominent eaves. Each house and its adornments looked almost obsessively pristine. "Are we there?" Leo said.

"I have brought you."

Diners sat under canvas awnings outside restaurants on the street Hanna turned along. A man raised a tankard in greeting, a gesture that passed to table after table. "That's very friendly," Leo said.

"You are the reason."

The condition of the streets and the amiable welcomes prompted him to ask "Did they have to rebuild much after the war?"

"It is as it used to be. Everything that was there is." Hanna eased the car to a standstill halfway down a residential street. "This is my home," she said with unexpected force.

She'd parked outside a broad three-storey house with a steep peaked roof. The panelled pine front door brandished a gleaming brass fist for a knocker, surrounded by a floral circlet like a wreath for a cranium. The entrance separated a pair of windows, the lower of two trios of them. Every window was graced with a balcony spilling masses of flowers that had been clipped severely regular. Leo was planting his case on the pavement when the door of the house lumbered open, releasing a man and a comparably barrel-shaped woman, both of whom resembled serious contenders in an eating competition. "Here is Leo Parker," Hanna said.

Her father stumped forward at speed to embrace Leo and thump his back, prickling the underside of Leo's chin with his close-cropped wiry hair. "Emil Weber," he said. "Many welcomes to you."

He made way for his wife to seize Leo by both cheeks and tug his head down so that she could plant a large kiss on his brow. Her cap of hair was softer but not a great deal more profuse than her husband's crop. "Thank you for being the friend of our daughter," she said. "Get her."

Leo held off answering until she stepped back. With some wariness he said "Forgive me, I don't think I caught that."

"There is no need to forgive. Gitte," she repeated. "Gitte Weber. I said thank you that you are her friend. You are the only one."

"Surely that can't be right."

"To keep in touch from your town, my mother wants to say to you."

Hanna's parents yielded to throaty mirth that quivered their expansive jowls and spread to all the features crammed onto their small squarish heads, and then they appeared to recall they were hosts. "You must come in," Emil urged, hoisting Leo's case.

"Yes, come immediately, Mr Parker."

He took Gitte and Emil to be competing at hospitality. "Do call me Leo."

"We are honoured," Emil said and bore the case into the house.

The soft plump white carpet in the hall reminded Leo of the wadding a jewel might rest in. The bristling doormat as wide as the passage was evidently where visitors removed their shoes, and he added his to a regimented rank of them against the left-hand wall. The walls gleamed with a discreet intricate silvery pattern that changed with every step he took. Emil stood the suitcase on the lowest of the blond pine stairs and rested a hand on Leo's name tag. "How was your travel?"

"I'm afraid I did some sleeping on the road."

"What have you seen?" Gitte said.

"Not much of the Alps just yet."

Leo had an odd sense that the Webers were waiting to see who would respond. "You will," Emil promised.

"At the least you have rested," Gitte said. "Shall you use the bathroom?"

"I wouldn't mind a shower."

"There is time. We shall wait."

Leo presumed she had dinner in mind. He followed Emil as he plodded up the stairs, propping the suitcase against his chest and most of his face with both hands. "Let me carry that," he protested more than once.

Emil blundered across the top floor to shoulder a door wide. "You will do enough."

A high ceiling slanted to a peak above a double bed. Three pudgy pillows leaned in a heap against the headboard. A fat white bathrobe lay on the floral quilt, its flattened arms aligned by its sides, its belt outstretched like the crosspiece of a crucifix, the gap that divided the front of the fabric perfectly central. An obese white bath-towel and its miniature sibling were stacked where any legs of the robe would have been. A pair of wardrobes snugly occupying alcoves framed a pine dressing-table and its attendant chair. "You must feel this is your home," Emil declared, lowering the suitcase onto the buxom carpet at the foot of the bed.

As Leo drew the heavy curtains he saw a sample of the Alps beyond the town. A last remnant of the sunset transformed a snowfield into molten lava. Expansive Alpine landscapes hung on the other walls of the room, which displayed the same muted changeable pattern as the downstairs hall. Leo undressed and donned the robe and took his toiletries to the bathroom, where he did his best to obey Emil's injunction. Three toothbrushes stood in separate glasses, leading a parade of jars precisely ranked by size on a tiled ledge beneath a mirror the width of the room. Three oval plastic carapaces – black, red, gold – presumably contained a trinity of soap. Beside a bath headed by a glass shower stall a toilet hid its shame beneath an immaculate shaggy white cover. Leo spent some minutes in the glass cell of the shower and felt bound to arrange his towels in a space on the rail once he finished drying himself. As soon as he was dressed he hurried downstairs to find the Webers waiting in the hall. "Come, Leo," Gitte said and opened the front door. "It is time you are shown."

"I didn't realise we were going out. Am I dressed for it, do you think?"

"You are suitable," Emil said from the street. "We shall foot it."

"You really should let me contribute. Just let me run upstairs and get some cash."

"You do not pay here," Gitte said. "You contribute yourself."

Hanna intervened again. "My father says we shall walk."

She shut the door with a decisive thud once Leo donned his shoes and left the house. "Walk beside us," Emil said.

This meant walking four abreast in the road, where Leo heard no sound of traffic. The mountains had put out the sun and its afterglow, clearing the sky for a moon bloated by a disc of luminous cloud. All the houses were aglow, entangling flowers in their own shadows, but none were lit from within. "Do people go to bed early here?" Leo said.

"Not this night," Emil told him.

"Why, is it special somehow?"

"You are, Leo," Gitte said.

He'd begun to hear the hubbub of a distant crowd beyond an alley crammed with eggs — no, with cobblestones gleaming in the dimness. Soon the alley swallowed the sounds, which grew audible once more as the Webers turned a corner. It brought Leo back to the street of restaurants, which was deserted now. As the family made for the unseen crowd they passed the alley again. "Wasn't that a short cut?" he said.

"We have no need."

Gitte seemed to think her husband's answer required explanation. "No need to go in the dark."

"I wouldn't have called that especially dark."

"You may," Emil said. "We shall have none of that here."

He was heading for the most extensive building, a beerhall that appeared to have captured all the interior light of the street, leaving every other window dark. It was audibly large enough to contain the multitude Leo had been hearing. "If you are ready," Emil said and hauled the massive oak door open.

The roar he loosed from the beerhall sounded like a celebration of a win. The onslaught was so overwhelming that Leo had to grasp it was simply the noise of a horde of drinkers. Hundreds sat on benches at long tables under equally bare rafters all over the extensive room, where waitresses whose uniform made Leo think of milkmaids were bearing handfuls of full tankards from the bar. The six women halted at the sight of the newcomers, and all the drinkers who weren't facing the entrance turned not quite in unison to them. The genial uproar subsided into silence punctuated by the thud of a drained tankard. "Here is our friend," Emil said.

Leo had time to wonder what response this might provoke before it did – the clenching of an army of fists. In a moment it developed into relentless thunder as the crowd pounded the tables to welcome him. It felt as if the bare boards across which the Webers led him were voicing an earthquake. The reverberation faltered as the party reached the furthest table, where the end stretch of both benches had been left unoccupied, and then the thunder merged with a different kind. Everyone had risen to their feet, and while Leo sidled into the space opposite Hanna the crowd began to sing. The words were almost familiar. "God save the gracious king…"

Appreciation overtook astonishment until Leo recalled the next verse. If everyone sang about enemies, how ought he to respond? The enemies weren't just made to fall, their politics were confounded and their knavish tricks frustrated. While he was sure nothing of the kind had to be dealt with in Alphafen, he felt relieved when the enthusiastic amateur choir omitted the verse. "Lord make the nation see – That men should brothers be…" Beethoven had expressed similar sentiments, and at once the anthem seemed less alien. As Leo saw all the Webers were singing he joined in, not too belatedly, he hoped. "And form one family

— The wide world o'er..." He let this prompt a smile at Hanna, since she was gazing at him, and in not too many moments she gave him the smile back.

The words and a renewed storm of table-thumping ended the performance. As everybody else resumed their seats, a bulky red-faced man topped with an impromptu tonsure stayed on his feet. "He is our mayor," Emil murmured.

"Welcome, Mr Leo Parker. You are welcome to Alphafen." As the massed fists began to pound out their refrain, the mayor held up a hand. "Enjoy every part of our town you like," he said, "and take our wishes home with you."

All the townsfolk raised their tankards as he did, which inspired Leo to brandish his before enacting a swig of lager. He seemed to be required purely to drink, and was applying himself when he heard a thin squeak threading itself through the renewed conversational uproar. A wizened thinly grey-haired fellow in a wheelchair was coasting down an aisle towards him. "Our oldest of the town," Gitte said shrilly enough to be heard.

The man swung the chair at Leo, halting just short of him. His pale eyes looked enfeebled but resolved to see. "Albrecht Richter," he said in a voice Leo had to lean sideways to understand. "I have lived to see you. It is good for all you have come."

"I'm glad you think so." This seemed inadequate, and so did "Thanks."

"I remember all."

Leo's reply would have felt awkward even if he hadn't had to shout it. "The bombing, you mean."

"I was here."

"At least you survived," Leo yelled, "but I'm sorry about everyone who didn't."

"You should not feel." As if to negate the reassurance Richter said "I have been in chairs since."

"I'll say sorry again. A lot of people think you should never have been bombed."

"Nor you neither. We were your Herr Churchill's mistake." Richter held out a shaky hand striped with grime from the wheel. "Across the sea," he said.

Presumably his brief grin underlined his familiarity with the phrase about hands. Leo grasped the proffered one, which felt tremulous and desiccated but immediately determined to be firm. Richter gripped Leo's hand and jerked it up and down while saying "Have no shame, Herr Parker."

Leo did his best to translate this into the exoneration Richter must intend, but he couldn't help feeling relieved when the old man trundled away, if only because he no longer had to strain to listen. The waitresses were bearing trays of bread and wurst and mustard to the tables. "Here is food," Emil bellowed, "so our celebration does not go too much to your head."

Did this reflect on Leo's behaviour somehow? "I hope I haven't let you down."

"You could not. You have only to be here," Gitte shouted, and everyone who heard raised their tankards to confirm her assurance.

CHAPTER NINE

sound he might have made himself roused Leo in the dark. As his eyes strained the room into shape he saw the walls were swarming with snails, and when he struggled free of sleep he found the invasion had coated the wallpaper with glistening tracks. No, those were its silvery pattern. How much had he ended up drinking last night? At least he didn't feel in need of the packet of paracetamol he'd left beside the bed. A drink of water might be advisable, and he groped for the capacious mug Gitte had given him. He'd fed himself a gulp followed by a lingering glug when he heard the noise again.

It sounded as though someone was struggling to cry out if not to breathe. It was on the top floor with him, which meant it must be Hanna in the bedroom opposite his. Could the snails be crawling up her bed and into it, perhaps even over her face? The irrational notion felt like wishing his uneasy dream on her, and he slapped his face to ensure he was fully awake if not to punish himself. He pushed away the comfort of the weighty quilt and padded across the room.

Hanna's door was open wide enough to let him see her room wasn't quite as dark as his, but the illumination was apparently unable to penetrate her sleep. "Hanna," he called just loud enough, he hoped, for only her to hear. "You're having a bad dream." Perhaps she didn't hear him, since her effortful protest didn't falter. He eased her door wider and took a step into the room, murmuring her name. Muffled moonlight through a gap between the curtains showed her lying on her back in bed. He was about to call to her once more when he saw an object creeping across the pillow towards her unhappily open mouth. Before he could warn her the intruder rose with a rapid tattered motion and flew across the room to blunder into his face.

He staggered backwards with a cry that appeared to release Hanna from sleep. He'd had no chance to distinguish the attacker's size or shape, but he felt it scrabbling at his eyes and glimpsed frantic blurred activity suggestive of scrawny fingers fumbling to find a way in. He batted it away with the back of his hand and saw it flutter jaggedly towards the stairs, shrinking as it went. Of course only distance was decreasing its size, and he lost sight of it as it flapped downwards. He heard a door open on the middle floor, and Emil's voice. "What has gone wrong?"

"Sorry if I woke you. It was just a moth. You can see it, I should think."

A light went on above the middle landing. "It is gone," Emil said.

"And Hanna was having a bad dream, weren't you, Hanna?"

"It would be her fear. As I have said, it is gone."

"Not about the moth," Leo said, only to wonder if he was presuming. "Sorry, Hanna, was that the problem?"

"My father said."

She sounded reluctant to discuss it, unless she was anxious to resume her sleep. Leo shouldn't aggravate any phobia she had. "Shall I close your door to keep it out?" he said.

"If you believe it will help."

However this sounded, she could hardly be indulging him. As he made to shut the door he caught sight of the view beyond her window, where a snowfield had borrowed moonlight to transform a mountain into a spectral presence. The vista seemed oddly familiar, and he loitered until Hanna raised her head. "What are you seeing now, Leo?"

"Just making sure you were all right," he said, closing the door.

"Enjoy the rest of your night," Emil said.

"It will be quiet now," Gitte called from the room behind him.

Was this a gentle rebuke? Surely it wasn't addressed to her daughter. "Good night, Hanna," Leo called in case it had been, "good night, everyone."

He was making for his bed when a sense of dislocation halted him. What had he almost seen? He switched on the overhead light and identified the oddity at once. Except for the absence of moonlight, the landscape above the headboard was the view from Hanna's window, which meant the painting was precisely lined up with the scene it represented. He took the sight to bed with him and was trying not too hard to establish what if anything it ought to mean when he fell asleep.

Voices at the limit of his hearing wakened him. Minutely delicate metallic sounds and tiny collisions of china let him know they were in the kitchen. His phone showed he'd left half the morning behind. He'd sent Ellen a message as soon as the plane had touched down, but none since. *Only just awake*, he typed now. *Seems as if I met the entire town last night. Thanks for making me come here.* He tapped the X thrice, producing an adult and its twin small offspring, and then headed for the bathroom.

Ellen had responded by the time he came back. *Happy for you, then. Keep up the sterling work.* Her trio of Xs had all attained maturity. Leo dressed and went downstairs, where the sound of rapid chopping brought him to the kitchen. Gitte was slicing apples to decorate three bowls of muesli. "Leo, you will have some," she said.

"My mother is asking you," Hanna told him.

"I understand. Just tense."

Emil frowned across the table, which was laid for breakfast – knotted pretzels, a rakish block of butter slouching in a dish, unlabelled jars of jam beaded with the berries it was made of. "Why will you be that?"

"No, I mean the language. The tense." Leo felt required to add "You're doing absolutely fine with it, all of you. You're putting me to shame."

"You need not feel that either. You are here."

Presumably he meant Leo ought to know by now his presence was enough. Hanna stood up to fill a mug from a percolator mumbling with bubbles. "I should have brought the coffee to your room," she said, "but we thought you should sleep while you can."

"Sorry if I've messed up anybody's plans."

"You can not. I should be the sorry one for disturbing your rest in the night."

"Honestly, don't worry. I got plenty of rest, and I was happy to help if I did."

"We are grateful," Gitte said, "that you take away the fear."

Did she intend to prove his point about tenses? Emil performed a long swallow of coffee and planted his mug on a coaster, covering a minified mountain. "What shall you see today, Leo?"

"What do you recommend? Maybe some Alps?"

"There are many."

Leo waited for someone to narrow this down, but none of the Webers spoke. "Somewhere I can walk. I know," he said. "Where you took the photo, Hanna."

Emil stared at her as if he should have been consulted. "What did she take?"

"A shot of your town to show me." Leo sped through Hanna's messages on his phone until he found the image of a distant Alphafen nestling among the mountains. Mist softened its colours and outlines, so that it resembled a dream of itself. "That helped to bring me," he said. "Where was it taken?"

"It is a restaurant," Emil said. "There is little of a walk."

"The walk is up," Gitte said and emphasised the warning by panting like an animal.

"I don't mind climbing. It'll keep me fit after yesterday."

"And there will be many people."

"If it's that popular I should think it must be worth a visit."

"It is as my father told you," Hanna said. "It is nothing but a restaurant."

"Then it's my chance to buy dinner," Leo said and heard someone release a defeated sigh, which left him feeling he'd triumphed in some way he couldn't even start to understand.

CHAPTER TEN

The car had left Alphafen well behind when Gitte said "The walk will be four hours."

"I didn't realise it would take that long. Will it be too much for you? You should have said."

"My mother says it will take hours. For them," Hanna said and pronounced gravely "Not phoo-er."

"Perhaps walking will be dark," Emil said.

"Would you rather I bought dinner somewhere else? I can always walk another day. Do you all have a favourite place?"

"It shall be where you are going," Gitte said.

"We must go," Emil said. "We are reserved."

"If you do not mind no walk," Hanna said, "there is a bus."

"Whatever's best for everyone."

"You are that." Gitte sent him an appreciative look from the back seat in the mirror. "Thank you also for the bus," she said.

No doubt the change of plan was why Hanna slowed down further. Presumably because her parents preferred not to travel too fast on the mountain roads, she was already driving at half yesterday's speed. At least the sun was well above the heights when they arrived at the bus terminal. As Hanna searched for a space in the car park her father said "No haste."

A bright red bus was receiving passengers as he led the way to the bus stop. "You should not hurry," Gitte said when Leo made to do so. "We must have tickets to go on."

Once Emil had bought them at the ticket office the party waited nearly half an hour for the next bus. A drive through pinewoods led through a tunnel to a revelation of the Alps, peaks rising behind peaks as the narrow winding road climbed above a valley. Beyond the terminus a lengthy passage ended at a polished brass lift in which elegant mirrors surrounded Leo with the Webers and himself. The lift raised them to a terrace that might have been presenting a panorama of creation for divine approval: lakes inset between mountains to capture samples of the scoured blue sky, sheer slopes furred with multitudes of pines, snowfields that appeared to be dissolving into skeins of cloud. Once Leo recovered from the first surge of awe he located Alphafen, displayed like a perfect miniature of itself between two distant ridges. He stepped over a supine pair of walking-sticks with the right angles of their handles overlaid to form an F if not more of a symbol, and held the railing while he savoured the view, which surely demonstrated why the town had been named an Alpine haven. "So why did you take the photo here?" he said.

When Hanna didn't answer he had the odd notion that he wasn't alone in awaiting her response. The man who'd just retrieved the sticks, a lanky long-faced fellow with a small precise moustache that underlined how extravagantly wide his nostrils were, had straightened up to gaze at her. "We had come to lunch," Emil said, and as if it were a natural progression "Shall we go in to dine?"

The Kehlsteinhaus was a broad low grey stone chalet overlooking the vista it hid from the terrace. Leo followed the family into the restaurant, a large resonant mostly wooden room. A waiter ushered the party to a table for eight, where a rucksack squatted like a pet dog on the boards beside a pair of German hikers at one end. As Leo sat next to Hanna another waiter seated a newcomer beside him – the lanky fellow from the terrace. He stowed the sticks under his chair and peered beneath his terse straight eyebrows at Leo but kept quiet while Leo considered the menu. As soon as Leo ordered – big noodle soup with sausages, schnitzel, a stein of beer – the man said "I'll be the same."

Despite the curious twist of phrase, he was audibly English. "Jerome Pugh," he said, extending his carelessly splayed fingers just far enough to suggest he was offering the hand. "Heartened to meet a fellow traveller up here."

"Leo Parker." Leo shook the hand, which clung clammily to his until he pulled back. "Have you come far?"

"Just from Chelsea. I'd have come a great deal further if there'd been the need."

"Settlesham, if you've heard of it. Not too far from Liverpool."

"Famous for the blitz, of course." As Leo wondered which place he meant Pugh glanced at the Webers, who were conversing with the hikers in German. "May I ask," he said, "why you were so interested in the view?"

"I'm staying there with my friends."

"Where exactly would that be?"

"Alphafen."

"Ah, I thought it might be. You may know it was the eagle's view."

"I haven't heard it called that."

"It should still be," Pugh said and peered at Leo's face. "How much do you know?"

"It looks as if I'm still learning."

"We all can, and it's important that we should." Pugh fell silent while a waiter planted a brimming tankard in front of him and served the Weber party. "Do you know the history of its construction?" he said.

"Alphafen? I know it was rebuilt after the war."

"Yes, we should remember. That raid was the grossest of our errors in the war. We sought to destroy but merely liberated." Before Leo could question this Pugh said "I wasn't speaking of Alphafen. I meant the eagle's nest itself."

"The Kehlsteinhaus."

"Precisely. The name it should still be proud to boast. Will you know its construction took twelve men?"

"Was that all? That's German efficiency for you."

Pugh allowed this a token laugh, apparently in case Leo had made a joke. "I'm telling you it killed them. That's one for each month of the process, and the thirteenth saw it finished. And the peak was struck by lightning twice during the construction. Make of all that what you will." As Leo failed to do so Pugh said "I believe they kept it from the birthday boy, though."

He'd adopted a tone of coy daring, like a child revelling in naughtiness. "I don't suppose it would be anything you'd want to advertise," Leo said.

"Indeed not. You had to take care what you said to him. Particularly here with his dislike of heights, though nobody would say he was afraid. He might not have used that magnificent lift if it hadn't brought him the view of your town."

"I wouldn't call it mine."

"Don't worry I'll think you're presuming. After your journey you've a perfect right to feel at home." Pugh's gaze strayed around the restaurant. "I wonder if these people know how special that day was," he said, "the presentation day."

"I wonder."

"You're aware what it was."

Leo felt found out. "Remind me."

"Not just his birthday but a night when the powers are at their peak."

Politeness prevented Leo from terminating the conversation, as he might have liked to. "Which?"

"What else but Walpurgisnacht. It takes on extra meaning here."

Leo had intended to learn which powers, but no longer felt the need. He saw the Webers glance at Pugh and then resume their chat. It seemed safest to say only "I didn't know."

"Will you know he visited Alphafen? It was more than just a view."

Leo's ignorance had begun to feel threatening. "Who did?"

"Who has been in our minds? The eagle. He flew high and saw far." When Leo betrayed no comprehension Pugh said "The leader."

Leo couldn't miss his meaning any longer. "You're talking about," he said and thought it best to lower his voice, "Adolf."

"By all means speak of him that way. We have no reason not to." As Leo sought to convey he'd simply tried to be discreet Pugh said "He was right in so many ways. He believed in the Alps."

Leo grew aware of a silence beside him. The Webers and the hikers were listening to Pugh. Emil beckoned a waiter over and spoke rapidly in German. "Sir," the waiter said to Pugh, "we do not encourage such talk here."

"Don't tell me you want to deny your own history."

"Are you a historian, sir?"

"Indeed I am, and it looks as though you need a few round here. This place wouldn't exist if it weren't for one of our greatest souls, and you should be celebrating that, not pretending he never lived."

"Sir, if you continue—"

"Don't bother threatening to throw me out. I've seen everything I need to see here. Let me just say you're an insult to your race." Pugh shoved his stumbling chair back and grabbed his sticks. "Don't miss the marble fireplace," he lingered to advise Leo. "Mussolini sent it for a present to our man."

As he marched out Leo was afraid he might perform a defiant goose-step. He refrained from doing so, and the arm he raised to salute Leo from the doorway wasn't quite as stiff as it could have been. "I can only apologise for all that," Leo said. "I didn't know what I was inviting. I wouldn't have let him go on if I'd known."

"You can invite and never know." As if this might have fallen short of reassurance Emil said "Now he is gone and forgotten."

"And you must forget," Gitte said.

Hanna leaned towards Leo, making way for a waiter to serve a salad. "And here comes a reason we brought you," she said, so emphatically she might have been heading off any question he'd wanted to ask.

CHAPTER ELEVEN

"Today all must work." Leo might have wondered whether this included him if Emil hadn't added "And what will you do, Leo?"

"I expect it's my chance for a walk."

"We are sorry there was not one yesterday," Gitte said.

"I was happy to come with the family. You keep saying I shouldn't blame myself for things, so don't you either."

"That should be so," Emil said. "There is no use in blame."

"I can drive you to a walk we like," Hanna said, "and then I will go to our shop."

"That would be great if you've the time." Leo bit into a pretzel spread with Alpine jam and dabbed his lips with an embroidered floral napkin that smelled reminiscently perfumed. "Do you mind," he said when he could, "if I just ask a question?"

"We shall hope not," Emil said.

"What that fellow was telling me yesterday, is it true?"

"We do not know what he told," Gitte said. "We heard only his last part."

"For a start, they built the restaurant for Hitler."

"It was not one then."

"Eerie," Emil said, "you would say, Leo."

"The eagle's nest, my father says," Hanna made sure Leo realised. "This has often been the name."

"The eagle's view as well, he said. Not your father, the man at the Kehlsteinhaus. He seemed to be saying it was built so Hitler could see Alphafen."

"He enjoyed views of our mountains," Gitte said. "He liked to have them from his favourite place, the Berghof."

"He would see the mountain where they say Charlemagne sleeps," Hanna said. "He could think the holy man would bring his knights to fight for him."

"So he believed in legends." Leo didn't mean to yield to the distraction. "But what was so special about Alphafen?"

"He thought much of the Alps," Gitte said with what sounded like diminished patience.

"Our countryside, my mother says."

Perhaps Hanna found the habit of translation hard to break. "I understood he visited your town," Leo said. "I wondered what he would have seen in it."

"What had you?" Emil said. "It fetched you to us."

"Let's say it helped." Leo was about to send Hanna a smile when he realised why her parents might be taking issue with him. "I hope you don't think it had anything to do with your Führer," he said. "If you heard that character assuming I was like him, he couldn't have been more wrong."

"Hitler is not ours," Gitte objected.

"And we do not dream he is yours," Emil said. "None of us were born, and we are not responsible."

"Now we shall forget," Gitte said, very much like advice. "We shall see you here for dinner."

As soon as Hanna's parents left the house Leo said "Tell me I haven't offended them."

"They are not easy to offend." Hanna tilted her head as if her faint grimace had tugged it awry. "Perhaps you have given them some guilt," she said.

"I didn't mean to. About what?"

"What has stayed from the past although they cannot stop it."

"They're no more responsible for the kind of person I met yesterday than I am." Leo finished the pretzel and took a last mouthful of coffee while carrying the plate and knife to the scoured metal sink. "Let me just wash up," he said, "and we'll be on our way."

"Guests do not work." Hanna held his elbows to move him aside. "You will do enough," she said.

He seemed to sense she wished she could rescind some aspect of her behaviour. Did she feel she'd gone too far by touching him – perhaps given him the wrong idea about their relationship? That would explain why she asked "Is anybody with you at your home?"

"There's Ellen. She has been for a while."

"You did not say." As he wondered if this was a gentle rebuke Hanna said "Mine is away to work, and so you will not meet her."

A minute let her deal the breakfast items a brisk efficient soap and rinse before striding to the Volkswagen. Some miles out of the town she halted by a pair of posts that framed the entrance to a path through fields. "Walk away," she said. "Call me when you want me and I shall collect you here."

As she swerved the car across the road and raced towards Alphafen Leo waved to her, ensuring that his arm wasn't too straight or his hand outstretched too high. He was turning away when he caught sight of a figure in the field she was passing, presumably some kind of scarecrow, since it seemed unlikely that anyone would keep so still with a flock of butterflies crawling over their face. Could they set off Hanna's phobia? Rather than risk drawing her attention to them he made for the path. Once he could no longer hear the car he looked back. Half a dozen butterflies were performing an intricate spasmodic dance above the field, but the figure was nowhere to be seen. It couldn't have been too secure if it had fallen in the grass.

The first mile of the gravel track led between meadows riotous with colours. The ascent was so gradual that for most of half an hour Leo failed to notice mountains had crept up from hiding behind the closer peaks. The open fields around him reminded him how alone he was, especially whenever he glanced behind him. Throughout the several hours that took him to a ridge from which he could survey the scenery he didn't meet a single walker. He perched on a rock cupped like a bucket seat and let his gaze wander the massive mountainscape. It would have enthralled him more profoundly if he hadn't felt an irrational need to keep looking over his shoulder. Once he tired of the compulsion he turned back along the trail.

As soon as he saw its end in the distance he phoned Hanna. "I'll be waiting when you're available."

"We are finished."

This sounded ominous until he realised "At the shop, you mean."

"For this day. I shall find you now."

Leo had been walking fast while they talked, and kept up the pace all the way to the end of the path. He was resting his hands on the pair of posts beside the road, a stance that made him feel like a hiker paralysed by having lost a route, when he saw a large white butterfly fluttering across the meadow he was in. Despite all the jagged airborne zigzags it described, it appeared to be heading for him. Sunlight set it shining like a patch of snow and trailed its unsteady shadow over the meadow. The wildness of the vegetation must be why the shadow kept changing its shape, while the swoops of the insect were making the shadow swell huge and then shrink, however unsynchronised Leo could have fancied the effect was. He'd grown so preoccupied with the phenomenon that he was wholly unprepared for the creature to settle on his face.

It felt like being robbed of half his sight. The blur that filled his left eye was fumbling at the eyeball as though searching for a way in. With a cry not merely of disgust he slapped it away and saw it plummet twitching onto the grass beside the path. When he finished furiously blinking he saw the butterfly had begun to crawl in a convulsive pattern like an obscure sign it was inscribing. At least one of its wings was broken, and he trod on it without a thought. As he stepped back he must have disturbed the grass, sending a sinuous restlessness through a thin line of stalks to disappear into the meadow. Or might he have startled a lurking snake? He was trying to decide, though not venturing to search for evidence – he couldn't even distinguish the remains of the butterfly now – when he heard a car on the road.

The Volkswagen halted by the path with an emphatic squeal of brakes. "Was your walk all that was wished?" Hanna said as he climbed in.

"I expect it was what I needed."

Leo was distracted by the sight the car had turned towards – the surroundings of Alphafen. Was he seeing what he seemed to be? As soon as they were back at the Weber house he went up to his room. He had indeed observed what he'd thought he had. He found the family in the kitchen, Gitte chopping sauerkraut while Emil attended to a pork joint and Hanna filled the percolator. "Surrounded by Alps," Leo said.

This paused everybody's actions as though a frame had frozen in a film, and he had a sense that each of the Webers was waiting for somebody else to respond. As they resumed their activities Emil said "Who is so?"

"Me in my room. Aren't those paintings exactly what I'd see if you had windows there instead?"

"Exactly."

This resembled an interrogation of the word, prompting Leo to ask "What's the idea behind those?"

"Nothing is behind them," Gitte said, apparently not as a joke. "It is only wall."

"It is what you think, Leo," Hanna said. "They show what you would say is there."

He was about to persist when Emil emitted an utterance in German. "My father forgot to buy wine," Hanna said.

"I'll go and get some, and I'll pay. You didn't let me at the restaurant," Leo said and left any protests behind as he hurried out of the house.

He'd noticed a wine shop next to the beerhall. As he made for the corner of the street he recalled the short cut through the alley. It let him see a vertical sliver of lit street at the far end, pinched thin by the curve of the passage. Apart from a bird that fluttered out of a niche in the wall, the alley was deserted. Whatever Gitte and Emil had said about it, their comments hardly seemed applicable, and Leo turned along it at once.

The light from the street he'd left gleamed on the rounded cobblestones. Walking on them was easy enough, at any rate to begin with. As he advanced between the towering walls of houses the cobbles seemed to grow more prominent underfoot, no doubt because his soles had begun to ache. Darkness closed around him well before he reached the bend, which proved to be sharper than it had looked and narrower into the bargain, while the street ahead remained more distant than he'd anticipated. He glanced back to confirm he couldn't have progressed as far as he'd thought, only to find the other street was at least as remote. The dark appeared to have stopped up whatever gap the bird had emerged from. Some instability of the light ahead must be causing the cobblestones to stir as if they were about to hatch. He couldn't see much light at all; the more he sought it, the more it seemed to hold itself aloof. He could only make for the street ahead, though the bend appeared to have lent the alley its narrowness. He wasn't really feeling the cobbles shift beneath his feet, let alone give way like trodden eggshells. How soon would the light from the street he was striving breathlessly to reach extend as far as him? Any diminution of the darkness he was trapped in would be welcome — at least, unless it showed him anything he might prefer not to see. He stumbled over stones that felt ready to come loose, to swarm clattering after him, perhaps. He clutched at the walls, which had grown a good deal closer than arm's length, unless this was the darkness that enclosed his vision like blinkers too impalpable to remove. At last the light ahead touched the cobbles and held them still, and the sight of a passer-by was a further reassurance. He glanced at Leo and then stared at him, and a frown dug shadows into his forehead. Before Leo could leave the alley the man strode heavily to block the way. "You are the English," he said.

"Just a representative. An emissary, if you like. Can I get by? I'm feeling a bit shut in."

The burly man stayed where he was. His substantial face looked flattened, even the broad nose, a process that appeared to have squashed his emotions so deep they needed time to surface while the fixed frown denoted them. "Maybe you deserve the prison," he said.

"Let me out and you can tell me what I'm supposed to have done." When this failed to shift the man Leo lurched at him, close to panic. He might have grappled with him if the fellow hadn't retreated a grudging step. Although Leo was tempted to ignore him, he felt provoked to ascertain "So what's my offence meant to be?"

"Maybe you remember Dietrich Gebhardt."

Leo was about to deny it when he had to admit "It does seem to ring a faint bell."

"He is here."

Leo glanced about before he understood. While the restaurants were busy, the street was deserted. "It's you," he said.

"You see me now. Maybe you don't find it is so easy to make threats."

"I haven't tried. If I've somehow given that impression—"

"You say hate speech in your country."

"I never do. Where on earth did you get that idea?"

"You call it so, what was written to me."

"Dietrich Gebhardt." The surge of memory was so forceful that it sent the name out of Leo's mouth. "Paddy Bloore wrote to you when we were at school," he said.

"Bloore, yes. I do not forget the name. And now you confess you knew."

"I give you my word none of us were involved. He wasn't meant to write to anyone when he felt that way. Didn't you get the apology the school made him send you?"

"Then it was not real, and you knew that also."

"If we'd apologised for him it would have been real. Look, let me do that now. If I'd known how you'd feel about it I would have then."

"It is too late. It always has been." Despite if not because of this, Gebhardt's frown had begun to clear. "What he wrote first," he said, "that was the real."

"Can you remind me? Then I'll know exactly what I need to apologise for."

"There will be more revenge." Gebhardt let this hover before following it with a laugh so flat it withheld its significance. "This is what your friend wrote," he said.

"In that case I do apologise. It wasn't necessary, and of course it isn't true." Having failed to rouse any expression on Gebhardt's stolid face, Leo said "But I should tell you he was never a friend of mine."

"Not necessary." Whatever this answered, a thought twitched up one corner of his lips. "The bombs were your mistake," he said.

"I wasn't born then any more than you were, and Bloore was just a kid when he wrote what he did. I hope he's changed by now. We all need to grow up."

"The English mistake," Gebhardt said as though Leo hadn't spoken. "Your bombs were meant to cast down Hitler, but they raised his spirits."

"How could they do that? I thought he was supposed to value your town."

"It was his vision. It was his comfort."

"Then why on earth would he want to see it bombed?"

"He saw it was a sacrifice. The people had to be."

Leo was about to question this when Gebhardt's gaze swerved past him. "Dietrich," a voice said.

The mayor had emerged from the nearest restaurant, wiping his mouth with a napkin. "What has caused an argument?"

Leo tried not to feel like a schoolboy caught squabbling. "We were remembering when your town was bombed," he said, since Gebhardt seemed reluctant to speak.

"It sounded worse." As Leo wondered how long he had been listening in the doorway the mayor said "Take away the badness." When this produced no result he turned his stare on Gebhardt. "Go now," he said.

Gebhardt returned the stare, but not for long. As he stumped away the mayor gave Leo all his attention. "You may as well, Mr Leo Parker," he said, and Leo couldn't judge whether he was meant to feel accused. Before he had time to reply the mayor turned his back. Perhaps he believed his town should have left conflict behind – believed Leo should have offered only peace. Surely this explained the terse encounter, but as Leo headed for the wine merchant's he couldn't help feeling in need of a drink.

CHAPTER TWELVE

Before she took Leo to the airport Hanna drove him and her parents to their shop. It was called simply Weber's, the name etched on the window in gilded Gothic script suggesting a bid to evoke a past before the war. "Is that the original building?" Leo wondered.

"Some things were not destroyed," Emil said. "They took a new life."

Leo trundled his suitcase into the shop and set about looking for souvenirs. "Have whatever you should want," Gitte urged. "You will be taking part of us home."

"Take some part you like," Hanna said.

Many items were too big for the space he'd left in the case: Alpine backpacks, tall lidded steins decorated with dancers, cuckoo clocks shutting up their tenants or allowing them illusions of escape…. All the books laid out on a table were in German except for *Old Tales of the Alps*. The volume had no jacket, just the words embossed in silver on the green binding. "I think this is for me," Leo said.

"We shall keep it here for you." Gitte took it to the counter while Emil made a phone call in German, apparently about a book. "What more will you choose?" she said.

"I'm after presents that will fit in my luggage."

"No need for fitting. We shall send to you."

Leo lingered at a display of carved figures – waiters, dancers, drinkers, walkers with knobbly sticks, musicians hefting tubas – in equally cartoonish painted wooden costumes. Some hung on strings attached to their scalps as though an unseen puppeteer were operating their brains. Outsize pretzels dangled too, and a heart encompassing a romantic couple lost in each other's eyes. Hoping Ellen wouldn't find it overstated, he transferred it to his wicker shopping basket and added gifts for his parents: a lidded tankard for his father, though not one depicting the Kehlsteinhaus; a bucolic magnet his mother could use to pin some of her many lists to the refrigerator. "I can take the book and the heart and the magnet," he told Emil. "Save some postage."

"You have already saved us," Emil said and sent a welcoming look past him. "Here is another customer. Guten morgen, Helmut. You may tell Leo Parker goodbye."

He was a tall man whose shiny egg-shaped cranium was so high it suggested an attempt to add an extra inch. "You are leaving us so soon, Mr Parker," he said.

"I said I'd just be here a week."

"Long enough, you say. Then I am sure it is. Allow me a handshake." Having delivered a vigorous version, he crossed to the table full of books and adopted a pose reminiscent of the double-handled steins behind him. "Where is the book that was in English?" he said.

"You must ask Mr Parker," Gitte said.

"I'm buying the one about the Alps," Leo told him.

"I had come to buy it for my children," Helmut said, "to aid them with the language."

"It will be the greatest favour, Leo," Hanna said, "if you let Helmut take your book."

"We will send all your basket today," Gitte promised, "and the other follows."

"Of course you will not pay for them," Emil said, "or sending either."

"Well, thank you." It seemed clear to Leo that he must accept the whole proposal. "I don't see how I can deny your children," he told Helmut.

"They will be just as grateful to you as the rest of us." Helmut barely touched the reader on the counter with his credit card. "Travel swiftly, Mr Parker," he said.

As he strolled away more slowly than he'd left the shop, bearing the book like a trophy in both hands, Gitte said "May you see your home soon."

"May your memories of us be pleasant," Emil said.

"I'll make sure. That's to say they are, of course. Let me pay for the heart at least or it won't be a gift from me."

"We understand," Hanna said.

"And I'll take it with me or I won't have anything to give her when I get back."

Gitte nested the heart in a padded box and secured a ribbon around it with a bow while Leo applied his card to the reader. Once he'd found room in his suitcase for the gift Hanna's parents saw him out to the car. Their last words had seemed oddly formal, close to ritualistic, and so did their farewell gestures: Gitte's kisses on his cheeks, Emil briefly gripping Leo's hand in both of his. "Thank you again for all you do," Gitte said.

Before Leo could protest he hadn't done much Emil said "May your flight be fast and safe."

They stood outside the shop to wave as they shrank in the wing mirror. Leo thought the mime looked wistful, even regretful. Hanna didn't speak until she had left Alphafen behind, but as the Volkswagen gathered speed she said "Will you need to make sure?"

"Of what, sorry?"

"Your memories are good."

"They mostly are." When she turned her head though not her gaze to him he felt compelled to add "I didn't want to trouble anyone, but the night I bought the wine I had a bit of a confrontation."

"With Hans at the shop? He should have been a friendly man. He sang at your welcoming."

"He was fine. That's how I knew which wines you all liked. It was somebody who stopped me on the way. Dietrich Gebhardt, if you know him."

"I do not know. What did he say to you?"

"One of my classmates wrote him a nasty letter when we were all corresponding, and Mr Gebhardt seemed to blame us all. We didn't even know the boy had written to him till the teacher called him out."

"You will say it is too long to keep a grudge."

"For either of them, but Mr Gebhardt said there'll be more revenge."

Hanna gripped the wheel and stared fiercely at the road. "He had no right to say."

"Maybe he was saying that's what was said to him. One thing he did say, and please don't think I'm endorsing it, was Hitler didn't care about the raid on your town. Mr Gebhardt said he saw it as some kind of sacrifice."

The car veered towards the wrong side of the road before Hanna recaptured control. "He ought never to have said such things," she protested. "It is wrong."

"I'm sure it must be if you say so. Forget him and I will."

He'd meant only to leave the subject behind, not to silence Hanna, but he contented himself with the Alpine vistas he'd missed on the outward trip. She didn't slow down until they had almost reached the airport, where she parked and climbed out as Leo retrieved his case. Overhead a plane was unzipping the sky with its vapour trail, which had parted in half. "Will you let me go now?" she said. "They will need me at the shop."

"Of course, and thanks for everything. Thanks for having me, and tell your parents too."

"They will not need."

Presumably this meant they knew he was grateful. The kiss she presented to his cheeks felt as formal as her mother's had, so that he wondered if he'd estranged her somehow. "If you feel like returning the visit," he said, "you know where I am."

"You will be visited." She seemed close to saying more, but dodged around the Volkswagen. "Do not miss your flight," she said more urgently than Leo saw the need for, and ducked into the car. In seconds she was speeding away without a backwards glance.

CHAPTER THIRTEEN

Once his suitcase had bumbled onto the belt behind the check-in desk Leo made for the security gates. He planted his shoes and phone and crumpled handkerchief and wallet fattened with cards on a tray, and was digging in his hip pocket for coins when an intruder squirmed against his palm. He closed his fist as he snatched his hand out and then flung the writhing object into the aisle between the metal counters. "What are you throwing away, sir?" the officer opposite him said.

"It must have been an insect. Didn't you see it? Don't ask me what it was doing in my pocket. Hitching a free flight to England, you might say."

As he managed to abandon babbling – his bid to placate the stare he'd invited – the officer said "I saw no insect, no."

"It'll be somewhere on the floor if it hasn't flown away. Can you see it anywhere? Let me look."

On his way to stooping he thought just in time to keep his fists clear of the floor in case he was suspected of jettisoning some drug. The man had called a colleague from directing travellers into queues for the gates. While Leo failed to locate any kind of intruder they conversed in German. "She saw you throw nothing," the man behind the counter said.

"I'm sure it was an insect. I felt it move," Leo insisted and opened his fists to show they had nothing to hide.

"She says there was nothing."

At last – not too belatedly, he hoped – Leo gathered she'd exonerated him. He finished loading the tray with a shrill scattered clatter of coins on plastic and headed for the electronic arch. He couldn't help anticipating the alarm he expected to set off, and when the arch kept its reaction to itself he released a breath he hoped nobody official noticed. As he padded shoeless to collect the tray he saw his wad of folded banknotes stir as if a lurker was preparing to emerge. Had the insect somehow hidden among them? No, the notes were unfurling by themselves. Once he'd unloaded the tray and slipped his shoes on he left security behind.

As he made for the duty-free hall he came to a bookshop. Much of its stock was in English, but he couldn't see the title he detoured to look for. As he tilted his head towards aligning it with a row of spinal titles, a young woman joined him. "May I assist?"

"Do you have *Old Tales of the Alps*?"

"There are a number."

"No, I mean the book called that."

"We have not. Let me make a search for you." She went to a computer terminal and typed at a speed Leo would have called feverish. "I am afraid it is discontinued," she said.

"Out of print, you're saying."

"Yes, that. May I find you something else?"

"It was just that book." Leo was surprised how much he regretted having yielded to the Webers' other customer. "Maybe I can buy it online," he said and made for the duty-free hall.

The extensive white-tiled space was considerably longer than its width. A maze of displays helped to hide the distant departure lounge, which appeared to be around several corners. Glass shelves taller than Leo and cabinets of equal stature surrounded the traveller with untaxed temptations. A confusion of scents from the perfume counters greeted him, and he thought they might have attracted the large black fly that was pressing its body against its identical twin as they climbed a mirror flanked by rampant lipsticks. Having completed their sluggish zigzag dance, it and its partner appeared to vanish into the frame of the mirror, no doubt crawling around the back. Leo was glad to leave it behind, but he was still among the cosmetics when he heard a child's voice close to him.

Although it was scarcely more than a murmur, he could hear the child's distress, not least because he understood some of the words – the

German for mother and father. Beyond a pair of cabinets he found a small boy confronting a mirror that towered over him. A similar mirror stood at his back, trapping him in a multitude of reflections. "What's the matter, son?" Leo said.

"Mein Mutter," the boy wailed, so that Leo wondered if the child thought he'd said the word. "Mein Vater."

Leo raised his voice. "Does this boy belong to anyone? Lost boy here." Several passing travellers glanced at him but gave no sign that they understood, and he couldn't see anybody working in the hall. "Let's find mother and father," he said, which appeared to make itself clear, since the boy clutched his hand, clammily but fiercely. Leo turned back to the concourse he'd just left, which was as crowded as ever. "Are this boy's parents here?" he called.

Most of the crowd looked at him, and quite a few people stared, but this was the extent of the response. As he thought of shouting louder, the boy tugged at his hand and pointed at the duty-free hall. "They went through there, did they?" Leo felt relieved to learn. "They must be looking for you. Let's go and meet them."

The perfumes were waiting for him. An impalpable mass of them trailed him into the first glassed-in aisle and its neighbour. He'd hoped to see a couple – just a man or a woman would do – searching for someone, but for the moment the hall appeared to be deserted except for him and his charge, him and his trusting charge, him and his trusting not yet tearful charge. Mirrors showed him all of those and more, but at least he couldn't see the fly. "Do you want to call them again?" he said as the end of yet another aisle exhibited him and his dependent companion. "Mutter, Vater."

He was only prompting, not adopting the words, but the boy's face wavered as if he thought Leo was preparing to betray him somehow. "Don't worry," Leo murmured, "we'll find them." Shouldn't he have outdistanced the oppressive scents by now? He didn't need to fancy he was trapped in the cosmetics section, because here were suitcases piled so high on either side of him they made him feel as dwarfed as he imagined the boy must feel. The heavy smell of leather fell short of ousting the scents, instead merging with them in a combination he found faintly nauseous. He was leading the boy around corner after corner, and near to growing desperate for an unhindered view of at least part of the hall, when he heard voices somewhere ahead.

They belonged to a man and a woman. "Das sind sie," the boy cried and hauled Leo in their direction. Leo was surprised how unconcerned they sounded, more like customers discussing a purchase, but he was happy to be led, however devious the route had to be. "Hello?" he called. "Have I got your son here?" Before he could locate them he heard an answer: a word, at any rate. "Nein," the woman said, precisely in the tone of a decision not to buy an item, and the couple retreated unseen.

Leo could no longer see either end of the hall. So many full-length mirrors cluttered his view that he was unable to determine which way he'd come in. He mustn't let them confront him with any of the panic he was trying not to feel. "I don't think that was your folk after all, son," he said as evenly as he could, but saw every copy of the boy's face grow uncomprehending. "Let's keep on where you thought they were."

Was his hand borrowing clamminess from the boy's? That had turned limp in his grasp. It felt robbed of conviction, but he mustn't let that affect him. As he urged the boy out of the crowd of mirrors he collided with a rack of T-shirts, which flapped like flattened overgrown insects while their hangers clanged on the rail. At least he'd escaped all the mocking reflections, but how had he managed to wander back into the cosmetics section, where a thick mass of scents ambushed him? He swung around so wildly that his elbow struck a glass shelf, setting jars and bottles tottering with a shrill clatter. For a moment he thought the entire display would collapse, showering him and the child with broken glass. "This way," he declared, unless it was a species of prayer, and did his desperate best to retrace his steps. Yes, he was back among the mirrors. He was striving not to let them bewilder him – they couldn't stop him finding his way out of the multitude of them, some of which had to be reflections, surely most of them – when he saw what they were showing him. While he was by no means alone, given the horde of him, he was by himself.

The frames of the mirrors were cutting off the boy's reflection. Before Leo could grasp this, the sight jerked his hand open. The boy let go at once and ran along a side aisle to disappear around a mirror twice his height as Leo lurched to detain him. "Don't run away," Leo shouted. "You don't want to get lost as well."

He meant as well as losing the boy's parents, but should he rather mean himself? When he sprinted between a pair of mirrors shivering like water into which a body had just sunk, he could barely see for panic. Had he somehow strayed back the way he'd come? Certainly the mingled smells of leather and perfume had returned to clog his head. The white light up above had become a glare that rebounded from every glass surface, rendering the riot of colours all around him agonisingly garish. For as long as he struggled to draw breath his brain felt incapable of comprehending where he was or even what it looked like in any detail. He shut his eyes so tight his vision flared as if their throbbing ache had been rendered visible. He had to clutch at the nearest mirror, bruising his hand on the frame, before he could risk even slitting his eyes. He glimpsed movement, but only in the mirror, where shapes were flocking through a vertical sliver of the glass. They were passing the far end of an aisle behind him.

The sight revived his hearing, which brought him the murmur of a crowd. They were in the departure lounge – he could see a sign above their heads, indicating the gates – and a small figure had just wandered into the aisle at his back. It was the boy Leo had tried to help. He ran to catch the child before he could vanish again – for a disoriented moment, ran at the mirror. "Wait there," he shouted and raced after the boy, hands outstretched.

He had nearly reached the concourse when the boy darted out of sight. "Don't run away again," Leo called and put on so much speed he outstripped his breath. As he dashed out of the aisle a woman demanded "What do you think you are doing?"

She was slim but muscular and tall enough to frown down at him. The boy had run to huddle against her, wrapping his arms around her long thighs. "Is," Leo gasped and had to find a breath, "he yours?"

A man answered, having interrupted his examination of a menu outside a bar. "He does not belong to you."

"No." The man was inches taller than the woman, but Leo didn't mean to let this daunt him. "Is he your son?" he persisted. "Just need to be sure."

"He is ours indeed," the woman said. "I asked what you have done to him."

"I didn't do." Leo's breath was lagging again. "A thing," he added when he could. "Helping him find parents."

"Why would anyone do so? He knew where we were."

"I'm sorry, but you're wrong there. He was lost."

"He was not. We knew where we would find him."

"Sorry again, but I doubt it. He was all the way back there." Leo turned to indicate how far this was, only to discover he'd just left a cosmetics section of the hall. Beside it gnomes with pointed hats as floppy as their bodies sent him wide fixed grins he could easily have imagined mocking him. "I'm telling you he was at the other end," he said. "He was in distress."

"He was where he had been put," the father said. "He was punished."

"Look, I had to bring him all the way through there. I'm certain he didn't know where you'd gone. Ask him."

"We shall do no such thing of the kind," the mother said.

The boy looked sleepily contented, close to smug. As his mother planted a possessive hand on the small crew-cut scalp Leo said "I just wanted to bring him to you."

"That is not what we saw at all."

The man stepped in front of Leo. "We warn you now, stay far from our son."

"He'll tell you I've been telling the truth," Leo insisted and made for the nearest departure board. It directed passengers for Manchester to wait in the concourse. He found a seat between a woman with a flattened Alpine backpack spread across her lap and a man who kept inspecting his haul of duty-free liquor as if unable to believe his luck. Leo was composing a message to Ellen – *At airport waiting for gate. Home soon. Many tales to tell* – when the German family strolled past him.

At least the seats across from him were occupied. A gate announcement cleared most of a row at the far end of the block, and the family sat opposite a departure board. Leo couldn't help hoping their flight would be announced before he had to walk past them, but they hadn't shifted by the time Manchester passengers were invited to the gate. Leo stood up, and the family did.

Might they be responding to a different announcement? He kept well back as they strode past gate after gate. When they came abreast of the matrix sign for Manchester he willed them to walk on, only to watch the father find them seats close to the desk. They didn't notice Leo hurrying to sit as far from them as the seating area permitted. If they boarded ahead of him, perhaps he could stay unobserved – but when an attendant at the desk named the section of the plane he would be sitting in, they rose as Leo did.

He held back from joining the queue until they passed the desk. While the attendant checked his documents the family vanished around a bend in the tunnel that led to the plane. On board he and the rest of the tail of the queue had to wait while passengers loaded overhead lockers or retrieved items from them. He couldn't see the family anywhere ahead, even when he made his way along the aisle. As he found his place, a window seat in the central exit row, the parents straightened up from stowing items on the floor. They were sitting behind him with their son directly at his back.

He looked away as he sat down, hoping the flight would let him and the family ignore each other. The hope didn't last long. Well before the aircraft even stirred, the seat developed an insistent tic that felt like a muscular spasm with which it was doing its best to infect him. The boy was kicking the back of the seat, but Leo restrained himself. At last he heard the father murmuring in German, and the repetitive impacts subsided, giving way to a brief wail of protest. When the plane commenced its timid advance towards the runway Leo willed this to offer distraction. He managed to relax as the plane took off, skimming its expanding shadow on the tarmac. The aircraft was ascending marble steps of cloud when a foot set about poking his spine. This was beyond disregarding, and he craned around the seat to find the father had replaced the son. The intrusion wasn't a foot after all; the man's knees were digging into the seat. "You have the room," he objected at once.

"Would you like to change seats?"

"You are too close to our son already. We shall keep you where you are."

"Then can you do something about the knees? They'll be a pain otherwise."

The man's legs gaped, pressing their knees against the edges of the seatback. "Will this satisfy?" he barely asked.

"I'm sure it should. Thank you very much."

When Leo settled back against the seat he felt as though he had to arrange himself between a pair of outsize calipers. At least they weren't physically troubling him, and he dozed until there was no queue for the toilet. Since it was next to the cockpit, he took the opportunity to visit the pilots, a treat he'd missed when he was the German boy's age. "It's got in," one pilot blurted, and Leo tried to feel she didn't mean him. It was surely more important to grasp how ominous this was – a warning of an imminent disaster. He dashed back to his seat and read the instructions on the emergency door as fast as his abruptly sluggish brain would let him. He was striving to free the handle – the glass in which it was encased felt soft yet impervious, yielding without breaking and then doggedly regaining shape – when someone unseen sought to restrain him.

"Stop it. Get away." Was this Leo's protest, even though his lips seemed to be clamped shut? No, he'd heard the passenger beside him, and he floundered awake to discover she was grappling with his arms, struggling to capture them. "Steward," she cried. "Some help here."

Leo let his arms go limp as his fists began to throb from punching the glass that protected the handle. "What has he been trying to do now?" the man at his back demanded.

"He nearly had the door open," the woman said and turned on Leo. "What's the matter with you?"

"No harm done. Just a nightmare."

"You are and no mistake."

"I'm saying I was trying to open it in my sleep."

Her cries had brought a steward. "What seems to be the problem?" he said to both of them.

"He nearly had this exit open. He says he was asleep, but now I don't feel safe."

"I'll swap seats with you if it helps," Leo said.

"That's the least he could do. Can you move him further off?"

"I'm sorry, madam, but we have no spare seats on the flight."

"Then just see he does what he said he would."

When Leo stood up she sidled around him as remotely as she could manage, miming distaste. The faces of the German family made it plain Leo had confirmed their impression of him. He took the middle seat, to find himself beside a man clattering a laptop and extruding bare elbows well out of his space. "Now you can have all the nightmares you want," the woman said as Leo sought refuge behind his eyelids, "just make sure you keep them to yourself," and he felt as if she was encouraging them to catch up with him.

CHAPTER FOURTEEN

s Leo retrieved his suitcase, which a baggage handler's
disembodied hand had propelled out of the wings like a director
urging a reluctant performer onstage, the German boy pointed at
him from the far side of the carousel. The parents leaned towards their
son to catch his words, and Leo tried to sound no more than interested
as he called "What's he saying about me?"

"He is speaking to us," the woman said.

"I can see that. That's why I asked."

"He is speaking just to us."

"Yes, about me. That's why I'd like to know."

"You will find out," the father said.

"If that's supposed to be a threat I'd like to hear what I'm being
threatened with. I give you my word I told you the truth before, and
I'm hoping he confirmed it, that's all."

"We are hoping you will be gone soon," the mother said.

The irrelevance provoked Leo as much as the wish. "You aren't
bound for Settlesham, are you?"

"We have never heard such a name."

"Then you won't be seeing any more of me, so if you could just—"

They were no longer looking at him. They and their son stepped
forward to detain their luggage, a pair of cases metallic as safes together
with their scaled-down scion. As the family wheeled them away, the
boy glanced back at Leo and made another comment to his parents.
"What's he saying now?" Leo demanded.

As the couple hurried their son out of the baggage hall a woman
waiting at the opposite side of the belt took pity on Leo. "I expect he
was showing them your friend."

There was nobody near Leo, and his unease left politeness behind. "What are you talking about?"

Apparently his curtness was her reason not to answer. More than one passenger beside the carousel sniggered at his bewilderment, and he was about to turn on them when another woman said "Have a look at your luggage."

Leo craned over his suitcase to see a large white butterfly clinging to his name tag. "Did anyone see where it came from?"

"Out of your pocket."

Leo recalled the sensation he'd experienced at the German security gate, the impression that he'd roused an insect from quiescence. He ventured to reach in his hip pocket, prompting further mirth. "Not that one," the woman said with ostentatious patience. "On your bag."

The zip from which the tag dangled had left the external pocket half open. As Leo stooped to investigate, the butterfly flew past his head, so close that he felt the whir of wings on his cheek. For a second he thought it had blundered into his ear. He unzipped the pocket all the way and tugged it wide to find it was empty apart from a flattened pack of paracetamol. He secured the zip and was heading for the unattended customs channel when the woman who had referred to his friend called "Don't you intend to deal with it?"

Leo's suitcase halted later than he did, tugging at his fingers. "Sorry, how?"

"You can't just bring insects into the country. It's your responsibility to see to it."

"I didn't notice where it went. Did you?"

"It wasn't up to me to do so. Please report the situation or I shall."

A pair of customs officers, presumably watchful despite their unconcerned expressions, stood next to the exits. "Excuse me," Leo said, "did you see the butterfly?"

Both men looked bemused if not amused. "Which would that be, sir?" one said.

"It was on my luggage. I may have brought it in without knowing."

"We'll let you off this time," the man's colleague said.

"Isn't it prohibited? It must still be in here somewhere."

"We'll keep an eye open."

"There are worse things you could have brought with you, if you even did."

Why should he feel accused? They weren't merely letting him go, they were exonerating him. He wheeled his case into Nothing to Declare and through the electronic exit that warned him he'd lost any chance to return. Among the passengers awaiting pickups he saw the German family, and couldn't help feeling they'd waited for him. "No, they didn't search my luggage," he muttered, and saw them wonder what he'd said. Let them suffer that frustration for a change, but he'd left himself wondering whether he should investigate the contents of the suitcase. He could once he was home.

A Superior Parker minibus was idling at a stop outside the terminal. Ellen's parents had selected the car park when they'd planned their latest holiday, having been amused by the name. Once half a dozen passengers followed Leo on board the driver set off, jettisoning the last inch of a cigarette. Several miles of winding lanes brought the bus to the car park. Leo collected his keys from a morosely monosyllabic guard in an unpainted hut redolent of stagnant tea and made for his car.

A pair of vapour trails crossed out the cloudless zenith. Halfway to the horizon the bright needle of a sunlit plane was threading a cloud. Other flights lingered over spreading heavy wakes of sound across the sky. Had the smell of cannabis that seemed to be loitering near Leo's car heightened his senses? It left him wondering how efficient the guard and his colleagues might be. He slung his luggage on the back seat and let himself into the car.

He was about to back out of the space hemmed in by hulking vans when he noticed the mileage on the dial. Could it really have been several hundred miles lower last time he'd read it? He wished he'd taken time to note the reading, because now he wasn't certain. At least the fuel didn't seem depleted. As he drove past the hut he peered at its occupant but couldn't be sure how determined the man was not to look at him.

Beside the motorway the landscape shone with spillages of yellow paint – fields of rape. Fat clouds had crumbed meadows with sheep. Beyond a stretch of tall wire fence Leo heard shouts of encouragement and frustration followed by a leather thump and the ascent of a football that immediately plummeted to earth. He passed a coach loaded with oldsters singing how they did like to be beside the seaside and the sea, to some extent in tune, which helped him feel he'd returned home.

By the time he reached Settlesham it was late afternoon. Shadows of houses had started to carpet the streets of the New Town. At the corner of Moss Row he braked to let a brace of policemen cross. They glanced at the car and then halted at the kerb, and he thought they were about to approach him. They conferred briefly before making for their vehicle, and he turned along his road.

He'd parked outside his house and was retrieving the suitcase from the back seat when a smell of cannabis assailed him. Behind the car it was stronger still. The boot was yet more odorous, though empty of anything unfamiliar. No wonder the police had been alerted, and he could only hope they'd thought the smell originated somewhere else. A slam of the boot sent a surge of it into his nostrils, and he hoped nobody wondered what his hand was warding off.

The stone jigsaw of the short path snagged the wheels of his case on the way to the front door. He left the key in the lock while he moved to silence the alarm, only to realise it was mute, which made the house feel indefinably invaded. "Anybody here?" he called.

"Who would you like to be?"

Ellen came out of the kitchen, modelling the chef's apron she'd bought him last Christmas. "Nobody but you," he said at once.

"Welcome home, then." She brought him a hug that left her floury hands outstretched, then stepped back from the kiss she gave him. "If that's how you feel," she said.

He hastened to renew their hug. "Whyever wouldn't I?"

"You seem a bit distant."

"I wasn't expecting you to be here when I didn't see your car."

"It's in for servicing. Are you sure that's all?"

Leo bumped his suitcase over the shallow doorstep before admitting "I think someone may have used my car to transport dope while I was away."

"Gracious. Have you told the police?"

"I should, and you'd better tell your parents to check their car when they get back."

"I will. Come and talk to me while I finish dinner."

"Just let me go in here first."

He meant the case as well as the front room. He dumped the luggage on the couch and found Ellen's present, its bow somewhat crumpled in transit, but no items he hadn't packed. Ellen perched on the edge of an armchair to linger over releasing the bow and parting the paper. "Someone's taken care over wrapping," she said.

"I won't pretend it was me. The lady of the house."

"Your friend, you mean."

"I hope they all were." When Ellen gave this a patient look he said "Her mother."

Ellen lifted the lid and gazed at the contents of the box. "That's sweet," she said. "I'll find a place for it at home."

"The shop didn't sell any jewellery," Leo felt he should establish. "It was the family shop."

"I expect you felt you should support them. You thought of me, and that's all that ought to count. Come and get us whatever drink you'd like."

"Tea will do to start with."

He followed her into the kitchen to find she'd made toad in the hole, sausages protruding from a bed of batter in a deep dish. He couldn't help wondering if she meant this as a reference to the cuisine she assumed he'd met abroad or to compete with it if not to oust it from his memory. As he switched on the electric kettle she said "So what are you going to tell me?"

"What do you want to hear?"

She set about flaying a potato with a peeler. "Whatever you think I should."

"To start with, they gave me a big welcome dinner."

"Your friend and her family. I hope mine won't suffer too much by comparison."

"Trust me, it won't. It wasn't just them. More like the whole town came to greet me. And one day I was taken to a restaurant that turned out to have been built for Hitler."

"You aren't saying that's why they took you."

"None of the family are into that stuff. We were just there for the view." Leo saw no reason to mention Jerome Pugh. "And there was a bus I took to explore the countryside," he said, "and I had a walk in the Alps."

"So it was all you were hoping it would be."

"Pretty well." Leo turned from dangling teabags in mugfuls of water to drop them in the pedal bin. "Except somebody went for me one night," he said.

"Leo." Her surge of concern sounded close to accusing. "What did they do to you?"

"Nothing physical. He was the chap I told you Paddy Bloore wrote to. He wanted to blame me and the rest of our class as well. I did my best to convince him he was wrong."

"You being there should have." Less fiercely Ellen said "Speaking of councillors, I was telling Louise Davies you were visiting our twin town, and she'd like you to give a talk."

"I don't know if I've got much more to say than I just did."

"You could tell them all about the town and your reception, and didn't you take any photos they can blow up?" When he yielded to agreeing Ellen said "I haven't heard much yet about your friend."

"There isn't much to tell. You've seen her photo."

Ellen turned down the flames under a pan of potatoes as the bubbling grew violent. "I hope she was livelier than one of those."

"She was, but a bit aloof too. Maybe she felt awkward meeting after all this time."

"What did you do about that?"

"Tried to put her at her ease. We ended up still friends, which is all we've ever been."

"Nothing wrong with friends." However she meant this, Ellen was quick to leave it behind. "Is it time to open a bottle yet?" she said, only to add "Are you making a call?"

"To let Hanna know I'm home, you mean? I suppose I should send her a message."

Ellen made her patience evident before she said "To the police."

"Let me just check what I'm going to tell them."

He was relieved to find the street deserted, though in any case the smell of cannabis had dissipated. He couldn't discern it when he reached the car – even when he opened the boot wide and stooped towards it. "It's gone. No trace," he told Ellen. "They'd only think I was wasting their time. Let's just forget about it, shall we? I've brought nothing bad home," he said and dug the corkscrew deep into a cork.

CHAPTER FIFTEEN

A nita Chattopadhyay sat in front of her desk as Leo took the armchair. "How have you been faring since I saw you?" she said. "I've had some thoughts I think may help."

She widened her eyes as though to pose a question she was too polite to voice, and then she asked it anyway. "Have you been able to return to your work?"

"My parents don't want me to till I'm sorted out."

"You feel you need their permission."

She opened her eyes further as if scrutinising his answer in advance. "It's their firm and besides, I don't want to worry them," Leo said, "especially my mother."

"Then might you find some other work in the meantime? Some job to occupy your mind and take it off your mental state."

Leo hoped she didn't think he'd looked away because he was averse to the suggestion. The intensity of her surveillance had begun to disconcert him, that was all, and he rested his gaze on the diplomas that decorated one wall of the placid blue room. "I've taken over doing the accounts for now," he said. "It lets my mother teach my pupils."

"You must be a good son." Before Leo could decide whether this was praise or an instruction Dr Chattopadhyay said "But you still wish to return to your original job."

He met her eyes, but not for long. He hadn't previously realised how protuberant they were. "That's why I'm here," he said.

"You were saying you had some ideas that might be helpful."

"I'm wondering if things that didn't seem important at the time have built up in my head."

"That can happen. What have you in mind?"

"I was in Germany last month, and maybe that's where it started."

"Do you speak the language?"

"I don't, and suppose I was so ashamed of not being able that it stuck in my brain and got in the way somehow? The last pupil I had, I ended up talking gibberish at her."

"You've remembered feeling ashamed."

"Not consciously, but don't you work on the principle that it's what people aren't aware of that affects them most?"

"That can be the case."

Her reticence made Leo glance at her. Surely her eyes weren't as extruded as the glimpse left him with the impression that they'd grown – were simply open wide. "Are there any other factors you believe you've identified?" she said.

"How they drive on the opposite side of the road from us. And the lady who was driving me, she went at quite a speed."

The doctor's silence drew his gaze. When had he last seen her blink? She must have done so while he wasn't looking at her. "What effect do you feel this may have had?" she said.

"Maybe when I had to teach people the opposite it made me too conscious of everything."

"Rather than doing it instinctively, I'm taking you to mean. Would you have been aware of the process when you started teaching?"

"I suppose I must have been."

"Did that inhibit you significantly?"

"Not that I recall."

"Then we'll need to examine why it would now."

"Maybe there were other things I brought home. One fellow took me for a Nazi and someone else thought I was glad the town had been bombed in the war. Maybe they confused me more than I knew at the time. I know I was confused on the way back."

"What form did that take?"

"I tried to help a boy I thought had lost his parents at the airport. All I did was get him more lost and me as well. It was a bit like the problem I had with my car."

"Did you drive home from the airport?"

"Yes, but I don't see—"

"Did you suffer from the problem then?"

"No, not till I was trying to direct one of our pupils."

"Did that feel related to the other incident?"

"No, but won't that be why I couldn't deal with it, because I didn't know where it was coming from?"

"I'm not sure how that could have been the source of your condition when you were able to drive with no trouble afterwards."

"These things can take their time, can't they? You deal with people who are suffering from stuff they've forgotten from their childhood."

"That's common, certainly. A cause as close to its effect as you're suggesting, not so much."

"It happens sometimes, though, you're saying."

"I'm afraid I'm really not. I'm sorry, but I don't believe we've found the root yet. I think we need to search further."

Worse than Leo's disappointment was the notion that her eyes had swelled in their sockets to watch his response. As he struggled to make himself look he seemed to glimpse them shrinking into place. He dragged his gaze towards her face and saw they were so wide it felt painful. "Excuse me," he blurted, "is there anything the matter with your eyes?"

"Just a touch of exophthalmos. Is it bothering you?"

"Not now I know. Look," he said and immediately wished he hadn't, "I honestly think talking to you today could have solved the problem. Maybe as you said I can still drive when I'm by myself. Maybe that'll be how I get my confidence back."

"You could try."

Leo told himself this was meant to convey encouragement, not skepticism. "I'll go and do that now."

Her eyes widened as if they had yet to reach their limit, and he looked away. "Is there anything else you would like to explore?" she said.

"I feel like we've finished for now." He did his best not to appear hasty in making for the door. "I'll let you know how I get on," he turned to say, then shut the door as swiftly as he could.

The receptionist glanced up from fitting syllables into a crossword. "Successful session?"

"I'm hoping so," Leo said and, more fervently than he'd spoken, did. He hoped he would have no reason to return – would find he could go back to work. However much she might have helped him, he wouldn't mind if he never encountered Anita Chattopadhyay again, even if he could hardly have seen what he'd fancied he glimpsed as he left her office. She must simply have been fingering her eyelids, perhaps because he'd left her feeling self-conscious. She couldn't really have been pushing her distended eyes back in.

CHAPTER SIXTEEN

A s Leo left the building he had to bat away a large black fly. Its shrill buzz sounded like a threat to return. Now he realised he'd heard it throughout his interview with Anita Chattopadhyay, where he'd taken it for some electrical activity outside. He hurried down to Lime Street, only to find his train was cancelled. By the time the next one showed up the platform teemed with commuters, and all the seats on the train were taken before Leo had a chance to board. It hadn't even reached the next station when it faltered to a halt, giving him a view of a back-garden swing as immobile as the carriage for nearly an hour. Long before the train crept forward his feet were aching. Each delay diminished the resolve he'd brought away from the session with Anita Chattopadhyay, and as he tramped through Settlesham the last of his determination to drive abandoned him.

Only the alarm was home to greet him. Ellen was away on a computer course in Manchester. He indulged in fish and chips from Cod Bless You up the road and then attempted to read *L'Étranger* before 1943 brought him *The Ministry of Fear*. The prose felt too remote for him to reach, a quality that seemed to have infected everything he tried to watch on television. In bed he lay awake trying to recapture the process by which he had rebuilt his confidence. "Feeling I ought to be speaking their language, maybe that stayed with me," he murmured and raised his voice, since there was nobody it would disturb. "How they spoke mine, maybe that did too. The Nazi and the fellow Bloore wrote to, they must have confused me. The boy at the airport did, and his parents made it worse. All that got to me, and no wonder."

He repeated the procedure whenever he awoke, until it resembled an elaborate mantra. It and the effect he was hoping it would have took him out of bed once the dawn below the horizon brought a pale hint of light to a low patch of sky. He roused himself further with a shower, still rehearsing his formula aloud, and then he went out to the car.

Beyond the Old Town and Settlesham Fields the lowest stretch of horizon was tinted a watery green. The street was deserted, and the only sound was the lowing of a milk float on its frequently interrupted travels through the suburb. The Fiesta dealt the road a momentary splash of its lights while emitting an avian peep. He mustn't let the dual controls suggest he'd climbed into the wrong side of the car. "No more confusion," he muttered. "Won't be confused."

As he twisted the ignition key he willed the car to start first time, not to offer him an excuse to quit. The engine came to life at once, and a sweep of the wipers cleared the windscreen of a tinge of mist. In films activating the wipers by mistake often signified a driver's inexperience, but Leo needn't feel this had happened to him. He turned on the headlights and peered at the mirror, an action that brought Lucy Fenton to mind. "Forget her," he said fiercely. "Just concentrate."

He indicated his intention to pull out even though the road was still devoid of traffic. The gesture left him feeling watched if not judged, acutely self-conscious at the wheel, painfully awkward in a way he hadn't suffered since he'd struggled to learn to drive. "Nobody's watching," he said and glared at the strip of his face in the mirror. "There's nobody to mess up your driving but you, and you wouldn't dare."

He depressed the clutch and snagged first gear and eased the accelerator pedal down as he released the clutch. The car began to crawl after the headlight beams it extended across the tarmac. Why was its progress so sluggish? Because he hadn't freed the handbrake. "That's all you're getting wrong," he did his best to vow. He shoved the lever supine and made himself accelerate as he engaged second gear.

Third took him to the end of Moss Row, and fourth along the next street. He was having to restrain himself to the speed limit by the time he finished exploring routes through the somnolent suburb. He'd been so preoccupied with reacquainting himself with the layout that he'd hardly noticed the return of his instinctive confidence. He drove out of Settlesham as fast as the limit permitted and picked up speed as he reached the luminously bedewed countryside. Now that he'd recovered his skills he was eager to celebrate.

He sped onto the motorway and raced the sun for half an hour before detouring onto a service area, where the Positively Piled Platter breakfast at a Frugiyum diner made a not entirely feeble bid to live up to its name. In the Gents he hosed away remnants of his predecessor's visit to the toilet before taking the considerable time required to determine the magical passes that would activate a hand dryer. He was about to start a second elated journey when he realised he ought to relieve his parents of the jobs they'd had to take over from him. He joined the morning trek on the far side of the motorway and drove back to Settlesham.

He was nearly at a bridge across the river when he saw a sign outside a house almost hidden by scaffolding: ANOTHER FENTON FIX. Workmen were posing on the structure like a diagram of snakes and ladders. He'd just passed the house when he heard a shout. "You. Stop there."

He thought Fenton was preparing to tell off an employee until the mirrors showed the builder marching towards the car. His eyes were redder than ever, and it wasn't only plaster dust that paled his face. He slammed a hand on the car roof and thrust his face at Leo's window. "Think you can dodge me? Don't try while you're living in our town."

"I didn't realise you were calling me. I do have a name."

"You've got one of them round here, I can tell you." The sight of the car stoked Fenton's rage. "All right driving now, are you?" he said like a wish for the opposite.

"You thought I should get help, and I did. We've sorted out my problem." A hope that he'd placated Fenton let Leo add "How's Lucy getting on?"

"Freddy Latimer got her through her test. Should have gone with him in the first place. Lucky thing for your lot we only made you give the money back. The wife was after compensation on top."

"Sorry, what for if you say Lucy passed?"

"For screwing up her head. Christ, don't you even know what you're doing?"

"I do remember. Of course I do. Please pass on my apologies, or I can. I still have her number."

"She doesn't want to hear from you. Try it and I'll lay you flat. Get her off your phone."

"I won't trouble her any more. You have my word." In a final bid to pacify Fenton Leo said "I'm sure she'll shine at university."

"Keep your word to yourself. We know what they did to her. Her trouble's worse because of you. She doesn't like driving much either." Fenton's rage was only growing. "Your firm had better do a better job than you," he said, "or we'll be seeing everybody knows."

"Look, I understand you're angry, you've every right to be and I wish I could make amends, but don't take it out on my parents. Now I think we've both said enough."

He was easing the car forward when Fenton thumped the roof so hard Leo could have fancied he felt it buckle overhead. "Get our Lucy off your phone," Fenton shouted. "I want to see."

Leo took the phone out to find a silenced message. *Your souvenirs are coming to you,* Hanna had informed him. *We are sorry that the book is not. It was for children anyway, just fairy tales.* He was reading the last words when Fenton came close to butting the window, having greyed a patch with his breath. "What are you hanging round for?" he demanded and saw the screen. "What's that? Is it from her?"

"Just a friend." Leo dismissed the message and brought up Lucy's number to delete from his contacts while her father watched. "Now you'll excuse me," Leo told him. "You said you don't want me hanging around."

The mirrors showed him Fenton's anger dwindling, unless only the reflections shrank. He should reply to Hanna – he'd left her daily messages unanswered for some days – but he was already later than he'd meant to reach his parents. He was relieved to see the pair of Pass With Parker cars outside their house, so long as this didn't imply they were losing customers. He'd made the pair into a trio when his mother flung the front door open. "Leo," she cried. "Have you driven?"

He couldn't tell whether she intended to express hope or joy or something else. "I'm back on the road," he said.

She turned away before he had a chance to read her face. "Leo's here. He drove."

His father emerged from the front room, swiftly by his standards. "So you just needed somebody to analyse your problem. I told you it was going to be fine, Bev."

"I didn't like to think of Leo needing that kind of treatment, that's all. If it worked, though, that's what counts."

"I pretty well treated myself," Leo felt he ought to reassure her. "It was mostly about thinking my way back to where the problem came from."

"Do you want to talk about it?"

"I did all I needed to."

"Don't if you'd rather we didn't know. So long as it wasn't our fault somehow."

"Of course it wasn't. Nothing to do with either of you at all."

"Just remember you can always talk to us about your troubles," his father said, "and we'll do everything we can to help."

"Another time, not that we're hoping there'll ever be one, perhaps you'll feel you can just talk to us. And Ellen, obviously."

"I'll remember. Aren't I invited in?"

"What a question, Leo. You never need to be." Less passionately his mother said "We're nearly off to start the lessons."

"Who are you teaching?"

"I've got Stanley Handley for my sins," Leo's father said, "and your mother's starting Tamara Bickerstaffe off."

"Tamara was going to be one of mine. I'll take her."

His parents glanced at each other, and his father broke the silence, though not instantly. "Then go ahead, old chap, and the very best of luck."

"That's it, you prove Ronnie Fenton wrong if you're confident you can."

"I am, and I won't be letting anybody change it." In case his mother took this as a gibe at her Leo said "I was taught by worse than me, and I passed."

"Are you talking about David Dent? It's the first we've heard you had any problem."

"It's a good job he retired. Denting people's confidence, that should have been his slogan. I'd never teach the way he did, and I'm sure you never have."

"We thought we'd only make you awkward if we tried to teach you."

"Maybe you would have." Leo wondered if he'd just worked through the confrontation Anita Chattopadhyay had suggested might be beneficial. "It showed me how not to do the job," he said. "Remind me of Tamara's address."

"Let him give it a shot," his father said as Leo's mother made to speak.

"I was only going to say I'm sure you won't do anything you think could let us down."

"You know I never would." Leo read the address his father sent to his phone and headed for his car. He was climbing in when his mother called "Make us proud again."

This left him feeling like a child encouraged to do well in a test, an impression he strove to outdistance as he drove to Settlesham Fields and parked outside the Bickerstaffe house. While he waited in the instructor's seat he sent Ellen a message – *Back behind the wheel* – and copied it to Hanna. It took him a minute to realise he ought to explain, but Tamara had come out of the house. He would have to clarify the message later. After all, how could Hanna know his job had turned into a nightmare once he'd returned home?

CHAPTER SEVENTEEN

s Tamara parked the car, having cured the indicator of its twitch, her mother hurried down the token path. "How did it go?" she was anxious to hear.

"Really very well for a first lesson. I'm looking forward to our next drive."

The woman laid a heavy gaze on Leo. "I was talking to my daughter."

"Like Leo says, mummy, it was fine."

"Well, if you both say so." Her mother's gaze relented, abandoning blankness. "Only I saw Mrs Vincent just before," she said. "She was saying his firm's been having problems."

"That was me." In case this sounded too much like a claim Leo said "I was the problem."

"At least you're honest. What sort of one?"

"Some things that happened to me had shaken up my nerves, and I'm afraid I passed it on to someone I was teaching."

"Lucy Fenton." When he acknowledged this, though mutely, Mrs Bickerstaffe said "You're telling everyone you're better."

"I'm saying so. Maybe Tamara can."

"You wouldn't know he'd been ill, mummy. I'll be telling people there's nothing wrong with you, Leo." As Tamara left the car she said "Have a good talk tonight as well."

She meant his lecture about Alphafen. He moved to the driver's seat and sent his parents a message. *Tamara very happy with her lesson. Any more for me?* In a minute, presumably because his father was between jobs, he had an answer. *Nothing else today but we'll fix you up for tomorrow.* Leo drove out of sight of the Bickerstaffe house so as not to appear to be loitering, and parked while he sent Ellen a message. *First day back on the job went well. Sorry you can't be here tonight to hear what I have to say about Alphafen.* The phone completed many of the words for him, and some he didn't even need to start to type. The only one it required him to spell out in full, as if it didn't believe such a place could exist, was Alphafen. He saw no reason not to send Hanna the message as well. If she needed any explanation, no doubt she would ask.

The responses interrupted his drive home. *I am sorry also, but our thoughts will be there. You will bring to your town what you can of ours.* Ellen's followed in a few minutes. *Just as sorry,* she assured him, which for a disoriented moment he imagined referring to Hanna's declaration. *Give them all you've got and break a leg.* He spent the rest of the day rehearsing his talk: how the reconstruction of Alphafen suggested a perfected version of itself, how the Alps added to the idyll, how the townsfolk had welcomed him and made it clear they didn't bear a grudge (no need to mention Dietrich).... Perhaps he shouldn't labour too hard over his language, in case it seized up when he came to speak. Surely he had no reason to fear that, and he did his best to force the notion out of his mind.

He drove to the town hall half an hour before he was due to speak. The wide high marble lobby announced him with a chorus of his footsteps, and so did a printout on a pole beside the broad stone stairs: LEO PARKER TALK ABOUT TWIN TOWN. He could have taken it for an exhortation. Its stubby printed arrow directed him into a room where hundreds of canvas chairs faced a stage on which a podium brandished a microphone at a glass screen on the back wall. The mayor and mayoress, informally disrobed for the occasion, greeted him at the door once its arthritic metal elbow gave way for him. "Get yourself some punch," the mayor urged, having delivered a plump engulfing handshake. "The lady's best concoctions."

A horde of plastic cups separated twin groups of glass bowls on an elongated trestle table, and Leo ladled punch out of a bowl tagged alcoholic. "Let's make sure you're matched up," the mayoress said and roused the screen with a remote control so that he could link his phone to the monitor. He found the Alphafen album the phone had assembled and brought up the first image, a shot of him with the Webers at the table in the beerhall, surrounded by townsfolk flourishing steins. "That looks like a good start," the mayoress said.

It stayed on the screen while the audience gathered. Leo's parents were among the earliest arrivals, and raised their cups of punch to him as if they were imitating the crowd in the beerhall. He needn't think that, and surely the sight of Parker pupils sending him the gesture could only be encouraging. "Top yourself up whenever you need to," the mayoress told him.

"I just need enough to loosen my tongue for now."

"Fair point. You don't want it too loose while you're giving us your talk."

"It won't have to be. Have not, I mean. It won't. Won't be."

Her gaze made each clump of words feel more cumbersome, which drove Leo to take a gulp of her punch. He refilled the cup from a teetotal bowl, where the fruit that blundered onto the ladle put him in mind of an enforced Halloween game. When the mayor approached him to suggest starting, Leo detoured to the Gents. At first he thought he wasn't alone in the windowless white-tiled space, but the shrill insistent trickle in a cubicle came from a cistern. Once he managed to relax enough to water a urinal he came close to scalding his hands with the only tap that deigned to work, and then spent time coaxing a succession of brief enfeebled tepid murmurs from the hand dryer. As he returned to the lecture room the mass of conversations sounded blurred beyond any recognisable language. The mayor raised a thumb to him and jogged ponderously up the steps onto the stage. "Ladies and gentlemen, please put your hands together for Mr Leo Parker."

Leo could have fancied the audience was being asked to pray for him until the mayor mimed applause and then produced some as clapping spread through the room. The acclaim subsided as Leo reached the stage, where the mayor was waiting by the podium. The ledge at the top was just wide enough to support Leo's cup. He risked letting go as the mayor said "I don't believe I need to say much about our Mr Parker."

Leo's gaze strayed over the audience, meeting unreadable blankness. Just his parents were projecting encouragement from the front row like a mother and father willing their child to succeed in a school production if not convinced he was the star. He resorted to fixing his gaze on the mayor as the introduction continued, often pausing to invite laughter or some other evidence of appreciation. "Mr Parker has been doing my job for me.... In fact he's been representing each and every one of us.... He visited the town we're twinned with in the cause of international friendship. That's just as important now as it was when we made up with them.... Anyway, you don't need me to tell you about it when he can from his own experience. Let's hear from Mr Parker," he said and flattened a hand towards Leo as though the proposal or its performer might be less than clear. "Mr Parker."

Leo watched the mayor head for the steps and descend them in a succession of jerks like jumps in an incomplete piece of film. Surely politeness required him to postpone his talk until the mayor was seated, and then he could speak. He wished the applause had been delayed so that it could fill the silence, which seemed to amplify the mayor's footsteps and a haphazard chorus of coughs suggesting a variety of comments. He avoided looking at his parents and tried not to wonder if they might be thinking how language had failed him after he'd returned from Alphafen. He wasn't being asked to perform much of a task; he just had to open his mouth and speak, to take a good breath and move his tongue and shape the words. He licked his lips to shift them as the mayor joined his wife on the front row, only to fear he appeared to have poked out a sly tongue at them. He lingered over standing his phone on the thin shelf that formed the lower edge of the podium, an interlude that felt like an obstacle he'd placed in the path of his bid to speak. He could only poke the phone to revive the first photograph from Alphafen. There he was with the Webers on the monitor, and the sight prompted him to face the audience. "That's how welcome they made me," he said and took a sip of punch to help him raise his voice. "Not just me but like the mayor says, everybody I was representing, and I'd like to think that's everyone in Settlesham...."

Did he hear a mutter of dissent? He couldn't locate the objector, even when the mayoral couple turned their heads to search. "You wouldn't know their town had ever been bombed any more than anyone would think ours had," he said and brought up the first of the shots he'd taken on a daytime stroll through Alphafen. He dallied over the image to point out architectural features, and was about to finger the next streetscape when a woman on the second row said "What's that?"

She was pointing past him. Why should this make him nervous? He turned to see exactly what he expected, a photograph of a typical Alphafen house with flowers overflowing down its frontage. "That's how they decorate their houses," he said.

"Not the flowers, the insect. Can you say what it is?"

It took Leo some time to locate a large white butterfly among the mass of flowers spilling over a balcony. What he'd taken for a pair of petals was a set of wings. "A butterfly," he felt superfluous for saying.

"You wouldn't have a name for it. Entomology interests me but I don't recognise the species."

"Maybe you only find it over there."

"I know their varieties quite well, and I wouldn't have said that was one."

"I nearly brought one home. You could have had a proper look," Leo said and sent the next photograph to the monitor. He was about to comment on the painted designs that bloomed around the windows of a house when the woman said "Even that's no help."

He stretched his arms wide to display incomprehension, or did he simply appear helpless? He didn't mean to prompt scattered laughter. "Now you're looking like it," a man called from the back of the room.

Leo swung around to see a gigantic butterfly at his back. The tips of its wings almost touched the sides of the street it was hovering in. Perspective was producing the illusion, of course, but how could he have failed to notice the intruder? It was on his phone as well. "I didn't even know I'd taken that," he said.

"Sounds like you should have been more careful."

The objection came from somewhere in the middle of the audience, but Leo hadn't time to identify the man. He put up the next photograph, which was greeted with a murmur that passed some way beyond appreciation. "There's another one," a woman informed anyone who, like Leo, hadn't noticed. The camera had indeed caught a butterfly in the act of fluttering along a street in Alphafen. "There it is again," the woman announced as soon as Leo changed the photograph. The show seemed to be turning into a game, members of the audience competing to be first to spot the winged visitor – not the same one every time, of course, however similar they looked. Was there even a distant butterfly in Leo's shot of Alphafen from the Kehlsteinhaus terrace? He thought it best to describe the vantage simply as an Alpine restaurant. His return to Alphafen ended a series of mountainscapes, and he was about to sum up his visit when the amateur entomologist protested "What on earth is that supposed to be?"

She and the rest of the audience were staring past him with expressions ranging from bemused amusement to dislike if no worse. As he leaned over to peer at the phone screen he had to grab the plastic cup, which his lurch had dislodged, spilling a trickle down the podium. What was wrong with the image of another flowery house? What was crouched among the blossoms on a balcony? Stooping closer let him see it was a cat, which nobody had any reason to find strange, even if he couldn't recall seeing any cats in Alphafen. It looked odd only because flowers were obscuring its face, and he turned to see how the screen made it look. Those weren't petals after all; a butterfly with pallid wings spread wide appeared to have perched on the cat's face, masking its features, as if the camera had caught it in an act of transformation. "Are you sure you haven't been shopping?" the woman said.

Leo was irrationally reminded of the book he'd failed to buy in Alphafen. "Shopping for what?" he swung around to demand.

"Not that kind. Photoshopping your photographs."

"I haven't touched them. They're what was there even if I didn't see it at the time. Why would I want to change that?"

"Maybe you don't want us seeing what it's really like."

This came from the man who'd counselled carefulness. The mayor glanced around at him and brought his hands together in a pudgy clap that might have been inviting more applause. "Have we finished with your photographs, Leo?"

Leo was grateful for the excuse. "I think so."

"You won't mind taking questions, will you?" As Leo shut off the photograph of the cat and glanced back to reassure himself the monitor had gone blank, the mayor said "Who has one for our diplomat?"

"Why don't you tell us about the restaurant you went to."

This sounded oddly flat, less a question than an observation. It came from the man who'd already spoken twice. "You saw it was a beerhall," Leo said. "I expect they wanted somewhere people go to celebrate so I'd feel welcome."

"Not there, and I reckon you know it."

The mayoral couple frowned at the remark. "I'm afraid I don't," Leo said.

"The place they built for Hitler. That shot you took from it of the town you're so fond of, that's what he liked to see. Some of us read up on it even if you didn't want us knowing."

"Councillor Bloore," the mayor said, "do we really have to rake that sort of thing up?"

At last Leo recognised his adversary, if only just. Dieting or exercise or both had reduced the obese schoolboy to an adult sketch of himself. "We've got a right to be told why he went there," Bloore said, "as long as he's saying he did it for us."

"I wouldn't say that was why I was there. As you said, it's a restaurant now, a tourist attraction."

"Some of us could wonder what kind of tourist wants to go where Hitler liked to be."

"Councillor Bloore," the mayor said, "is there a point to this?"

"Some of us can do without your Mr Parker making out he went because of us. We're glad we got out of Europe and took our country back. Never should have cosied up to them in the first place. Don't let them kid you they've got any love for us."

"Well," Leo said and saw insufficient reason not to add "You haven't changed much."

Bloore clamped his hands on his knees and hunched forward as if he was preparing to rush the stage. "What are you trying to make out about me?"

"You can't have forgotten the letter you sent when we were at school."

"I won't be forgetting. It's your sort that does and tries to make the rest of us as well."

"Then you should be pleased to hear they haven't forgotten you in Alphafen."

"They better hadn't. Who's been saying what?"

"Dietrich Gebhardt. He remembers you quite well."

"Never heard of him."

"You have, you know. He was the boy you sent your declaration of war to."

"I said we weren't going to forget what they'd done to our town."

"As I recall you said more than that." When Bloore's face stayed doggedly defiant Leo said "So that's why he thought we all agreed with you. I don't believe any of us did, but he collared me in the street because of you."

"You're telling us he roughed you up."

"He might have if I hadn't managed to convince him you were nothing to do with me."

"I've got more to do with you than any foreigner, and we all just heard you prove it."

"I think you're by yourself on that. Go on then, tell everybody how."

"You just told us one of the lot that's supposed to love us so much nearly knocked you about in the street."

"Well, that's an original take." Bloore's unforthcoming stare provoked Leo to add "It's as blinkered as I'm afraid you are."

"Sounds like he gave you some of his hate. Thought you weren't meant to bring back any bad stuff."

As Leo took a breath before retorting the mayor said "Thank you both for a stimulating discussion. Does anyone else have a question?" Several hands waved or groped as though to find an answer in the air. The questions felt like compensation for confronting Bloore, and Leo dealt with them readily enough. The mayor thanked him for an informative presentation and invited him to reward himself with punch, but Leo was anxious to examine how he could have overlooked so many details in his photographs. "You did well," his father said as Leo left the stage, and his mother didn't lower her voice to declare "Better than somebody deserved." Leo murmured without making his agreement too explicit and retreated to his car, where a streetlamp provided the seat beside his with an insubstantial luminous antimacassar. He took out his phone and opened the Alphafen album. At least, he tried while the streetlamp seemed to probe his vision with an increasingly fierce glare as he searched, but his efforts were useless. Somehow the phone had erased every photograph he'd taken during his visit to Alphafen.

CHAPTER EIGHTEEN

Bid for Peace Leads to Town Hall Conflict

On Tuesday evening a packed town hall enjoyed a talk on Settlesham's twin town. Leo Parker of the Pass With Parker firm illustrated his lecture about Alphafen with photographs of the town and the Alps, including local fauna. His visit was the outcome of a lifelong correspondence with a German friend. Their relationship began under the Pals For Alps scheme organised by Mr Basil Turvey at Settlesham Grammar as a means of furthering international relations and repairing breaches caused by the last war.

After the talk Councillor Patrick Bloore spoke from the floor. Best known as a persistent campaigner against unity with Europe, Councillor Bloore frequently raises arguments and objections in council. He criticised Mr Parker's mission to Alphafen as unnecessary and warned against trusting Europeans, while Mr Parker felt his visit had helped maintain international friendship. Mayor Bill Dainty thanked Mr Parker for an instructive lecture and for strengthening the bond with Alphafen.

It was clear that the reporter liked neither Bloore nor his behaviour. The report had appeared not just in the *Settlesham Sentinel* but on its website and Facebook and Twitter. Leo only wished his German photographs were somewhere online. He'd told Hanna of their disappearance but hadn't bothered mentioning it to Ellen. Presumably Hanna had memories in mind when she responded that he'd brought more than photographs home with him.

At least he was back at his job. This afternoon he'd worked on coaxing competence out of Lionel Bartlett, a pensioner who'd decided it was time he learned to drive. Leo's mother had found him so difficult she had turned him over to her son. He delivered orations while driving, by no means always on the task at hand. He made it plain that sitting for the entire hour of a lesson was a burden, and today he'd sped undirected out of Settlesham Fields into the open countryside to seek relief behind the nearest roadside hedge. "Would that one could contain one's age," he'd commented while laboriously reinserting himself into the car.

The furtive lengthy release had left him more loquacious still. He provided a commentary, mostly anticipating where he planned to chauffeur his wife, all the way back to their cottage in the Old Town. "Give my good wishes to the mater," he said as he clambered out of the car, gripping the edge of the doorframe so hard the action diagrammed the way his knuckles worked, "and my commiserations for having to put up with the old reprobate," which had to mean him, not Leo's father. Leo resumed the driver's seat and was about to move off when his phone proclaimed an unknown caller. He was hoping for an extra pupil as he said "Hello?"

"Laurie calling for Anita."

Leo tried not to feel disappointed, let alone annoyed. "Wrong number, I'm afraid."

"I'm seeing the right one on my screen."

"Take another look. There's no Anita here."

"That's right, she's here. Sorry, though, she isn't."

Leo had begun to suspect a prank. "Could you make your mind up, do you think?"

"She's at home just now. That's why she's asked me to call round."

Was this some form of scam? "Call round where?" Leo challenged him.

"To you. To everybody on her list."

"List of what?"

"Her clients. This is her secretary, Mr Parker."

The use of Leo's name seemed to render the voice more familiar. "Anita who?" he wanted to confirm.

"Doctor Anita Chattopadhyay. I'm afraid she may have to cancel her appointments for a while."

"I'm sorry to hear that. What's the trouble?"

"An issue with her eyes. She's had it in a small way but it's turned much worse."

Leo was ambushed by the glimpses that had disturbed him during their last session. "Please tell her I hope she's better very soon," he said.

"I'll give you a call as soon as she's seeing people again."

Leo wasn't sure he wanted to see her. After all, their last meeting appeared to have cured him. He thanked Laurie and was laying the phone on the dashboard when it detained him with a clank, alerting him to a message from his father. Was it offering him another pupil? No, it said *Someone here for you at the house.*

Who could make him so untypically coy? Leo could only think of Hanna, but why would she have come unannounced to Settlesham, and how should that make him feel? He found no answer to either question on his way to the house. The slam of the car door brought his mother to the front-room window and then the hall. "We've been having a good chat with your friend," she said. "You can tell when somebody's a lecturer."

This left Leo feeling less informed than ever, and he had to restrain himself from sidling if not pushing past her. As he followed her into the house she said "Here he is for you, Jerome."

The visitor was lounging on the white leather sofa, staining it with a faint surreptitious shadow. His long face boasted a smile Leo found insufferably smug. His eyebrows remained as straight and terse as his moustache, and his wide nostrils flared to greet Leo, much as they had at the Kehlsteinhaus. "Jerome has been telling us how you met," Leo's father said.

Leo succeeded in swallowing enough of his shock to ask "What has he been saying?"

"Just how you'd gone up the mountain for the best view," his mother said.

At least they seemed not to have connected this with Bloore's diatribe at the town hall, and Leo turned on Pugh. "What are you doing here?" he said, withholding a good deal of fierceness.

"I'm lecturing in Liverpool and thought you would be worth the detour."

"Why?"

"To finish the talk we were having. I don't care to be silenced."

This sounded like a threat, not least of letting Leo's parents hear, which Leo hoped to head off by saying "I'd like to know how you found me at all."

"You told me whereabouts you lived, if you remember. I was reading up on your town when I came across the report of your talk that told me who you work for. I hadn't realised you were a fellow lecturer as well."

"That's because I don't claim to be one."

"What subject do you teach, Jerome?" Leo's mother said.

"History to anyone who'll listen, but not the kind that's presently in fashion."

"I'm sure that must be very interesting."

"It's a pleasure to meet people who still want to keep their minds open. We have a duty to ensure we're not bred out, would you not agree?"

"I should think so."

"I take it you share your son's attitudes."

"Pretty much," Leo's father said.

"For clarity, which would those be?"

As Leo made to interrupt if not to terminate the interrogation, his mother said "We don't want any more wars. We want peace wherever it's possible."

"Indeed so, and we should embrace everything that's best from elsewhere."

Leo was nervously aware what Pugh might have in mind. In a bid to keep it unspoken he said "If everyone will excuse me, I have to be off to a lesson."

"We didn't know you had another yet," his mother said. "Who's your pupil?"

Leo tried and failed to invent a name. "I'll tell you later."

"Will you come back to us afterwards?"

He imagined her keeping Pugh in the house until he returned –

imagined what Pugh might say in Leo's absence. "I'm not sure yet," he had to say. "I'll take Mr Pugh with me."

"Surely he'll be in the way," Leo's father objected.

"And won't he have his own car anyway?" Leo's mother said.

As Leo realised desperation had prevented him from grasping this, Pugh said "I walked from your station. I like to get a sense of anywhere I visit. I think your town has kept its purity. As far as I could see its Englishness hasn't yet been spoiled."

Leo felt he should have headed most of this off. "I'll run you to the station," he said.

"It's a pity you have to leave us so soon, Jerome," Leo's father said. "We enjoyed our talk."

"Perhaps we'll be seeing you again now you know where we all are."

"I would hope Leo will keep you informed."

Leo stalked as far as the hall to encourage Pugh to follow, but Leo's mother said "Do you mind if I make just one comment, Jerome?"

"That's a lady's privilege."

"I hope you won't feel insulted." With a prefatory apologetic laugh she said "Don't you think that moustache makes you look a tiny bit like someone we're all glad to be rid of?"

Pugh gazed at her until Leo had to remind himself to breathe. He was opening his mouth when Pugh said "I'm not insulted, no."

"I need to be moving," Leo said. "We can talk in the car."

"Perhaps I may just leave your parents with a thought."

"We're listening, Jerome," Leo's father said.

"Whatever your beliefs, you've raised your son well."

Leo saw his parents fail to grasp the basis of the praise, and hoped they wouldn't ponder it too much. He didn't speak until Pugh was in the car and fettered with the safety belt. As Leo's parents at the gate dwindled in the mirror he demanded "What do you actually want?"

"I thought you might still be interested in the conversation we weren't allowed to finish."

"You sound as if you're surprised you weren't. They didn't like you talking that way about Hitler, and they aren't the only ones."

"Have you tried to enlighten your parents?"

"They're as enlightened as I am. I don't know where you got the wrong idea about me, but you need to realise I don't share yours."

"You seemed receptive enough at the eagle's nest."

"That's because I didn't understand what you were going on about."

"I see." Pugh turned his head to weigh his gaze on Leo. "Perhaps you were prevented," he said.

"You were right before. My parents brought me up well, and I'm glad they kept me clear of your sort of thinking."

"They aren't who I had in mind."

Leo nearly didn't ask, not least because he felt he knew the answer. "Who, then?"

"Your friend from Alphafen."

"I already said why he had you shut up. He didn't want them thinking anyone with him agreed with the stuff you were saying."

"What do you imagine that was?"

"Defending the character you think was such a blessing to humanity, as if you needed to be told."

"But I'd finished discussing the leader. That isn't what your friend was so anxious for you not to hear."

"I think it was, you know." Leo could only wonder how Pugh planned to convince him otherwise. "What are you saying you'd started to say?" he barely bothered asking.

"I'd just begun to tell you what the leader believed."

"That sounds as if you hadn't given up the subject at all."

"Your friend knew what I was setting out to tell you."

Leo wished they weren't still minutes from the station, where the dogged dialogue could be brought to an end. "How on earth can you know that?"

"Perhaps you remember what I'd just said that made him call the waiter."

Leo tried, but not too hard and not for long. "I really can't while I'm driving. Do remind me."

"I would have asked what Alps mean to you."

This felt like very little of an answer. "Somewhere to visit," Leo said. "Very beautiful, and I'm glad I went, but that's all."

"Not the place." Pugh added a noise like a search for a laugh. "Its creatures," he said.

"The people, are you saying?" When this earned a dismissive headshake so vigorous Leo saw it without looking he said "The wildlife."

"Wilder than you could dream of." Pugh found his laugh, which proved to contain meagre mirth. "Or perhaps that's exactly what you can do."

"I've no idea what you're talking about. We're nearly at the station, so if you've anything to say worth hearing, better make it clear."

"Perhaps the mountains were named after them, out of fear of them. You might notice how alp resembles elf."

"I shouldn't think even you believe in those."

"The leader did." Quite as haughtily Pugh said "He believed they could have been his secret weapon."

"And how was that supposed to work?"

"He would have sent them to confound the enemy. An agent posing as a defector would have carried the infection. Once the enemy was infiltrated the sendings would have started to invade their minds."

"They'd have had elves on the brain, you're saying."

"Perhaps you will find reason not to scoff, Mr Parker."

"If that's meant to be a threat, don't bother. I'm not impressed."

"I would not wish it on you, but someone may have."

"That's an accusation, is it?" Leo halted the car while a line of children sheathed in yellow trooped after a teacher across the road. He hardly heard himself demand "Who's the guilty party going to be?"

"I should not blame anyone for seeking to defend themselves and those who are dear to them."

A second teacher finished the procession, and Leo sent the car forward. "Defend them from what?" he made himself ask.

"It's said that anybody born where the alps make their lair can never leave. Legend has it the first settlers were drawn there so that the creatures could feed on their fears."

None too soon Leo saw the pointer for the station. "Do you honestly believe any of that?" he said.

"I have good reason to."

Pugh's voice had sunk as if he wanted only Leo to hear, but Leo might have preferred it to have grown inaudible. Anger at his own reaction provoked him to retort "What kind of reason's that?"

"I visited Alphafen after we met in the eyrie. I should have liked to see what inspired the leader, but I wasn't ready to encounter anything. I'd thought they came only in the dark. I have to think the sacrifice gave them more power."

Leo could see the station at the far end of the road. He was nearly free of Pugh, which let him say "Which sacrifice?"

"The raid Churchill meant to undermine the leader's confidence. The creatures must have taken all those deaths for nourishment. That's how the old powers are said to work."

Leo didn't speak until he pulled up outside the station entrance, above which a matrix sign listed arrivals. "Your train's due," he was glad to confirm.

"We have a minute. Let me answer your previous question."

"I've heard all I want to, thanks."

"It will do you no harm." Too close to a contradiction Pugh added "Being as prepared as can be possible."

"Isn't that your train now?" When this failed to shift him Leo said "I'm afraid I don't think there's anything I need to be ready for."

"I thought so too until I had the encounter. I'm sure you must acknowledge my mind is all my own, but not that afternoon. I saw the creature fly at me in one of the shapes they adopt, and then I was its puppet for as long as it amused it. It might as well have been for all eternity. Losing control of my mind is my only fear."

Leo thought Pugh had. He watched the man haul himself out of the car and sprint into the station as the train coasted alongside the platform.

Pugh's dash through the short passage that contained the ticket office and its watchful occupant roused a sparrow or its like beneath the roof. Was the bird uncommonly small? Perhaps it was young, although adept at flying; it could scarcely be shrunken by age. Leo lingered to establish that the train took Pugh away, and saw the bird again as Pugh made his way through a carriage. The creature could hardly be fluttering after him along the aisle; it must be reflected in the window. As the train crept away Leo saw Pugh march past a succession of windows enclosed by the station entrance like images on film drawn through a projector. Was it just the framing that suggested the resemblance? Before the train carried Pugh out of sight Leo could have thought he was advancing like a figure in an imperfectly projected silent film, marching jerkily and stiff-limbed as a marionette, a helpless parody of himself.

CHAPTER NINETEEN

Leo didn't feel he needed to tell Ellen about Pugh, and by the morning he'd decided against asking Hanna about the Alpine legend. He hardly even knew why he wanted to investigate. Perhaps learning about the tradition would help him put Pugh's delusions in perspective, although surely they were already there and remote from Leo too. Still, he had an hour to play with before collecting his first pupil, and he set about consulting his phone once Ellen left for work.

What should he search for? *Alp tradition* fetched references to a Tyrolean folk museum and a style of jacket and a technique for milking cattle. *Alp stories* produced a list that included accounts of an adult learning project and a Japanese cartoon series and reminiscences by mountaineers. There were fairy tales as well, but none like the tales Pugh had cited. Didn't this prove he was even more deluded than Leo believed? Just the same, frustration made Leo type *Alp legend* in the search box, which brought him some at once.

German folklore cited the alp as a nightmare creature, and he dabbed the excerpt from the Splendid Superstitions site with a fingertip as if he was trying to squash a small insect. In a moment the paragraph filled the screen. While the alp might be related to the elf, its antics were a good deal more demonic; indeed, some folklorists thought the elfin image had been created to placate it. It was said to fasten on unwary Alpine travellers. It delighted in inflicting nightmares on its victims – alptraum was the German word for nightmare – and its power was reputed to reside in its headgear, a notion Leo found comfortingly absurd. A woodcut showed a diminutive humanoid shape confronting its audience with a malevolent smirk and a savage stare from its perfectly circular eyes beneath the brim of a drooping conical hat, although the lore claimed it could adopt many disguises: insects, birds, animals, mist or fog.... An eyeless head emitting a trio of crescents from its rudimentary mouth stood beside the creature's name. When Leo tapped the icon, an asexual artificial voice prolonged the solitary syllable until it resembled a plea for help. He returned to the list of sites, not that he needed further confirmation that Pugh had convinced himself of nonsense. He wouldn't have touched Daoloth Reveals except for having time to waste.

The site showed him depictions of nightmares, a series of increasingly monstrous grotesques perched on the chest of a sleeper or looming over their victim. He recognised some of the images, not least the famous Fuseli, and was reflecting that none of the creatures sported the supposedly crucial headgear when he found an explanation in a sidebar. *Just as the elf is an idealised version of the alp, so paintings such as these and the very notion of the alp veil its true form.* Perhaps this was illustrated by the flaking mural reproduced beneath the lengthy stack of words. The remnants clinging to a wall appeared to sketch a vaguely manlike shape perched on the chest of a supine woman. The creature had hunched forward to reach for her cranium with the top of its head, elongated into a sinuous cone twice the length of its sloughed-away face. *Even the alp's cap is a euphemism*, the commentary added, *for the appendage with which it may invade the victim.*

Leo's eyes strayed to the next paragraph. In mediaeval times and even recently, sorcerers and their like had allegedly tried to send alps to defeat or otherwise trouble their enemies. Perhaps this had given Hitler ideas, which hardly made them less nonsensical. Leo left the site and was about to end his search when it occurred to him that he had one more quest to try. *Old tales of the alps*, he typed in the box.

The solitary listing took him to the German site of Amazon. The book was unavailable, with no suggestion when or if this would change. Leo activated a translation of the brief descriptive paragraph and read it twice before returning to the image of the cover. It was indeed the volume he'd yielded to the children's father in the Webers' shop, but it was unquestionably a folklorist's account of the alps and their legendary iniquities. The description left Leo in no doubt that the book wasn't meant for children.

Surely Amazon might have matched it with the wrong description. Even if Werner Hausgard was an academic, he could have written a book for younger readers. Leo retreated to the search box and typed the author's name. It revived the Daoloth Reveals site, where Hausgard was credited with relating the alp to another traditional source of nightmares, the incubus. The site suggested a connection, linguistic if not occult, between the incubus and incubation, but Leo was distracted by a sidebar. Werner Hausgard was indeed a noted authority on European folklore. Just one of his books had been translated into English: his seminal analysis of the lore of the alp, now out of print – *Jagen der Alp*.

Leo was staring at the title as if this might alter its significance when the doorbell shrilled and the front door reverberated with a triple thump. He was only just in time to see an inexplicitly uniformed man dash through the gates while typing on a minute monitor. "Parcel for you," he shouted without looking back, and drove off in a grimy whitish van.

The writing on the package propped against the doorsill seemed elusively familiar. Yes, it was Hanna's, which Leo hadn't seen since they'd begun to communicate online. It had grown less gleefully cursive than he recalled. He used the kitchen scissors to slash the tape that bound the parcel, and the contents of the carton bulged forth. It was stuffed with a large squashed jellyfish – with translucent wadding that squeaked beneath his fingernails. More of it filled the tankard he'd bought, which proved to contain the magnet that depicted an Alpine tippler, having made the journey while it hid inside its host. He ought to let Hanna know the souvenirs had arrived – and then he saw they were his excuse to speak to her. Just now he felt the need.

At first her number offered him a distant silence, and then the phone informed him the call couldn't be connected. It made him feel abandoned if not tricked. Could she have blocked his number? He hadn't seen a word from her for days. Why would she cut him off? There ought to be another way to contact her, and he searched online for the Webers' shop. While it had no website, he found a listing for the number.

He'd begun to think he'd mistaken the hour in Alphafen when Emil answered. "Morgen."

Mightn't he have wished the caller a good one? "Morning," Leo said like a translation.

"You are English."

"That's me."

"You are here in Alphafen."

"I was."

"But you have gone elsewhere."

Leo quelled the notion that he'd heard a hint of urgency. "You saw me go, Emil."

"Leo. Leo Parker." The expansion was audibly directed at someone in the shop. "Leo," Emil said as if to fix him or his situation somehow. "Why have you called?"

"I've been trying to reach Hanna. I haven't heard from her in a while."

"You can not."

Leo tried not to feel this confirmed a suspicion. "Why is that?"

"She is below."

"Below what, sorry?"

"In the cellar where we keep more things. Where your phone will not reach." Still surely as an observation rather than a prohibition Emil said "You will not want to speak to her."

"I can speak to you instead."

"If there is something to say."

"First of all, thank you for the parcel. I'll say again it was very kind of you."

"We were glad to send you."

This sounded like an aside to a listener, presumably because Emil was including Gitte in the comment. "I was just wondering about the book I meant to buy from you," Leo said.

"We have not forgotten."

"I gather there isn't much you can do about it."

"It can not be had any more. Helmut and his children have been grateful to you. If you will like we shall find you a better book."

Leo felt entangled in tenses. "I'm still after that one."

"What can it mean to you?"

"It was meant to be a souvenir of staying with you." While this was no longer the whole of the truth, it made Leo add "After all, you're a souvenir shop."

"That is our purpose."

In a moment Leo was troubled by the implications of a memory. "Didn't I see a bookshop in Alphafen?"

"It will not have the book you wish for."

"I wasn't going to ask that. I was just wondering why your friend Helmut came to your shop."

"We hope it will satisfy the customer."

"Yes, but why did he come to you for the book?"

"He said this to you. For his children."

"Why would he look in a souvenir shop? I'd have gone to the bookshop myself."

"We could say you ought to have if you wished a book."

Leo heard Gitte appreciate her husband's wit with a laugh that sounded oddly like their daughter. "You have said he is our friend," Emil seemed to find it important to remind him. "Perhaps you can think he saw the book another time he visited."

"Then why didn't he buy it then?"

"Can you think he goes home to ask the children if they will like the book?" As Leo allowed this was possible – he didn't know their ages or abilities, after all – Emil said "We shall remind Hanna she must send you her messages."

"Give her my best and say I'm thinking of her."

"You may do that."

"And a return visit could be an idea."

"You are not returning here."

This had to be a question, however its abruptness made it sound. "No, I was saying Hanna could come here," Leo said. "She could be your ambassador."

"She does not travel."

"What, she never does?"

"Not as far as you. It makes her ill."

"I'm sorry to hear that. I'm surprised she didn't mention it when we were discussing our trip. Well, if she's still not there," Leo said and waited in vain for any hint of the opposite, "I'd better let you get back to work."

"We shall send a book for you to like."

"Could I ask for the same kind as the one I didn't get?"

"We shall find one. There are many that will tell you of the Alps."

A question struggled in Leo's mouth until he loosed it. "What kind of alp?"

"Why, you will know. Our mountains where you walked."

"You're saying that's all that book was about."

"Yes, but for children. We shall send you one that is for you."

Leo quelled a retort, because he wanted to be alone to think. "Well, thank you in advance," he said. "I'll look forward to seeing what comes."

"So goodbye, Leo."

"Goodbye," Gitte called so enthusiastically she might have been drawing support from a second voice.

Leo was about to echo the farewell when a thought overtook him. "Did you phone your friend Helmut after I chose that book?" he blurted, but only the drone of a terminated connection answered him.

When the home screen reappeared he saw he hadn't time to ponder after all. He was nearly due to pick up his first pupil. However much his conversation with Emil had disturbed him, he mustn't let it affect his work – mustn't let himself grow nervous that it would. His resolve saw him through the first lesson and the one that followed, both successful. Now he would have a chance to reflect until mid-afternoon – at least, he thought he would, but then his phone announced his father. "Can you take a few more pupils for a while?" his father said, sounding wearily bewildered and struggling to overcome it. "Your mother's taking on the rest for now. I'll be sorting myself out, don't anybody worry about that, but some wretched thing has sapped all my confidence."

CHAPTER TWENTY

I *am sorry to miss you. My father says you came back to me. I have not been in touch because I did not hear from you for some time. I sent no texts in case you have not liked the ending of your visit. We will be glad to see your messages again. My parents always look forward to hearing of your news. We hope the sending will continue. What is your life being like now?*

"When did you go back to her, Leo? I don't understand how you could have."

"I left and that was the end of it. She isn't talking about that. I—"

"You didn't have a fight or anything like that and then try to make it up to her."

"We got along perfectly well. All she's saying is I phoned their shop yesterday because I hadn't had a message for a while."

"It bothered you so much you phoned abroad."

"I thought she might be ill."

Ellen's gaze fastened on the phone between them on the kitchen table. "Is she saying you were sorry you came home?"

"Where on earth are you seeing that?"

"She says you wished your visit didn't have to end."

"She doesn't say that either. I had the kind of time I told you, but I'd rather be home." Not too belatedly, he hoped, Leo added "With you."

"Then what is she saying you didn't like?"

"How we parted, I suppose. That's all it could be."

Ellen raised her eyes to study his. "How did you?"

"She dropped me at the airport and then she had to rush off without a proper goodbye."

He was making to explain what he meant by proper when Ellen said "Anyway, she's missing you."

"She doesn't mean that. She wasn't there when I phoned, that's all."

"No need to be so fierce about it. She can miss you if she likes. It doesn't bother me, or does it bother you?"

"I don't know if it would or not. Look, her English can be a bit eccentric. You'd almost wonder if she writes like that to confuse us."

"I wouldn't wonder that myself. Are you going to send them a message, since they're so eager for you to?"

"I can't say I understand that. It's not as if I ever tell them much."

"I expect it shows how much they think of you. You must have made quite an impression. Shall I leave you to it while you think?"

"Not even while I text. No reason you can't see."

"I wasn't implying there might be."

Leo couldn't judge whether he'd made her suspect the opposite. He retrieved the phone while he tried to find enough to say. *Glad you're okay*, he typed. *Nothing much happening here* was less of a truth. *Ellen and I are off to dine with my parents*, he appended before displaying the message to Ellen. "You don't need my approval, Leo," she said.

"I wasn't asking for it. Anything you think I ought to add?"

"It's your message. You don't want it to be mine." As Leo sent the text she said "You didn't have to mention me."

"Was there any reason why I shouldn't? Why wouldn't you want me to?"

"I only wondered why you felt the need."

"Because it was true," Leo said and hid the phone in his pocket. "Shall we brave the dinner?"

"Let's try and think it may not be so bad and then maybe it won't be."

While he realised Ellen meant well, the proposal simply aggravated the confusion he'd yet to resolve since talking to Emil Weber. Just now other troubles seemed more immediate. As he and Ellen left the house he said "I should tell you my father's having problems driving."

"Oh dear, what kind? You aren't still, are you?"

"I'm fine. I've taken on some of his pupils. I feel as if I've transferred my problems onto him. I imagine he'll be telling us what kind."

Ten minutes' stroll, which Leo told himself didn't feel reluctant, took them to his parents' house. As he opened the gate a cat leapt out of the garden onto the wall like a wave surging over a promenade. He glanced back while he turned the house key in the lock, but the cat was nowhere to be seen. When he opened the door a large fly as black as the cat had been buzzed past him, despite his efforts to bat it out of the hall. "We're here," he called.

A timid aroma met them, a thin smell of soup that promised little of a taste. In a moment or rather several, his father emerged from the kitchen with a pair of wineglasses dangling head down from each hand. "Here's the rescue," he said.

His wife appeared behind him, cradling a capacious wooden bowl heaped with salad. "I hope nobody needs rescuing from my dinner."

"Of course they don't, Bev," Leo's father said with a gesture like a hug cut off by the handfuls of glasses. "I mean Leo's helped save our business."

"Just like we had to do for him."

"And you've been doing it just as much, if I even need to say."

Leo heard the final or perhaps not final reverberations of an argument. "Here's some wine," he said, hoisting the carrier he'd brought, "and presents from Germany to cheer everyone up."

"Does everyone need cheering?" his mother said.

"Not when we've your dinner to look forward to," Ellen told her.

"Shall we eat while we talk?" Leo's father said. "I wouldn't mind a bit of a distraction."

"I hope that isn't all my cooking is," his wife protested.

"What did you just hear Ellen say? She was saying it for all of us."

Leo saw his mother send this a searching look. "Would you like your presents first?" he said.

"That was understood, old chap. You mustn't think we were turning them down." Low enough to pretend not to want to be heard his father said "Too many people ready to jump on everything you say round here. Not what anybody needs right now."

He trudged around the dining-table to pose the glasses on their coasters while Leo produced the packages he'd wrapped. "Thank you for the thought," his mother said, having unboxed the magnet. "Very useful."

His father made the lid of his tankard clack like a wordless chattering mouth. "There's my excuse to drink," he said, "while I'm getting myself back together."

"What seems to be the problem, Brian?" Ellen said.

"I'll tell you."

Leo might have thought he'd decided against it, instead retreating to the kitchen. Perhaps he simply meant to fetch a bottle, which he uncorked while his wife pinned a list to the refrigerator with her magnet. "Bring the soup, Leo," she said once she'd poured the pale cloudy liquid swarming with noodles into a tureen. In the dining-room she ladled bowlfuls as her husband finished off the bottle by topping up his glass. "Here's to success," he said, inviting a communal clink.

"For us all," his wife said.

"You were wanting to hear about my issues, Ellen."

"If you think it'll help."

"You're hoping it can fix me the way it fixed Leo, are you? Right now I don't know what else could." He took a sip of wine as if to demonstrate restraint, only to yield to a mouthful. "I can't tell how far away anything is when I'm driving," he said. "I've started seeing danger where there isn't any, or maybe there is and I can't tell that either. I feel as if it's all been creeping up on me since that day we went out with Leo driving. It's just a blessing for everyone you've got your skills back, son."

"You've seen him do it," Ellen said. "That means you can too, Brian."

"So long as I don't start losing mine as well," Leo's mother said.

"You won't, Bev. We'll make sure you never do. Let's forget about my pickle now and just enjoy your dinner."

Leo hoped she didn't think this sounded like a ruse to shore up her confidence. The meal – soup and cold cuts with salad – was so untypically straightforward that he wondered whether she'd designed it to ensure none of it could go wrong, in which case when had she begun to doubt her abilities? "We'll definitely do that," he said and plunged his spoon into his soup.

Collecting a spoonful proved to be a task. The extravagantly lengthy noodles persisted in floundering off the spoon, taking most of the sample of broth with them. He considered taming a bunch with a fork, using the tines to twirl the noodles into submission, but he would look too much like a child bereft of social graces. His father appeared to have solved the problem, since he was emitting sounds of suction close to slobbering. "For pity's sake," Leo's mother said, "have you lost your manners as well?"

The silence this engendered felt as if nobody dared speak or look at anybody else. At least it gave Leo time to think of a solution he hoped his father might imitate. He used his spoon to slice a mass of noodles into manageable lengths and lifted a triumphant spoonful. The soup seemed determined to make him guess its flavour. He supposed it was hinting at chicken, and weren't pale fragments of fowl afloat in the bowl? His father was copying Leo's method, chopping up noodles with vigour if not vehemence. "That must be how men deal with things, Ellen," Leo's mother said. "Brute force conquers all."

Meeting his father's eyes rewarded Leo with a surreptitious wink he thought was warning him not to let himself be goaded. It left him afraid that if his mother was watching them both she might assume he hadn't finished his mouthful because it was unpalatable if not inedible. He swallowed the noodles, and then the spoon in his fist rattled against the bowl as he struggled not to gag. He couldn't really have felt the strings of pasta writhe in his throat as though a worm too thin to notice had been lurking among them. He dug the spoon into a tangle of noodles, telling himself that only his action had sent a spasm through them. Perhaps he hadn't quite hidden a grimace, since his mother said "What's wrong with my soup?"

Leo stopped short of feigning relish of a mouthful. "Not a thing," he said and made his gaze convey the same.

"I'm glad if yours is all right. Something's up with mine."

"What do you think is wrong with it, Bev?"

"So yours is too, Brian. You tell me what is."

"I wasn't meaning that at all. I'm asking why you don't think it's up to your usual standards."

"Perhaps I've had the pasta too long and it's gone off. I can see you're agreeing with me, Leo."

This made him reluctant to open his mouth, either to speak or to take a demonstrative spoonful of the contents of his bowl. "I'm sure he's not, Bev," his father said. "Nobody is."

"You listen to Brian, Beverley."

"Well, I'm not having any more," Leo's mother said and released her spoon to loll among the noodles squirming in her bowl. "Don't anybody else just to be polite."

"We aren't, Bev. It's absolutely fine."

"Do you say that even when it isn't?"

"Of course we don't." Ellen seemed to feel compelled to turn this unambiguous. "It never isn't, that's why," she said.

"I'm clearing this away," Leo's mother said with some defiance.

"Let me, dear," her husband said and stood up.

"You see, you can't pretend you want any more. Just dump your helpings in here and we'll hope I've done better with the main course."

She emptied her bowl into the tureen and stared at the diners until they complied. "Please try and be more honest with me," she said with a sardonic twist of her mouth.

Leo's father hefted the tureen and jerked his head, gesturing Leo and Ellen to bring the bowls. "Do your best to buck her up," he murmured once they were in the kitchen. "She's already worried about having to fit in so many of my jobs."

"I've room for a few more," Leo whispered. "Let me tell her."

"Don't do that yet, son. We don't want her getting the idea she can't cope. Let's just make sure she doesn't start thinking the rest of her dinner's no good."

Leo felt entrusted if not burdened with the responsibility for maintaining her belief in herself. He was first back to the table, where he set about loading his plate. A lettuce leaf unfurled as he transferred a clump of salad, and stayed restless while he added cold cuts – an uneven slice or rather wedge of beef, a variously brownish slab of chicken presumably related to the samples in the soup, a strip of ham sufficiently pink for a plastic imitation. Once he'd returned the elegant tongs to the equally silver oval dish he could only reach for his knife and fork, leaving eagerness behind. The gesture failed to satisfy his watchful mother. "Don't you want it?" she said.

"Just waiting for everyone else."

Waiting had to give him time to convince himself nothing was wrong on his plate. He'd disturbed the sprawling lettuce leaf as he'd dropped the meats beside it, that was all. He hadn't glimpsed a translucent greenish grub squirming into the curled edge of the leaf. Surely someone else would have noticed so plump and vigorous a grub, but he flattened the leaf with his knife to be certain. While he found no sign of life, as he cut into the thicker edge of the slice of beef a twitch passed through the pieces of meat on his plate. His action must have shifted them, and he was holding his utensils still to confirm that nothing on the plate would stir when his mother said "Oh dear, what's the matter with that?"

"Nothing is. Nothing at all," Leo vowed and yearned to believe, but her question had made him jerk the knife and fork. That must be why the pieces of meat had shifted, slithering apart as if they'd gained some travesty of life that rendered them averse to one another. He hacked at the piece of beef so furiously that the knife screeched against the plate – he could have felt he was ensuring the meat stayed as lifeless as it ought to be, though the noise might have suggested it had found an anguished voice – and then the phone rang in the hall. "I'll get it," he said at once.

"You enjoy your dinner. I'll see who doesn't want to let us," his father said and stood up with untypical alacrity to head him off. The pulse of the phone bell set the pace of his tramp into the hall. "Parkers," he said. "Yes, Brian Parker…. Ah, that would be my son…. Yes, he's here as well…. I expect you can. I'll just take you to him…." He reappeared carrying the receiver, which he deafened with one hand. "One of your Germans for you," he said.

Instinct more than thought prompted Leo to switch on the speaker before laying the phone on its back beside the salver spread with cold cuts. "Hello?" the phone was protesting. "Hello?"

While the man's voice sounded familiar, this didn't lessen Leo's puzzlement. "Emil?" he said.

"Not Emil, no. We are not all called Emil. This is Fredrich Schmidt."

"Forgive me, I don't think I know the name."

"But we know yours, Mr Parker. We made it our business to know."

Should Leo hear a threat? "How's that?" he said.

"We saw it on your tag."

"What tag?" Leo's mother objected. "Our son doesn't have a tag."

"Ah, has he drawn his family around him? Then I want you all to hear. He had one at the airport on his luggage."

By now Leo had recognised the voice. He was about to demand the reason for the call when his father said "Why did you go to so much trouble, Mr Schmidt?"

"It was little trouble. We saw the name of Parker, and he told us where he lives. You are the only Parkers with a number in that town."

"That isn't what I'm asking. Why did you want his details in the first place?"

"Because he interfered with our child and nearly killed us all."

"That was never Leo," Leo's mother cried.

"Leo Parker. Thank you for that information. It may be very useful."

"If you're trying to threaten our son, I wouldn't. Just remember we're witnesses here." Not much less ominously his father said "What exactly are you trying to make out he did?"

"He made our son lost at the airport while we were coming here."

"Is that all?" Leo's mother said with a laugh that multiplied the syllables, then jettisoned her mirth. "You need to watch your language, Mr Schmidt. That isn't what we mean by interfering with a child."

"It is not all, no."

"That's right, you said he tried to kill you. What on earth makes you say that?"

"He was trying to open the door while we were in the air. He had to be moved away."

"That part's true," Leo said. "I was doing it in my sleep."

"Don't say you're having sleep problems again." Louder to the phone his mother said "It sounds as if you're too fond of exaggerating, Mr Schmidt."

"And I told you at the airport," Leo said, "I didn't get your son lost. He already was and I was trying to find you for him."

"That is not how he describes it."

However irrationally, Leo felt betrayed. "I thought you weren't going to ask him."

"You would wish we had not, would you? He was put where we could find him and you led him astray."

"Your language is letting you down again, Mr Schmidt," Leo's mother said. "Maybe your English isn't quite as perfect as you think. In case you're wondering, we believe Leo."

"We're sorry if there's been some misunderstanding." Apparently his father was including Leo in the placation. "But I've got to say," he said, "I for one don't understand why anything you've told us made you want to track him down."

"I have said that is not all."

A nerve began to pluck at Leo's left eye, which must be why he seemed to glimpse the cuts of meat surreptitiously fidgeting on the salver as if they'd grown desperate to regain some form of life. When he tried to fix his attention resolutely elsewhere he saw Ellen and his parents gazing at him, delegating if not urging him to answer Schmidt. "What else, then?" he couldn't very well not ask.

"You have left our son afraid of being lost. He will go nowhere without us."

"Couldn't that be quite a good thing?" Leo's mother said. "You were saying you like to know where he is."

"Is this some kind of an English joke? We have had to take him to a doctor."

"Well, he's not the only—"

"It sounds to me as if your son already had the problem," Leo's father interrupted in some haste. "If Leo couldn't help, let's hope the doctor can."

"So you are a joker too."

"Could we ask just what you want, Mr Schmidt?" Ellen said. "We're supposed to be having our dinner."

Leo did his utmost not to fancy this had sent a responsive convulsion through the contents of the salver, let alone that some of the restless slices of flesh had set out to crawl over one another. "Then I must wish you a good appetite," Schmidt said. "You should enjoy it while you can."

"What are you saying is going to stop us?" Leo's mother demanded. "If you've anything else to say to Leo, we'll hear it as well."

"I believe I have spoken enough."

"I hope you don't mean you're planning worse," Leo's father said.

"Perhaps I have done sufficient for the present. Now you know how your son behaved. You know what he is capable of doing to others. Perhaps it is only some of what he does."

"I'll tell you what we do know, Mr Schmidt," Leo's mother began to retort, but the handset answered with a monotonous electronic moan. "Rude man. Are they all like that over there?" she said but didn't wait for Leo to respond. "Do you think you may have got a little bit lost where he said?"

"Yes, when I was trying to take their son to them. He was calling to them when I found him, whatever his father says."

"But you're over it now. It won't affect your driving."

"Maybe it did, the way you saw." Leo wished her words could fend off any implications of the phone call, but those were only being postponed. "And you're right," he hoped aloud. "It's dealt with."

He was about to make the phone call his excuse to admit he wasn't hungry when his mother said "Then let's forget him and go out for dinner."

"Not when you've done all this for us, Beverley," Ellen protested.

"I should have seen it wasn't good enough for guests. I can tell nobody really wants it. Own up, now, don't keep being so polite. I don't think much of it myself. See, Leo can't even bear to look at it."

At the edge of his vision Leo saw the fleshy slices on the salver flop inert as if their antics had exhausted them. Of course they could never have moved, and he made his eyes turn to them. "I certainly can," he said.

"Let's go out anyway. I fancy an Indian. Put everything you haven't touched back where it was and the two of us can see it off tomorrow."

Leo had begun to hope her proposition could stave off everything he'd just experienced, however temporary the salvation might be, when his father said "Is that the end of them now?"

"Who?" Still more reluctantly Leo added "What?"

"Your lecturer friend and now this fellow. Are they all you've brought over?"

"They must be," Leo said, only to wonder why his words felt like a plea he didn't understand if not a desperate denial.

CHAPTER TWENTY-ONE

As Laura Frost turned the car homewards Leo's mobile uttered a clank. He experienced an inexplicable twinge of nervousness until he saw the phone was offering him an upgrade to the latest model. "Don't let your phone distract you while you're driving," he said, only to wonder why the offer seemed so tempting, close to crucial.

He hadn't grasped the reason by the time they reached her family house, one of a terrace of timidly individualised clones in the middle of Settlesham Fields. She turned her large dark eyes on him and pinched her top lip beneath its equally pink twin before asking "Do you mind if I say something, only please don't tell your father?"

Leo couldn't help feeling wary. "I'll try not to mind."

"Only I'd rather have you teaching me than him."

"I'm glad you're happy with the service," Leo said and wished he didn't have to add "What was wrong about him?"

"Last time he didn't seem like he could concentrate. He kept looking for some kind of insect he thought was in the car. That wasn't what I meant, though. I'd rather have the way you teach than his way. You make me feel you know how hard learning can be and you're making sure it's not for me."

"I didn't have the best teacher. They weren't either of my parents, I ought to say. Do keep on driving with yours between lessons and you should be ready for your test next month."

He heard himself clutching at professionalism, pretending all or at least most was well or would be. He hadn't realised so much had gone wrong with his father. As he headed for the Mean Caffeine coffee shop in the New Town to give himself a chance to think, the phone released another clank. He pulled over to read the message outside a butcher's displaying a flypaper encrusted with insects. *How was your dinner with your parents?* Hanna appeared to be anxious to learn. *What are your plans for your day?*

Went for dinner at the Jabs of Punjab, Leo typed. *Teaching now until tonight,* although he wasn't for an hour. *Taken on some extra pupils for a while.* The phone seemed eager to see the message sent, completing most of the words for him and fleshing out the final phrase from the initial letters as if to reassure him how temporary his father's lapse was. He could have fancied the device was urging him to acquaint Hanna with at least his general situation, and he was about to loose the message when the sense of haste caught up with him. Why did it make him feel he should be wary? Before he knew why, he'd deleted the message. *What are yours?* he typed and then erased that too. He needn't let Hanna know he'd read her questions, even if he wasn't sure why he was demurring. Instead he brought up her previous message.

I am sorry to miss you. My father says you came back to me. I have not been in touch because I did not hear from you for some time. I sent no texts in case you have not liked the ending of your visit. We will be glad to see your messages again. My parents always look forward to hearing of your news. We hope the sending will continue. What is your life being like now?

A nightmare, he was tempted to reply. For a moment this felt more honest than the response he'd sent. Of course it wasn't true, not all the time. There had only been a few occasions when he could have thought he was living a bad dream, and now wasn't one of them. Losing his way at the airport, Lucy Fenton's lesson, his drive with his family, his final encounter with Anita Chattopadhyay, his most recent dinner with his parents: these were surely all, and why should recalling them feel like a threat of worse? He needn't be afraid to ponder them, he simply had no reason to linger over them – and then, with a lurch of awareness that felt like a punch to the stomach, he saw what nearly all the incidents had in common. Making the Schmidt boy fearful of losing his way, robbing Lucy of her confidence, leaving his father incompetent, imagining the doctor had developed an ocular problem, only for it to overtake her: in every case he'd infected someone with dread.

He shouldn't give in to such fancies. The boy at the airport had already been lost, whatever his parents were determined to believe. Lucy had a history of difficulties, which must have resurfaced in a somewhat different form. Anita Chattopadhyay's trouble had preceded Leo's visits, and it had just grown worse. Perhaps Leo was to some extent responsible for depleting his father's self-assurance, but that mustn't mean it had gone for good. Most importantly, his delusions about dinner hadn't inhibited his mother's appetite at the restaurant. Didn't this prove his fear was nonsense? No doubt it had its roots in the comment he'd found online about incubation, along with Jerome Pugh's rant about nightmares. To suffer those you had to be asleep, and Leo wasn't that sort of sleeper.

Still less was he the other kind, the sort you saw in spy films, posing as ordinary citizens until the time came for them to perform some insidious task. Often they didn't even know this was their function, which had to be triggered by some form of message. Certainly Leo had received nothing of that nature – and then a thought overtook him. Suppose the messages mattered only because of the information they secured? *What are your plans for your day?* In every case he'd answered some such question before his situation had turned nightmarish.

No, that wasn't true, he thought with breathy relief. He'd received no message at the airport, and so his notion was as absurd as it was grotesque, evidence of how shamefully stupid his brain was capable of growing if he let the likes of Pugh infect his thoughts – except that Hanna wouldn't have needed to ask where he was going to be, since she knew.

The realisation seemed to shatter a barrier, loosing an onslaught of insights. As he stared in dismay at yesterday's message, sentence after sentence revealed a new significance. *We will be glad to see your messages again* – in other words, the information Hanna tricked him into supplying. *My parents always look forward to hearing of your news,* and now he saw why: so that they knew which situation they could render dreadful. *We hope the sending will continue* – not Leo's messages but the terrors they enabled to be sent to him. He remembered Emil saying at the Kehlsteinhaus "You can invite and never know" and the mayor of Alphafen exhorting "Take our wishes home with you." How many of the townsfolk knew how Leo would be used to take their revenge on Settlesham? His confrontation with Dietrich Gebhardt came back to him: not just the man's assurance "There will be more revenge" but the mayor's directive "Take away the badness." At once Leo wondered whether this had been aimed not at Gebhardt but at him.

All this might almost have made him wish he'd temporarily lost his mind, but it left him feeling he'd found it at last. He would have panicked if he hadn't been offered a means of protecting himself, of ensuring he infected no more victims. He wouldn't be safe until he made himself unreachable, and he phoned his next pupil. "Could we possibly postpone until next week?"

"That's a hell of a wait. Have you nothing sooner?"

"I could make it shortly after six tonight if that's any use, Mr Fowler."

"Do," his father's pupil said and rang off.

The Grown Phone shop was just a minute's walk from a car park in the New Town. From the entrance Leo saw several empty spaces sketched with white paint on the tarmac. When he drove at the barrier the jointed metal arm ignored him. Had he approached too fast, provoking a robotic rebuke? He inched forward until the hood almost touched the barrier, which remained unmoved. Was something determined to hinder him? Could he have let his plan be guessed somehow? He reversed at speed out of the entrance and then drove with painful slowness at the barrier. Of course, in his eagerness to park he'd neglected to take the ticket that would raise the arm. The stubby metal pillar he'd just passed stuck out a derisive cardboard tongue again, only to withdraw it except for a narrow scrap protruding from the expressionless slit. He would have backed up to snatch it if a car hadn't turned in behind him. He ran the window all the way down and strained to reach the ticket, scraping his armpit on the corner of the window frame and nearly ripping the crumpled ticket against the edge of the slit in his haste to retrieve it. He twisted to face the barrier, only to find it hadn't stirred. Had he removed the ticket too belatedly? He was jerking out a hand to poke the button for his hazard lights when the barrier yielded to a twitch before setting out to stagger relatively vertical. The instant the way was sufficiently clear Leo sped to the nearest vacant space. Once out of the car he checked his phone, which appeared to have been inactive while he was distracted. "You've played your last trick," he vowed, and the driver who had followed stared at him.

Less than a minute's sprint took him to the phone shop. A pair of electronic gateposts greeted his arrival with an amiable beep, and an assistant accosted him at once. "How can we help you today?"

The badge pinned to his lapel named him Phil Networker. Dozens of images of mobile phones plated his T-shirt like a suit of armour. He looked too young to be much of a knight, with pimples punctuating faint lines on his forehead while a frame of timid stubble seemed designed to lend his limp mouth strength. "You've invited me to upgrade," Leo said.

"Which phone do you have?" When Leo produced his Frugimob the assistant said "You'll be happy."

"I'm hoping so, but why?"

"Better camera, for one thing."

This reminded Leo of the vanished German photographs. Could they still be lurking in his phone? He wouldn't need to be concerned about that much longer. "I'll just get your new one," Phil said, "and then we can see to the paperwork."

While awaiting his return Leo scrutinised the phone screen. It betrayed no activity, but suppose simply rousing it put him at risk? Could the phone be maintaining some secret connection? That might explain his delay at the car park. He switched off the phone and was consigning it to his hip pocket when Phil reappeared, offering the contents of his hands. Both were empty. "Sorry for this," he said. "Could you wait for the upgrade?"

Leo's fist clenched on the phone as though he could crush it. "I have to be back at work soon. How long?"

"We had a new one left, but we must have sold it while I was on my break. We should be getting more in tomorrow."

Leo let go of the phone, which had begun to bruise his palm. "I can't afford to wait that long."

"We guarantee the cost won't go up on the plan you've got. We'd give you today's price even if it did."

"I mean I don't have the time. I need to change it now. Not just the phone, the number."

Phil's forehead grew more ruled, underlining the pimples. "We're supposed to ask why."

"I have my reasons, and I don't believe they're anybody else's business."

"Head office says we have to ask."

"I don't want someone being able to reach me, all right? Call them a stalker if you like."

"That's bad. Have you told the police?"

"I can deal with it myself. That's what I'm here to do."

"Okay, we can put a new card in your old phone now and transfer it to a new one tomorrow."

"I've already said I want to change the phone as well." Not knowing how thoroughly it might be infected brought Leo close to panic. As he stared about in search of a solution he caught sight of a Frugimob – the latest version – perched on a shelf. "There's one you missed," he said with the breath his surge of relief left him. "I'll take it even if it's shopsoiled. It'll do for me."

"We aren't allowed to sell display models."

"Then sell me a different phone, for Christ's sake. Recommend one and I'll take it."

"There aren't any better than the new Frugimob. Seriously—"

"Then give me one that's just as good. Jesus, even give me one that isn't. You sell all kinds, don't you? You have to think they're worth it or you wouldn't be selling them. Just give me a new phone."

"I was going to say you don't have to change your phone to make sure somebody can't contact you. You only need to change your card."

"I want a different phone as well. I want it right now." Leo no longer cared how childish he might sound. "Never mind what you think," he said. "It's my choice."

"Are you sure you don't still want your upgrade? They might have the new one at Own Your Phone. I can call them if you like."

"Don't bother. They're too far. I'm parked here." Leo suspected the assistant had grown eager to be rid of him. His clenched fists felt capable of grabbing Phil to shake obedience into him. He shoved them in his pockets to restrain them, and his knuckles collided with the phone, which gave him a desperate inspiration. As he insisted "My contract's with you" he snatched out the phone to drop it on the linoleum.

Had he let it fall face up by mistake? At first the reflection of an overhead light made it impossible to judge. Would he have to feign losing hold of the phone a second time? No, it had landed on its face, and surely this had done some damage. When he picked up the phone he found the screen had developed a gratifying diagonal crack. "That's the end of that," he said. "Even you'll have to admit I need a new one now."

Phil was staring at him not quite in disbelief. "Did you just drop that deliberately?"

"I'd be careful what you're accusing people of. Do I get a replacement or not?"

"We can put a new screen in for you. No charge. It's included in your insurance."

"I don't want a new f—" Leo barely managed to truncate the expletive, which might have seen him expelled from the shop. "You know what I want," he said, "and I'm the customer."

"Have we a problem, Philip?"

The stout man was at least twice Phil's age but similarly armoured. According to his badge his two-tier name was Terence Manager. "He came in for an upgrade," Phil complained, "but now he's asking for a different phone."

"As the gentleman says, he's the customer. Allow me to deal with this."

Leo wasn't sure whose permission the manager was asking, if anyone's at all. As Phil swooped to welcome a newcomer Terence said "Existing?"

"They haven't stopped me yet."

"Ha, ha," Terence remarked like a dutiful substitute for a laugh. "Are you a customer of ours?"

"Didn't you hear? That's why I thought I might be treated better."

"I believe Philip followed all our guidelines, but if you wish to make a complaint—"

"I don't. I haven't time." On the edge of panic, Leo stared at the displays and made an urgent choice. "I'll take a Friendliphone," he said.

"Let me see if we have one in the back."

"Don't you know? Haven't you got anything you're meant to sell?" Leo muttered for nobody else to hear and then raised his voice as Terence headed for the stockroom. "If you've none of those," he thought it best to shout, "anything will do."

This merely made Terence duck as though to avoid a missile Leo had flung at him. While the phone in Leo's hand ought to be as good as dead, he was anxious to be rid of it. He might have shied it into the street if he could have trusted the traffic to pulverise its works. He stowed it in a hip pocket and was striving to ignore its chilly weight when the manager emerged from the stockroom, brandishing a boxy handful. "You're in luck," he said. "Just the one left. Take a seat and we'll set you up."

A round big-eyed cartoonish face smiled at Leo from the box. No doubt it was meant to look welcoming, not secretly amused. "May I take your name?" Terence said.

"Leo Parker."

"And the address."

There was so much more along these lines that Leo started interrupting questions with the answers. He tried anticipating what he would be asked until he found he was offering the information out of order, which apparently contravened the guidelines of the business. "Sorry to rush you," he said, although he wasn't and indeed had failed to do so. "I've got to pick up a driving pupil soon."

"Ah, you're that Mr Parker."

"One of them." His inability to judge the tone provoked Leo to enquire "What have you heard?"

"Just that your family teaches driving round here. I understand you're quite good."

"We're better," Leo said, only to hope his father was. "Is that all?"

"I can't say I've been told anything else."

"No," Leo said and thought he felt the phone crawl deeper into his pocket. "Have you got all the details you need?"

"I believe so. Please excuse the hindrance. I needed them to set up your new contract. Now let's make friends with your new phone."

Presumably the turn of phrase went with the brand of mobile, but it made the phone sound more sentient than Leo liked. When Terence activated the device it greeted Leo with the round face from the packaging – perfectly circular eyes and nose, smile fixed in friendliness. At last it displayed the home screen and its flock of icons, and Leo was about to stand up until Terence said "Just let me make your transfer."

Uncertainty arrested Leo in a crouch. "What transfer?"

"I'll copy all the data from your phone for you before you trade it in."

"I'm taking it with me."

"I've given you the discount for the trade."

"How can you do that without asking me first?"

"As I understood it you wanted to get rid of the phone. I thought the saving would be appreciated."

Terence sounded disappointed if not aggrieved, which left Leo's nerves feeling scraped, and the behaviour of one of the luminous tiles overhead didn't help. It had begun to buzz like a swarm of flies. "You still ought to have asked," he insisted. "I've things I need to do before I'm finished with it."

"So long as you'll be bringing it in I can let the discount stand."

"I won't be. I can't." He couldn't leave the phone anywhere in Settlesham when it might still harbour some nightmare infection. "You wouldn't want it," he said. "It'd be no use to you by the time I'm done with it."

"Then I'll need you to sign for the cancellation of the discount."

Was he hoping this might seem so onerous that Leo would relent? Leo slumped on the chair as if the phone in his pocket had dragged him down. "Better be quick, then."

The manager took so long to adjust the transaction that Leo could have suspected him of slowing down the process with pique. At last the printer stuttered out a page. Leo scribbled his signature on the hot paper and lurched to his feet, only for the buzzing overhead to seize him by the nerves. "Shouldn't you have that seen to?" he said.

"It's from keeping the door open. All sorts get in."

Had Leo been hearing flies after all? He hadn't time to look. He ran back to the car park, where he jabbed the ticket followed by a credit card into a pay machine so vigorously that for a protracted breathless moment he was afraid he'd bent the card beyond repair. He dashed to the car and threw the old phone in the boot, willing the impact to damage it further but knowing that wouldn't be enough. He had to leave the phone incapable of doing any more harm, and he couldn't achieve that in Settlesham.

He would have no chance to drive far enough until the day's lessons were done. Every emergency stop roused a clatter in the boot, so that he could have fancied the phone was eager to wreak more havoc. He was tempted to put off Mr Fowler's lesson once again, but he mustn't fail his parents or the firm. He found Mr Fowler loitering truculently outside his cottage in the Old Town, hands clamped to his hips while his elbows enclosed his impatience in quotes. "I thought you'd let me down again," he made certain Leo knew. "Your father never has. I take it whatever was so important has been dealt with."

"Most of it," Leo said and strove to put the rest out of his mind. Otherwise he might have felt the hour he devoted to his father's pupil would never end. In sixty prolonged minutes – three thousand seconds and six hundred more, all of which he felt aware of – it did, only to let him realise he couldn't leave Settlesham yet. He still had to deal with what might prove to be the hardest task of all.

CHAPTER TWENTY-TWO

"Hello?"

The greeting was so curt that Leo felt found out before he even spoke. "Ellen," he said.

"Leo? Is that you?"

"It's me all right. Only me."

"Where are you?"

"I've just dropped off one of my dad's pupils, and I was wondering—"

"No, I meant where are you calling from."

Too late he realised more explanation was required than he'd manufactured in advance. "My new phone," he said while he tried to fabricate a reason.

"When did you get that? You didn't say you were going to."

"I didn't know I was until you'd gone to work. The old one went wrong all of a sudden, so if you were trying to get in touch, that's why you couldn't."

"I haven't been. What was so wrong with it?"

"They couldn't tell me at the shop. I expect we'll never know."

"So you had to replace it. I can understand that."

"I knew you would." He needn't have said so – perhaps he shouldn't have – and he hurried to add "I was going to ask—"

"But why have you changed the number?"

"That was part of what was wrong. The card was corrupted."

"I thought you said they couldn't tell you."

"They told me that much."

"You could have just replaced the card, then."

"It had messed the whole phone up somehow. That's what they didn't explain."

"Well, I see why you got yourself a new phone, but I don't see why you had to change the number."

"Because there was a new card in it."

"You can still keep your old number. You just need to say you want it transferred."

"Can you? They didn't ask me and I didn't think. I was between pupils and I didn't have much time."

"Maybe you can get your old one back if you go into the shop."

"It's done now. I've bothered them enough. Look, what are we arguing about? This isn't why I called you."

"Sorry if you think I haven't let you speak. That's a point, why are you calling? Shouldn't you be home by now?"

"I was wondering if dinner could possibly wait a bit longer."

"If it absolutely has to, I suppose. What's the delay?"

"I'd like to see off one more job."

"A pupil, you mean." When Leo let her think so Ellen said "Is all the extra work getting the better of you?"

"If my mother can take it, so can I. I just want to get this out of the way."

"Leo, I wasn't thinking. Did having to change your phone throw you off your schedule?"

"It took nearly an hour." However guilty accepting her suggestion made him feel, at least it relieved him of the need to invent any more excuses. "So can we dine late?" he said.

"I've already turned it off for now. Will you let me know when you're on your way?"

"That's a promise. I'll get going right now."

So lying to Ellen was easier than he'd feared it would be, although wasn't this in itself something to fear? As soon as he left Settlesham behind he put on all the speed he felt able to risk. Before long he was in open countryside. At least, he'd always thought it was, with scattered buildings adding to its charm, but he'd never realised how few fields weren't overlooked by farmhouses or solitary cottages. Hedges might hide him while he threw the phone in a ditch, but he was afraid someone would find it and pick up a lurking infection. When he caught sight of a glint of water in a meadow he slewed the car onto the verge of a bend. The nearest house was at least a mile away. He braked beside a stile and ducked out of the car. The low light of a molten silver sun glared across the fields into his eyes, and he could no longer see the pond. When he warded off the glare he found there was no pond, just a supine sheet of metal, part of a selection of litter that had been dumped in the grass. If he drove much further Ellen might wonder where he'd gone. As long as there was nobody to see him he could bury the phone by the road.

The phone was slouching on the far side of the boot, hiding its face against the wall behind the rear seats. He needn't imagine it was trying to stay out of his reach, let alone that while he was driving it had risen up to nestle as close to him as it could manage or even spy on him. His last stop must have thrown it upright, that was all. He took it to the driver's seat and told himself he mustn't hesitate, however ominous the chilly metal slab felt. He had to switch it on.

The scrawny button bruised his fingertip as he held it down. The phone took quite a time to regain its kind of life, greeting his face with an upsurge of icons. When nothing else surfaced he was able to let out a breath. Even if he'd found a message from Hanna he wouldn't have responded, but he was glad to feel Alphafen was presently unaware of him. He stood the phone on the dashboard, only to realise how much of a chore lay ahead. He would have transferred his contacts list from the old phone to the new if he hadn't feared that something else might take advantage of the process. All the email addresses were stored on his computer. Surely copying the phone numbers wouldn't take too long once he settled into the task.

He tapped the first listing to display the information, which he used his new phone to photograph. Five seconds to do that and return to the list, another two while he identified the next listing: tap the cracked screen, take the shot, tap again to bring the list back…. Soon the actions grew virtually automatic, but they still consumed most of half an hour. He stabbed the image of a button with his throbbing fingertip to take the final photograph, and then he grabbed the doorframe to speed himself out of the car, only to falter and shout a collection of words he seldom used. He'd brought nothing with which to dig.

He could use the phone itself. He knelt on the grass behind the car and tried to poke the phone into the soil. Weeks of sunshine had hardened the ground, but the corner of the phone should do the trick, and perhaps it would have if it weren't so rounded. Twilight and the increasingly vague shadow of the hedge merged around him as he tore at the grass to clear it away while he scraped at the earth. A smell of petrol caught in his throat, and his aching hand grew prickly with sweat before he'd managed to dig an inch deep. He wanted to believe this would be enough, but he ought to separate the card from the phone to disable it further. He was levering a last paltry layer of soil out of the hole, and feeling like a child employing a toy spade that was unequal to the enterprise, when he heard a car on the road.

While he couldn't see it, it sounded too imminent to leave him time to extract the card. He dropped the mobile in the meagre trench and set about refilling the hole. Most of the soil he'd succeeded in removing was scattered over the grass, and he hadn't managed to gather much with the sides of his hands when the car swung around the bend ahead. As he staggered to his feet the car halted opposite him. "What have you lost?" the driver called. "Hold on and I'll help you look."

"Thanks very much, but please don't bother. No point looking. Can't be helped."

None of this prevented the man from clambering out of his car. He was a smallish fellow, and Leo couldn't have said much more about him. The twilight added to his anonymity, tinting most of him close to colourless. "No bother whatsoever," he assured Leo, flourishing a flashlight the length of his forearm. "You can't be seeing too well just now. Let's find out what this can do."

"No, I mean you needn't help me." Leo showed the man an earthy hand he immediately clenched in case the dusk failed to hide its emptiness. "I found it," he said.

This didn't halt the man's advance. For a moment Leo thought he meant to shine the flashlight on the hand. "What did you nearly lose?" the man said.

"A phone. Just my phone."

"We'd be lost without them, wouldn't we? How did you manage to lose yours?"

"As I say, I didn't. Just dropped it, that's all."

The man raised the flashlight but seemed to think better of switching it on. "Will you be all right to drive?"

"Certainly I will. Why do you ask?"

"I only wondered if you aren't seeing too well. I shouldn't have thought it would have taken so long to find something that big, even in this light."

"It didn't take long. It isn't that big." Leo shoved his fist into his pocket and brought it out no emptier. "You'll have to excuse me now," he said. "I'm supposed to be home."

The man stepped back but watched Leo climb into the car and clean his hands with chilly gel. Leo was easing the car into a turn when the man paced forward as if to stop him. He peered both ways along the road and then beckoned Leo to continue, which required Leo to steer around him. "Thanks," Leo said but didn't feel. Was the fellow making sure Leo was fit to drive? He was still standing in the road when Leo turned the nearest bend.

Once the man was out of sight Leo tramped on the brake. *Fifteen minutes*, he typed – at least, accepted the suggestion his phone made before he'd completed the first word. He sent Ellen the message and was planting the phone on the dashboard when the mirror showed him a bird hovering above the stretch of road beyond the bend. Did hawks normally fly so late? Presumably this one did, and Leo sped after his headlamp beams into the dusk.

He reached home soon enough not to render his message too approximate. As he let himself in Ellen emerged from the kitchen, wearing her chef's apron. "Were they grateful?" she said.

For a confused uneasy moment Leo wondered why the Webers would have been – was afraid his plan had gone wrong somehow. "Who?" he said more fiercely than he thought Ellen deserved.

"I don't know, do I? You didn't tell me." As Leo tried to grasp the accusation she said "Whoever you've been putting yourself out for."

"Of course, them. I don't think anyone's to blame but me. As I said, I had to change the schedule because of the phone."

When Ellen opened her mouth he was afraid she meant to ask for a name. Would mentioning an actual pupil or inventing one be more of a risk? "So long as everything's dealt with now," she said.

"I can't think of anything that needs to be," Leo said, hoping he'd thought the truth.

"I've done my best to see the bourguignon's not reduced too much. Open a red while I dish."

As Leo unscrewed a flaking cork from the opener in the kitchen, Ellen's phone rang. The ladle lounged against the rim of the saucepan with a clank while she said "Hello?"

"Ellen, it's Brian Parker. Sorry to trouble you. I can hear you're busy. Has anything happened to Leo, might you know?"

"He's here with me. I'd say he was fine. Why do you ask?"

"I've been trying to get him on the phone for a good while and there's no response."

"He's here at home. He bought a new phone earlier. He's been so busy he didn't have a chance to tell us. Shall I put him on?"

"I'd appreciate it." With barely a pause to let Ellen hand Leo the phone his father said "Don't do that sort of thing too often, will you, son? I'm worried enough as it is."

"I've no reason to do it again. I didn't mean to worry you. Why, what else is wrong?"

"I'm trying not to think it's your fault, but I still need your help."

"I've room for a few more pupils till you're more yourself again, and I'm sure you will be soon."

"We aren't talking about me. It's your mother."

"You mean I'll have to take hers on as well?"

"Not at the moment." As Leo admitted relief to himself his father said "I can't talk long. I've just stepped out of the house."

"Then tell me what the problem is."

"Her driving's just the same. Nothing's happened there, and I pray this won't affect her confidence." Leo was making to prompt him more urgently when his father said "I need you to come here when she's out so we can discuss the situation. You know how much she enjoys her food, but now she's eating hardly anything at all."

CHAPTER TWENTY-THREE

"**B**rian said he wouldn't blame you, Leo."

"Maybe he should. I just don't understand why he wants you as well."

"Would you rather I didn't come with you?"

"I wasn't saying that. I only—"

"Sometimes you don't have to say. Is there something you'd prefer me not to hear?"

"I won't be saying anything you can't. I can't understand why he wants you there and not my mother, that's all. I can't see what sense that makes."

Leo had to hope other things did. If he was indeed responsible for his mother's problem, it must surely be the last case of the incubation – the way the contagions he'd brought home delayed infecting their victims. Surely now he'd severed every contact with Alphafen he was no threat to anyone, and mightn't his victims recover? To some extent Lucy Fenton had. "There's only one way to find out," Ellen said.

Once he disengaged himself from his thoughts he grasped she meant they had to listen to his father. The Pass With Parker car outside the family house was bereft of its twin, its triplet if you counted the vehicle Leo had left at home. His mother would be tutoring a pupil on the road for most of the next hour, presumably long enough for his father to make himself clear. Leo unlocked the front door and followed Ellen into the house, which had grown ominously odourless. "We're here, Brian," Ellen called.

Leo's father strode out of the kitchen at once. He looked determined to be untypically nimble, so relatively swift that he'd left any expression behind. "Come in," he said as if they hadn't, and Leo saw his bid for terseness referred to the kitchen. "Coffee," his father said more like a requirement than an invitation. "Be quick and sit down."

"Are we in a hurry?" Leo felt provoked to ask. "I thought mum was out for an hour."

"I want to get this done well before she comes back." Nevertheless his father paused while he lifted the percolator off its stand. "She could have done without not being able to call you," he muttered at the bubbles as they subsided. "I can tell you that didn't help."

"I didn't know she'd been trying to get in touch."

"You wouldn't when you hadn't told us how to."

"No, I'm saying nobody let me know after you could."

"She wasn't trying. She saw I was and I nearly had to tell her why. We don't want her more worried than she already was. We don't want her worried at all. I've spent half my life seeing she's not, and I don't thank anyone for making her."

"I did say Leo was busy with his pupils," Ellen said.

"And mine as well, you're thinking. Believe me, I'm doing everything I can to get back to being some use." He planted mugs in front of her and Leo so emphatically the coffee made leaps to escape, only just contained. As he sat facing them across the kitchen table and gripped his own mug with both hands despite how hot the contents were he said "All right, talk to me. I want to hear the truth."

Leo felt interrogated in advance. "I don't know what you're saying hasn't been."

"Tell me honestly, both of you. I promise you I have my reasons. What do you think of Beverley's cooking?"

"I'd call it adventurous," Ellen said.

"And what exactly does that mean?"

"She tries recipes I'd never think of trying. She uses her imagination."

"You aren't saying you've not tried them because you never would." He transferred his scrutiny to Leo, though not at once. "You're staying quiet," he said.

"Ellen's more the chef than me. I wouldn't question her judgement."

"That's very diplomatic. Do you want to hear mine?"

"Whyever wouldn't we?" Leo tried to make this sound like a declaration, not a query, just as Ellen said "Of course we do, Brian."

"I've put up with her cooking and been polite about it, and I think you both have. I've been doing it since before we were married."

"I'd never have known," Ellen said, "and I'm sure she doesn't either."

"Thank you for understanding. Thank you for keeping it up, but now I'm afraid she knows."

"Has she said so?"

"I know what's in her head without needing to be told. I expect it's like that with you two."

"Sometimes I wonder."

This dislodged Leo's nervous muteness. "Why, what do you—"

"Let's not get distracted," his father said. "What were you thinking last time you were here?"

"About what? I'd quite a few things on my mind."

"Why did you let your mother see you didn't want her dinner? Why that one out of all of them? Even she couldn't get that wrong. Couldn't you be bothered any longer?"

"I really don't think Leo meant to give her that impression. He was just upset by that phone call."

"Maybe we should wonder why."

"Because the person was accusing him of leaving a child in a state."

"And now he's left his mother in one. He's done that to too many people lately."

"As Ellen says, I've never meant to."

"After all the care I've taken with your mother all these years. Shall I tell you something you don't know or maybe you've forgotten? If she loses any of her confidence the chances are the rest of it goes too. It's like every bit's propped up by the rest of it. I nearly saw it all go once."

Leo felt more accused than ever. "When was that?"

"When you used to keep waking up at night talking gibberish. She started saying she was no good as a mother because you were a disturbed child. The doctor told her it was just a phase you'd grow out of, and I thought you did, but I had to spend weeks convincing her she hadn't done anything wrong. All that kept her going was she didn't want to let her pupils down. I'm not saying you knew what you were doing to her." As Leo allowed himself to feel pardoned his father said "But you didn't bother hiding how much you enjoyed your Indian."

"It was her idea to go to the restaurant, remember."

"So Leo was really doing it for her. He mightn't actually have liked it so much."

"You're a loyal lady, Ellen. I'll give you that." Leo's father was still staring at him. "Don't ever do anything like that to your mother again," he said.

"You ought to know I've always tried not to."

"Well, now she needs you to try harder. Convince her she's the best if you want her back how she deserves to be."

"I can as well, Brian."

"I was asking you both. That's why you're here," Leo's father said, and then his gaze veered past her. "What's that?"

A sound of scraping suggested an intruder was eager to join them. Realising a key was fumbling at a lock didn't reassure Leo much. He heard the front door open, and his mother called "I'm back, Brian."

Leo wished this could mean she was restored to her old self, but his father plainly didn't think so. "Why are you home so soon?"

"My one o'clock had to cancel. Family emergency. No problem, is there? Don't say I've caught you with your mistress."

"It's only me, Beverley," Ellen called.

"And me," Leo thought he should establish.

His mother's haste along the hall seemed to multiply her footsteps. "What's brought you two here?"

When Ellen didn't answer, Leo felt required to. "We just want you to know how much we like coming round to eat."

His father gave him a look that impaled Leo's impulsiveness. Had he been too eager to persuade her? He could only continue as he'd begun. "That phone call put me off last time," he said, struggling to forget how he'd seen the food grow restless with insects if not of itself. "I just didn't want you to think it was anything else."

"Remember how much we were all enjoying your dinner," Ellen said, "and then that spoiled it for everyone."

"It's kind of you to come round just to say so." Leo's mother halted in the kitchen doorway while she waited for them to turn their faces to her. "It was thoughtful, wasn't it, Trevor?" she said.

So the extra footsteps hadn't been illusory, and their perpetrator appeared at her back. Leo found his expansive placid ruddy face a little overstated, not least its look that seemed always to challenge the world to surprise him. "I don't think you've met our neighbour, have you, Ellen?" Leo's mother said. "Inspector Trevor Kerr."

"Have a seat, Trevor," Leo's father said. "Will you have a coffee too?"

"If you've finished saying anything you wouldn't want to say in front of me, Brian."

"I can't imagine what that could be, Trevor," Leo's mother said. "You're an old friend and always welcome. What did you want to see us about? Sit down while I get us both a coffee."

"I won't say no. You know my style."

"Two sugars and a glug of milk. Let's have it in the front where we can all be comfortable."

Leo sensed the policeman wasn't quite. Kerr stayed on his feet, an awkward presence that seemed to shrink the room, while she filled two mugs and handed one to him. "As you say, let's go and sit down," he said. "I'm here mostly as your neighbour."

"What's the rest of it?" Leo's father said.

Kerr responded by turning to Ellen. "Do I take it you and Leo are together?"

"They're more than friends," Leo's mother said. "Why do you ask?"

"Because what I came to tell you concerns him."

Before anybody could speak Kerr made for the front room. By the time everyone followed him he was seated in an armchair, his arms folded as though to demonstrate patience. Leo found himself isolated in the other armchair while Ellen and his parents occupied the couch.

Having watched the process like a judge, Kerr said "I should like it to be clearly understood that I'll be speaking off the record. I trust everyone knows what that means."

"We can't tell anyone what you say," Ellen said.

"If anybody does there could be serious consequences."

"We'll keep it in mind, Trevor." Leo's father might have been attempting to revive their neighbourly relationship. "Can we hear what you want now?" he said.

"I'm afraid your fleet may be missing a car for a while."

Leo's mother gave a laugh that sounded unsure of its reason. "Well, I wasn't expecting that."

"What were you expecting?" his father demanded.

"Nothing Trevor would have been involved with. Leo's never been in trouble with your people, Trevor. Are you saying something's wrong with his car?"

"It may have to be impounded for investigation."

"Investigating what, for heaven's sake? Can't you just give him a caution or whatever you do if something needs to be fixed?"

"We believe it may have been used to transport drugs."

"That's utterly ridiculous." This time she didn't bother to reach for a laugh. "Who's been saying that? They want to be careful what they're saying."

"I'm afraid it was a member of the force."

"I don't care who they were. What right have they to say such a thing?"

"They were passing the car and they smelled it. They wouldn't be mistaken."

"Well, I think they were." Just as doggedly she said "When's that supposed to have been?"

"The day Leo returned from abroad."

Leo couldn't play dumb any longer. "I think someone may have used the car while I was away."

"Well, you certainly never told us," his father protested. "Who are you saying did what?"

"Someone involved with the airport car park. I noticed the smell when I picked the car up, and I thought the mileage was higher than it should have been."

"Did you report this?" Kerr said.

"I was going to, wasn't I, Ellen? Only when I went to do it the evidence was gone."

Kerr's face remained placid except for the eyes. "Which evidence?"

"What you said your chap spotted. The smell."

"You could still have alerted us to the situation."

"It's all very well blaming Leo, Trevor," Leo's father said. "Why didn't your fellow investigate at the time? Leo could have told him what he suspected then."

"In these cases we usually wait to gather more evidence."

"Well, you'll get no more on Leo," his mother said, "and it sounds if there ever was any it's gone."

"I'm afraid there's more, Beverley."

"What are you trying to say about him now? What else can there possibly be?"

"I shouldn't think you'll be aware of the situation with his phone."

"He bought a new one, if that's what you mean," Leo's father said. "Last time I heard we're allowed to do that in this country still."

"Do remember I'm acting as a friend here, Brian." Kerr laid a heavy look on top of the rebuke before saying "He seems to have been very anxious to get rid of the old one."

"The shop couldn't salvage any of it, that was all," Ellen said. "Where is it now, Leo? You can show him."

"You can let Trevor have it if that's what he wants, can't you?" Leo's mother said. "Have you left it at home?"

As Leo searched for an answer he could risk letting anybody hear Ellen said "Wait a moment. How did you know about it, Mr Kerr? Why would the shop have told you?"

"I haven't said they did. I'm sure you understand I can't give out that kind of information. In any case they didn't need to alert us. Someone else did."

"Who could have?"

"Someone who found it after Leo tried to bury it."

Leo felt as trapped as the breath he sucked in. He'd found no words by the time his father spoke. "I'm surprised at you, Trevor, believing anything like that. They must have it in for him, if you ask me."

"I can understand how you might want to think so, but—"

"As long as you're telling us stuff off the record, can I guess who it was?"

"You can't, so please don't start thinking you can."

"Fred Latimer."

"Not Mr Latimer. I'm sure he would never slander anybody here."

"I wouldn't be so sure. Ronnie Fenton, then. He seems good at bearing grudges."

"Are you making an official complaint about him, Brian?"

"Depends what he's been saying about Leo."

"He's said nothing I'm aware of. Please don't continue this. I've no reason to believe the informant knows any of you. That's what makes him a disinterested witness."

"Maybe he's a friend of one of them. Are you absolutely sure he couldn't be?" When Kerr fended the suggestion off with a saddened look Leo's father faltered, and then he thumped the arm of the couch hard enough to dent the leather. "Brian," Leo's mother cried without managing to interrupt him. "Hang on there," he said. "If whoever it was doesn't know any of us, how did he know it was Leo?"

"Because Leo was driving the car we've been talking about," Kerr said. "I'm afraid he didn't realise he was advertising himself."

"Who says I didn't realise? More like I'd no need to care." Leo had found some words at last, mostly to head off his father from blundering further. "He couldn't have seen me burying the phone," he said before he knew where this would take him.

"What do you claim would have prevented him?" Kerr said.

"Because I didn't do that. I just threw it away."

"Leo," his mother protested. "We brought you up never to drop litter."

"I'd had enough of the wretched thing letting me down. It made me so angry I couldn't help chucking it. You know that isn't usually me."

"Well, I don't blame whoever had to pick up after you. I don't even blame them for taking it to the police, Brian. They couldn't have known there was nothing suspicious about it." For a moment Leo thought she'd finished chiding him, and then she said "Where did you throw it away?"

Too late he realised where he'd led himself. "Nowhere in particular," he desperately hoped was enough.

"Outside Settlesham." Perhaps Kerr imagined he was being helpful. "About twenty minutes out," he said. "Yesterday evening, when he might have expected the road would be clear."

In a bid to forestall any thoughts this might prompt Leo said "Anyway, you've got it now. I can promise you won't find anything."

"Information isn't so easy to erase as some people think."

"I'm sure Leo means there's nothing to find," his mother said.

"That's exactly what I mean, because it's the truth."

At least, it was in terms of Kerr's suspicions, but could some infection be lying dormant in the phone? If the investigation roused it, how might it affect anyone involved? He was feeling too helpless even to speak when his mother said "Have you finished with him now, Trevor?"

"You'll appreciate I wasn't expecting Leo to be here."

"I'm glad he was. I'd have known you were wrong even if he hadn't been here to defend himself, but now we all know he's done nothing you could prosecute him for." The maternal gaze she was training on Leo took on a tinge of reproof. "Unless you think you should fine him for littering," she said.

"That isn't my department, but I fancy they may let it slide. I'm afraid the rest of the inquiry will have to take its course."

"I'm sorry you haven't more serious things to investigate."

"Perhaps we will have. We've seen too many odd incidents locally of late."

"I hope you're going to tell us now you've said that much."

"They're like nightmares, but the victims aren't asleep." Kerr sounded angry, though it wasn't clear with whom. "One lady kept thinking her house was infested with insects," he said. "Not just her house. She felt them crawling in her mouth and anywhere else they could get in."

This silenced Leo's mother. "That's certainly a nightmare," Ellen said.

"It's a good deal worse. The lady has been sectioned."

His muted vehemence hushed Ellen too. It was Leo's father who declared "At least you can't blame Leo."

"Some people might."

"Then they'd better be damned careful what they're saying." His rage seemed to leave him few more words he could utter. "Who?" he demanded.

"You know I can't name names. People who were at his talk. It's been suggested the punch was spiked."

"Then everybody should be feeling the effects. You were there and I saw you take some. How's your brain now? Maybe that's why you've been talking so much nonsense."

"Brian, don't," Leo's mother said. "I think Trevor's trying to help."

"It looks as if all those affected took a drink after the talk," Kerr said.

"What's that meant to mean except nothing at all?" Leo's father retorted.

"Leo didn't have much, and he went nowhere near it when he'd finished talking. Some people thought they saw him try to spill his drink on the stage."

"Let's be honest, shall we, Trevor? Are these people you?"

"I hope you don't think I'm in the habit of rushing to judgement. That isn't how I do my job."

"It sounded as if you were judging more than a bit to me."

"I'm sorry you've formed that impression. I was simply trying to advise you as much in the way of a friend as I could."

"So what are we supposed to think you've told us?"

"You should have a sense of how investigations may proceed," Kerr said and slapped the arms of the chair like a displaced punishment. "Now if you'll all excuse me, I think I've said rather more than enough. Please make sure it stays here and nowhere else."

Leo saw his mother had to rouse herself to say "Thank you for doing your best for us, Trevor."

Nobody else seemed willing to risk a remark, and she saw Kerr to the front door without speaking. As she returned at a pace expressive of reluctance Leo's father said with determined optimism "At least we won't need all the cars just now if they insist on taking one to check."

"Wasting their time and ours when they'll find nothing, will they, Leo?" When he agreed with all the vehemence he couldn't use to say much else his mother said "We know you wouldn't do anything like that to us."

"To anyone. You ought to know that too."

"Of course we do. That isn't why these things are happening to us."

He found he was unwilling to ask the question Ellen asked. "What things?"

"Maybe the sort Trevor was talking about. Brian's driving and the way I am with food just now, and the trouble Leo had as well. I'm just glad it's left you alone, Ellen."

"I don't think those are quite the same as Mr Kerr had in mind, are they?"

"Mine is. I'm like the lady with the insects." Leo saw her have to swallow before she could go on. "I keep thinking they're in all the food," she said. "I keep almost seeing it move."

CHAPTER TWENTY-FOUR

A s he turned away from his parents' house Leo said "I think the sandwich may have done the trick."

His father had made one in front of them all, just a thin sample of ham between two slices of a fresh loaf. He'd performed every stage of the process in plain sight like a worker in an open kitchen committed to reassuring the public about hygiene and not, Leo did his best to think, a conjurer concealing a secret. He'd cut it into quarters and encouraged everyone to take a piece, murmuring "That's for you, Bev. You've seen exactly what's in it." She'd watched him and their son and Ellen bite into theirs, miming hunger like a troupe of mutes or a team of adults formed to urge a reluctant child to eat, and then she'd gnawed off a mouthful so resolute Leo feared she was overstating her courage. She'd taken some moments to make her jaws move, a paralysis that had felt ominously infectious, but eventually she'd begun to chew, and when the task was completed at last she'd worked her throat to swallow. "Thank you," she'd said so indistinctly it wasn't clear to whom, gazing not much better than blankly at the portion she had yet to conquer. "Finish yours and you can leave us to it," Leo's father had advised him and Ellen. "We'll be in touch." It was clear that he wanted to be alone with his wife while he dealt with whatever might transpire. "We'll see you very soon," she'd called after Leo and Ellen, as much like a plea as a promise.

"Let's hope so," Ellen answered Leo, but he could hear it was a preamble. "And what tricks have you been playing, Leo?"

"It's more like they've been played on me."

"I don't know what that means, but you know what I do."

"I'll tell you if you'll let me. I haven't known how to, that's all."

"Try just telling the truth for a change. Why don't you start with the name of your pupil."

"Which would you like?"

"I don't like it at all. Is this another game you're playing? I really wouldn't do that. If I can't trust you there's no point in going on."

"I honestly don't know what you're asking."

"Who you went to see when you made me delay dinner."

"You know the answer to that. Nobody at all."

"Are you certain that's really the truth now? You're not telling me another lie?"

"I wouldn't have told you that one if I could have thought how to explain."

"Then you'd better try doing that now. What were you actually up to?"

"Getting rid of my phone."

"Why did you have to go all that way to do it?"

"I thought it would be safest."

"Safe from what?" Ellen halted by a postbox with an imperfectly inserted package for a fat brown tongue and scrutinised Leo's face. "Was Mr Kerr right after all?"

"I can't believe you'd think that. If it's my fault I'm sorry." All this postponed having to admit "Safe from anyone I didn't want to get to me."

"Such as who? Get to you how?"

Leo shoved the package into the gaping straight-lipped slot while he tried to find an answer Ellen might accept. The elongated parcel was softer than he'd anticipated, unnecessarily reminiscent of an overgrown grub, but there was no need to imagine it squirmed as it plunged into the dark to land with a muscular thump. "Look, I want to tell you everything," he said, "but I need to show you something first I hope will help you understand. Shall we wait till we're home?"

"If we must, but then let's be quick."

She was already marching towards the house, but the sight of his Pass With Parker car made Leo falter. Why couldn't he have seen the logo would betray him to any witnesses? He loitered to sniff at the vehicle, detecting no smell. "They'll find nothing," he said and thought it best to add "Because there's not a thing to find."

By the time he reached the house Ellen had let herself in. "Where are we going?" she was impatient to establish.

"The kitchen if you'd like a drink."

She strode into the front room at once. "Just show me what I'm meant to see."

When Leo joined her on the couch she made all the space she could for him. He brought up the Daoloth Reveals site on his phone, which he planted in her outstretched hand. He wouldn't have retreated if she hadn't said "Don't crowd me. Just let me read this."

She did so more than once. He watched her recall the paragraph about the Alps, scrolling up and down as if this might dislodge some significance. Eventually she dropped the phone on the unoccupied third in the middle of the couch. "What am I supposed to make of all that?"

"It's what they believe in Alphafen, but they don't want you to know."

"I'm not surprised. I should think they'd be embarrassed to admit it."

"It isn't just embarrassment. It's their secret. A secret weapon, if you like. I think I brought it home with me."

"I don't understand what you're trying to say. What did you bring?"

"Some kind of infection. Call it psychological."

"You're saying something affected your mind while you were over there."

"Not just mine. My father's ended up with my driving problem. My mother thinks something's got into her food, and I did last time we had dinner with them. My words started going wrong when I was giving Lucy Fenton her last lesson, and now she's had trouble with her language. I'm infecting people, don't you see?"

"Leo, I didn't realise you'd been blaming yourself like that. You really mustn't. There's no need."

"There's every need. I had to understand what was happening or it might never have stopped."

"I'm saying there's no need to bring those fairy stories you showed me into it. Lucy Fenton was dyslexic, wasn't she? Maybe she affected you instead of the other way round. And I know your parents made you learn to drive with someone who gave you a hard time. Do you think Brian may feel guilty now you've told him and that's why his driving isn't up to scratch just now?" When Leo shook his head while he searched for words Ellen told him "Maybe Beverley thought you didn't like her dinner, but there wasn't anything not to like, was there? As you said, that phone call put you off. I'm sure she sees that now and you've stopped her going off her food."

"Haven't you heard anything I've said?" Every bid she'd made to reassure him aggravated his desperation, not least because he'd previously clung to the ideas himself. "You heard the phone call," he insisted. "I infected that boy at the airport as well."

"Why do you want to believe all this? How can it help?"

"Because it's the truth you asked for. The truth they tried to hide from me in Alphafen. They had a book about alps, the kind you read about just now, but Hanna's father tricked me out of buying it. He made me think one of his friends wanted it, but then I realised I'd heard Emil phoning him."

"In German, Leo?"

"Yes, in German. I understood enough to figure out he'd told his friend to come and buy the book so I couldn't."

Had he convinced Ellen at last? Certainly he'd prompted her to think – and then she said "What has any of this got to do with your phone?"

"Hanna kept asking what I was doing. All she really wanted was to find out what they could turn into one of their nightmares.

I thought I'd brought those back with me, but now I think they needed her to send them. Or maybe they were inside me and had to be set off."

".Leo." Ellen reached across the dormant phone to grip his hand so hard he felt captured. "Shall I tell you what I think is wrong? You stopped seeing your analyst too soon."

"Believe me, seeing her wouldn't help. She was another of my victims. I made her eyes start coming out of her head."

"You can't be telling me she thinks that."

"Her secretary rang me up to say they were. Shall I phone him? You can listen in."

"If she's ill that doesn't mean you're responsible. You can always find someone else."

"I don't need that kind of help. I just need you to believe me. You said you wanted trust. Don't you think I do?" At once he had an inspiration he hoped wasn't simply desperate. "If you won't listen to me," he said, "will you listen to somebody else?"

"It depends what they're saying and who they are."

"A lecturer. An academic. I can't tell you what they'll say. I'll find out when you do. Promise you'll listen and I'll track him down."

Ellen gave a nod not entirely unlike a drooping of her head and released his hand, perhaps just to let him use the phone. "If you think it's going to help somehow," she said.

As Leo set about searching for a number he remembered there were three universities in Liverpool. How much of a story might he have not just to invent but repeat? The topmost listing brought him an efficient slightly Scouse voice that announced the institution and then enumerated options before making way for him to jab the digit for the operator. "I need to contact somebody I think may have given you a talk," he told her. "He forgot to let me have his number."

"Can I get a name?"

"Jerome Pugh. That's him, you understand, not me."

"And who is calling?"

"I'm from—" Leo had to think fast. "Speech Unlimited," he said. While this earned him a sharp look from Ellen, it seemed to satisfy the operator. "You'll want external speakers," she said. "I'll put you through."

A tinny lump of Mozart furred with static and doggedly trailed by a repetition of the random sample of the concerto preceded the next voice. "External."

"Is it right you had Jerome Pugh as a speaker recently?"

"Right in what sense?"

"I mean did you hire him?"

"May I ask who wants to know?"

Leo didn't look at Ellen as he told the woman "Speech Unlimited."

"Ah, I should have known."

With no idea what response he was inviting Leo said "You've heard of us, then."

"I'm saying I'd expect some organisation of the kind to have an interest in Mr Pugh."

"I was telling your operator Jerome forgot to give me his number so I could get in touch."

"I take it you want him to speak to your people."

"That was the idea."

"You're welcome to him. Perhaps you won't have as much trouble as we did."

As Leo made to hasten past this Ellen said "What sort of trouble?"

"Is that another member of your group?"

"Just someone who's here with me," Leo said and quite as swiftly "Could you give me Jerome's number?"

"The union caused the trouble. Students opposed to his being heard. Let me see if the details are to hand." Before Ellen could speak, as she plainly meant to, the woman said "I have them here."

Leo typed the digits in his contacts list as she dictated slowly enough to be instructing a child. "I hope your event goes as well as it deserves," she said and ended the call. Just as immediately Ellen said "Who exactly is this person you want me to listen to?"

"I told you, a history lecturer."

"So why wasn't he welcome there?"

"Some people don't care for his ideas."

Leo did his best to head off any further discussion by fingering Pugh's number. He felt Ellen's gaze gathering on him while the indeterminately distant phone rang. As he gave her a grin he hoped needn't be apologetic she said "Don't get too good at lying, will you?"

"You heard I had to," Leo said as the phone fell silent. He thought the connection had been severed until Pugh spoke. "Who's there?"

The challenge sounded uncharacteristically edgy. "It's Leo Parker," Leo said.

"Why, Mr Parker. I wasn't expecting to hear from you. What do you want of me now?"

"Just some confirmation of what you were telling me last time we met."

"Confirmation? I've enough of that to spare. How much would you like?"

He mustn't let Pugh's aggressive tone deter him. He was about to introduce Ellen when Pugh demanded "How did you get hold of my number?"

"I asked the university where you told me you were speaking."

"So I did. Silly me," Pugh said, adding a pinched solitary laugh. "Calling to check how I've fared since we met, are you?"

"No, I've got someone who'd like to hear what you have to say."

"Then they're one of the last of an endangered species. What will I want to know about them?"

"My name's Ellen, Mr Pugh. As Leo says, I'm with him. That's really all there is to know. Tell me about yourself."

"I'm a historian. The sort too many people these days would like to shut up. Apparently they think silencing my kind will make the past go away, but I guarantee it won't. It'll grow stronger and make itself felt. I'm sure your friend Mr Parker can tell you all about that."

"I'd like you to if you don't mind. You lecture at a university, do you?"

"For the moment, but who knows how much longer if some people have their way." Pugh seemed to be enacting a version of the hindrance, straining his voice. "I can only be grateful for friends in high places," he said. "Even if they don't agree with me, a few still think I should be heard."

"I told you Ellen does. You ask him, Ellen."

For a moment she seemed to have decided against it, and then she said "Tell me what you told Leo, Mr Pugh."

"About what in particular?"

"Alps," Leo said. "You know which I mean."

"All too well, but I believe you can tell your friend everything she needs to know about them."

"I really would appreciate hearing it from you," Ellen said.

"You want to know what it's like, do you? That's why Mr Parker is putting me on show."

"How's Leo doing that? I thought you said you liked to be heard."

"So I did." Quite as bitterly Pugh said "Can you hear now?"

"Perfectly well." Either Ellen didn't notice how effortful Pugh's voice had grown or she found this insignificant. "I want to know what you put in Leo's head."

"You think I put it in there, if that's even where it is."

"Didn't you tell him about some kind of legend?"

"Alps are no legend. They're more than that, and worse."

"What are you saying is worse?"

"Their nature and their purpose. They're the essence of the dark. They come up from the caves under the mountains and bring their darkness with them. Not a dark you can see, one you can feel. It feels as if you're trapped where there's never any light with things that need the dark to live in, and they delight in making you more afraid. It's what they feed on."

"You can't tell us that's not a legend, unless you've made some of it up."

"You need convincing, do you? Hasn't Mr Parker done his job as well as he'd like to think?" With a surge of triumph that sounded close to its opposite Pugh said "Would you care to see?"

Leo found this ominous beyond defining. "See what?"

"You'll see."

Pronouncing even such a short phrase appeared to be a task. In a moment an icon appeared on the phone screen to signify a video call. "Take it, Leo," Ellen murmured when he hesitated. "I wouldn't mind seeing what he looks like."

Leo's finger shivered as he touched the icon. Could the screen really feel as cold as the wall of an unlit cave? The image the icon summoned didn't reassure him. It displayed just the ceiling of a room, as if it was reluctant to show what else was there. He heard an indistinct fumbling as a fleshy blur filled the screen – a hand that was groping to reposition the phone. It took some seconds to tilt the phone downwards and show its owner.

At first Leo thought a faulty connection was infecting the image with a stutter. Then Pugh's hands jerked up to twitch their fingers on either side of his face. He looked close to scrabbling at it like a mime depicting an appalled inability to remove a mask. "Here's what he's given me," he barely said.

Not just his voice put Leo in mind of a ventriloquist's. Pugh's lips had turned unyieldingly straight and seemed scarcely able to open. The small moustache had grown raggedly unkempt, while the large reddish nostrils appeared to be gaping in search of breath. The wide eyes looked desperate to close, and raw with insomnia. "That's one way to stop me being heard," the cramped voice complained. "I haven't been able to lecture all week."

While Pugh spoke he staggered backwards as if his body no longer obeyed him. His hands fell away from framing his face, and Leo saw the man's limbs were as rigid as a wooden puppet's, only just able to bend at the joints. He remembered seeing Pugh strut along the railway carriage like a marionette, a condition that had plainly grown more chronic. Pugh glared at the phone while he clutched at the desk to steady himself. The spasmodic action unbalanced the phone, which gave Leo and Ellen a glimpse of diplomas on a wall before clattering onto its face. "Seen enough?" Pugh demanded offscreen.

"I can see you need help," Ellen said, "and you really ought to get some if you haven't, but I don't see how you can possibly blame Leo."

"He's the carrier."

"I've no idea what you mean by that."

"The kind the leader would have sent against the foe. What they would have brought is here now, nearly a century too late."

Saying all this required audible labour, like a last resolve to be heard. It prompted Ellen to retort "By the leader you mean—"

"I'm sure Mr Parker will tell you. Now I think I've exerted myself enough on everyone's behalf. Don't blame yourself too much, will you, Mr Parker? I should have known better than to visit you after you returned from Alphafen."

His face loomed at the screen, and the skin around his eyes jerked as if they were struggling to blink. A shaky blur groped at the image, and then he was gone. "What was he talking about, Leo?" Ellen said at once.

"Me. What I've done to him and everyone. You must have got that."

"He said too much about you, but I wasn't asking that. Which leader?"

"I'm afraid he's a bit of a Hitler fan."

"How could you get involved with anyone like that?"

"He was at the Kehlsteinhaus and he heard I was English. He started telling me about the alps until Hanna's father had him thrown out, and don't say you don't wonder why he wanted to get rid of him, or can you guess? And then Pugh tracked me down to tell me the rest after I came home. But listen, his politics aren't the point just now. Don't you see—"

"I think they are. I think they show how dangerously obsessed he is, and coming to find you certainly does. Shall I tell you how I see the situation?"

"So long as you saw what's happened to him. He was nothing like that the first time I met him. I saw it start when he was leaving here."

"I think meeting him may have made things go wrong, but not the way you've convinced yourself."

She was aggravating Leo's distress at Pugh's state, and he could only say "So tell me how."

"I think you want to feel responsible. I understand why, but you need it too much. You're saying all this started when you went abroad. I think you were ready to feel guilty because you'd never really stopped deep down."

"Guilty of what?"

"For your friend who was killed when you were at school. You could say that was brought over from there, couldn't you? So you already felt guilty of bringing it. And then you meet this Pugh person and all his nonsense gets mixed up with it in your head. You think people can be infected psychologically, and that's exactly what he's done to you, but you can overcome it just like you did when you were having therapy. Maybe you don't need any more of that if you see what I'm saying is true. Even your Mr Pugh said you shouldn't blame yourself."

"You've only heard what you wanted to." In growing desperation Leo said "He told me I'd done that to him. Just because I didn't know what I was doing doesn't mean I'm not responsible."

"You want to feel you are, and it's past time you stopped. It can't bring your friend back. I can prove you wrong if you'll listen to me."

Leo did his best to sound receptive even as his nerves contradicted him. "I'm listening."

"If you've been making things happen to people, why hasn't anything happened to me?"

For the duration of the breath he took Leo was tempted to offer her all the suggestions he could find: that the effects were unpredictably random, that his concern for her might have shielded her somehow, that he hadn't contaminated most of the people he'd met since returning to Settlesham, at least as far as he knew. He'd infected Pugh before disposing of his old phone, but he'd experienced no daylight nightmares since replacing it, and some of those had taken time to affect their victims. Surely all this was as much as he needed to know. "You're right," he said as persuasively as he could muster. "Nothing will, I promise."

CHAPTER TWENTY-FIVE

"Do give the senior my wish for a speedy recovery."
Bernard Whitley's drooping jowly face suggested this
contained if not concealed a mournful quip. "We're hoping he'll
be back on the road very soon," Leo said.

Mightn't his father's problem dissipate by itself, given time? Nothing
in the legend said the nightmares persisted as long as their victims lived.
He scheduled the retired headmaster's next lesson and watched him trot
through a doorway moustached with drooping vines into his cottage.
Leo was still in Settlesham Old Town, heading for a coffee break before
he picked up his next pupil, when his phone shrilled on the dashboard.

It couldn't be Hanna Weber. There was no need for his nerves to
make him jerk the accelerator and the wheel. In the midst of ringing,
the phone told him the caller was his mother. Why should this leave his
nervousness untouched? Suppose Hanna had searched out his parents'
landline so as to hunt him down, as Schmidt had? Leo veered into the
nearest space he could find, leaving his father's car at an extravagant
angle with the kerb, and jabbed the phone screen. "What is it, mum?"

"Sorry, are you on the road?"

"Not right now. I mean, I am, but parked. You go ahead."

"Just a bit of news for you, that was all."

"Yes?" When this prompted no reply Leo said "Is dad fit to
drive again?"

"Not quite yet, we think. Slowly making progress. It's the thing
about walking before you can run."

Leo tried to avoid hearing how inappropriate this sounded. "You're
eating properly again," he hoped instead.

"Same answer, Leo. Just for now."

"Keep trying, both of you. You mustn't let it get on top of you."
This was all he felt he could risk saying except "So what's the news?"

"I happened to see Trevor Kerr in the street and we were talking about you."

"Tell me they've finished with my car."

"He didn't mention it, but they have with your phone."

Leo waited but had to urge "And?"

"They couldn't find anything bad. Of course that's because we know there never was."

"So do I get it back?"

"I wouldn't know that. I thought you didn't want it any more."

Her bemusement showed him how careless his question had been. "Thanks for letting me know," he said. "We'll see you both soon."

"I'll make myself make dinner. I'll tell myself you told me to."

This ought to be positive so long as he managed to be, Leo resolved. Might the nightmares be persisting because the phone was still in Settlesham? Even if the police had found it innocent, it could still harbour elements they would never discover. It had to be destroyed, and he backed the skewed car out of the space to drive to the police station.

The anonymity of the hulking concrete block in Settlesham New Town resembled a disguise. Token windows slitted by plastic blinds relieved the flat white frontage. The glass doors seemed reluctant to admit him. A clump of grubby fingerprints clustering around a virtually invisible hint of a slit demonstrated that at least one visitor had lost patience with the mechanism. Beyond the doors a counter shielded by plate glass stretched across the width of the reception area. Leo rang the bell beside it and eventually, despite the notice specifying just a single ring, again. This summoned a policewoman from the crowded room beyond the counter. "May I help you?" she said, by no means wholly in the manner of an invitation.

"I believe you've got my phone."

"Do you know when it was handed in?"

"You've been searching it for evidence. You couldn't find any. That's to say there was nothing to find."

"Have you been advised of that?"

"Inspector Kerr said so."

"And he told you you could pick it up."

"He didn't say I couldn't."

Leo wished her eyes weren't so glassily blank. Perhaps a reflection on the window was coating them, but it felt like being scrutinised by a doll. "May I take your name," she said, not even slightly as a question.

"Parker. Leo Parker."

"Please wait there, Mr Parker."

She marched back to the inner room as stiffly as she'd emerged and shut the door, cutting off a mumble of discussions. The wait let Leo notice how the far side of the counter was more than an arm's length from the glass, which was breached only by a pair of gaps not much bigger than a hand. Even if this hadn't been designed to make the public feel criminal, he did: more dangerous than he cared to be, and displayed like a specimen in a glass cage. He was wondering whether any of the muffled discussions concerned him when Kerr said "Leo Parker."

It was more a statement than a welcome. He was standing in a doorway on Leo's side of the glass, having eased the door open unheard. His face looked laden with dispassion, more immune than ever to surprise. "Come through here," he said.

He led the way along a boxy concrete corridor, but not far. When he gestured at a room Leo thought he was being ushered into an office, but the windowless room contained just a bare table bolted to the floor and flanked by two straight minimally cushioned chairs. "We shouldn't be interrupted in here," Kerr said, indicating the further chair.

Leo hadn't anticipated much conversation, and hoped there wouldn't be. As Kerr shut them in Leo made to inch the chair on the far side of the table forward, only to find it was secured to the floor. "Some things have to be made safe," Kerr told him.

He sat opposite Leo, leaning forward to rest his folded forearms on the table as if to demonstrate its correct use. "I'm told you're looking to reclaim your phone," he said.

Why did his eyes give a secretive flicker? The pair of fluorescent tubes overhead had momentarily faltered. "My mother says you've finished with it," Leo said.

"You gave me the impression you had."

"It's still my property, though, isn't it?"

"Nobody doubts that, but I should like to know why you want it returned."

"Just to be sure." When this earned a fixed stare Leo said "I'd just like to know where it is."

"I may as well inform you I am not entirely satisfied."

The walls shivered, because the light had, and Leo could have thought the room was sympathising with his nerves. "Why not?" he protested.

"You insisted you'd thrown it away."

"Because that's what I did. If I hadn't that fellow couldn't have found it, could he?"

"Mr Parker. Leo." The diminution of the name sounded less like a friendly gesture than a bid to make Leo feel smaller. "Every hole in your phone was full of soil," Kerr said. "That could only be the case if it had been buried."

"All right, I did."

"You'll need to tell me why you didn't say so when you were asked."

Leo glanced up at the sputter of the tubes in the hope of finding time to think. He was about to declare that the lie didn't matter when he thought of a better response. "I didn't want my parents knowing I had."

"I can understand that, but not why you did it."

Leo wished he hadn't looked away from his interrogator, because lowering his eyes brought an impression that the room had surreptitiously shrunk. "I wanted to be certain it was got rid of."

"What reason did you have?"

Leo felt as if he wouldn't escape the windowless cell until he succeeded in satisfying Kerr. "I picked up a stalker," he tried saying, "when I was abroad on everyone's account."

"Did you report this?"

"I didn't think it was that serious." At once Leo saw how this undermined his explanation. "I mean she was a pest like you wouldn't believe," he said. "She was getting on my nerves so much I wanted to be sure I wasn't even aware of her any more."

"You seem to make something of a habit of not reporting offences."

"She was only offensive to me." Leo saw his lurch at wit fall short of the listener. "I told you," he said, "I didn't want my parents to know when it really wasn't that serious. Even if I'd reported it, what could you have done about it? She isn't in this country, remember."

Kerr laid a weighty gaze on him as though to hold him in the chair and straightened up. "Please wait here while I fetch the phone and the documentation."

Leo watched the door judder shut, leaving him alone in the room. No doubt the movement of the door had grown momentarily intermittent because the light had, and he needn't imagine the flickering was able to accomplish worse. If the walls appeared to jerk inwards with each stutter of the tubes, this couldn't mean the room was almost imperceptibly shrinking, and he mustn't imagine the door was twitching smaller too. Was it even reasonable to wonder if the jerky light was meant to wear down suspects who'd been brought in for interrogation? This might imply Kerr had left him while the sly strobe worked on him. The light snatched the walls closer again as he heard footsteps rescinding the retreat they'd made along the corridor, but why were they taking so long to return, as if the room had shrunk away from the rest of the world? A spasm of the light greeted Kerr, so that Leo wasn't sure he'd glimpsed the policeman ducking into the room. "Do we have to do this in here?" Leo blurted.

The snug thud of the door was the immediate answer. Kerr laid the phone in a plastic bag and a form beside it on the table before he spoke. "What issue do you have with it?"

"I'm finding it a bit oppressive."

"Some people do." Kerr gave him time to guess the kind they were supposed to be. "I've had a touch of claustrophobia myself on occasion," Kerr said. "The sooner you complete the receipt, the sooner you'll be dealt with."

The sheet of paper was a mass of cramped rectangles demanding information: name, address, phone number.... Each time the light convulsed, the spaces to which Leo was struggling to restrict his details appeared to dwindle while flickers plucked at the cheap ballpoint and the walls edged towards him. He scribbled his signature and the equally constricted date at last and shoved the page across the table, rucking it up. Perhaps this was one reason why Kerr met it with an unfavourable look. "That's barely legible," he said. "You can't hide, you know. You should have realised that by now."

"I wasn't trying. Your light's getting to me, that's all."

"I wouldn't say it was too much of a problem. If it's making you nervous, I wonder what else may be."

When Leo suppressed any answer Kerr slid the phone across the table. The crumpling of plastic sounded excessively loud, forced closer by the walls. "I believe that will do for today," Kerr said.

As Leo shoved the phone in his pocket with a rustle reminiscent of a creature burrowing in rubbish he said "What's the situation with my car?"

"What do you feel it should be?"

Leo felt as if the antics of the light had snagged his eyelids, jerking their nerves. "How much longer is it going to take them to find out there's nothing to find?"

"As it happens I was advised while I was fetching your phone."

Leo waited, to be rewarded only by a furtive shifting of the walls. "Advised of what?" he appeared to be required to ask.

"The vehicle has been given a clean bill of health."

"I'm glad to hear it. Where do I pick it up?"

"At the pound as soon as the fee has been paid."

"Which fee? Who's paying?"

"That will be you, Mr Parker."

Leo no longer knew whether the light was twitching or his eyes were, if not both. "You're telling me I have to pay even though I've done nothing wrong?"

"You wouldn't expect the good people of Settlesham to foot the bill."

"I'm one of them and I don't expect it either."

"I can't help you any further, I'm afraid. We don't make the rules. You'll need to pay the price if you wish to recover your car."

"I'd say I've paid too many prices as it is."

Kerr's weary look was the response, faltering only because the light did. Leo was about to stand up when the policeman said "One more word before you leave us."

"Won't it wait till we're outside?" Leo came close to pleading.

"It may not take long. I told you I'm not completely satisfied." Kerr leaned over his folded arms to scrutinise Leo's reaction, and Leo felt as though the walls had advanced on him as well. "Your mother wanted me to know she has been suffering from hallucinations," Kerr said.

"What's that to do with any of this?"

"She thinks it shows how stress can affect people. How it has locally of late."

"And what do you think?"

"I believe more is going on in Settlesham that requires investigation."

His unrelenting gaze together with the stealthy agitation of the room provoked Leo to blurt "It is right now in here. Can't you feel it? Can't you see?"

"Whatever you may have been doing to people, it won't work on me."

"I don't want to do anything bad to anyone, can't you understand? If you think I am, tell me how."

"I've said the issue warrants further investigation."

The phone as well as the light was making the walls judder, Leo thought but couldn't say. He shoved himself off the immovable chair, only for a thought to arrest him. "What's anybody doing about the parking people at the airport? I told you how they used my car without my knowledge."

"They are under investigation too."

Leo could have done without Kerr's last word. He was alongside the policeman, having crossed more space than he'd felt was there, when Kerr stood up. He looked ready to detain his captive. "You aren't planning any travels soon, are you?"

"I wish I hadn't planned the last one. I don't think some of the people over there are as friendly to us as they'd like us to imagine."

"They certainly seem to have kept it to themselves. Are you saying they didn't with you?"

Leo's inability to explain helped urge the walls closer. "They kept pretending," he said desperately but inadequately. "They nearly had me fooled."

"Then let me offer some advice as a friend of the family."

Leo lurched to throw the door open. "What is it?" he said from the corridor.

"Don't be in such a hurry. You may be glad of my concern." Kerr halted in the doorway, gripping both sides of the frame as though to hold them apart. "Best keep your thoughts about your visit to yourself," he said low.

"I've no complaints. I know you had to do your job."

"Your visit to Alphafen." Kerr's stare made it clear he didn't welcome even an inadvertent joke. "We don't want you stirring things up unnecessarily," he said.

"I don't," Leo said more passionately than he could expect Kerr to understand. "I never did."

Kerr took a step out of the room at last, and Leo could have fancied he'd been hindered from emerging. "You distracted me from what I meant to say," the policeman said. "I take it you've no reason to leave Settlesham in the near future."

For an instant Leo wondered if he had, and then the possibility deserted him. "Not that I can think of."

"That will need to be seen to." Kerr was staring at the defective lights, which had begun to emit a buzz like a fly caught in a cobweb. "Please make sure you're available if necessary," he said.

Leo mumbled an approximate undertaking as he left the corridor behind. He had to destroy the phone as soon as he could – before he dealt with his next pupil, because it might infect them. It had plainly affected him in the interview room. He dashed out of the police station to fling the bagged phone into the boot of his car, where the crumpled plastic began to unfurl with a shrill whisper as though its contents were making a bid to escape. As he took refuge in the driver's seat he realised his next pupil was Mr Fowler, but he couldn't let this matter. "Yes," Fowler said, silencing the second repetition of the bell, and immediately "Yes."

"It's Leo Parker, Mr Fowler."

"Let me guess. You propose to let me down again."

"I hope you won't see it that way. I do apologise, but I was wondering if I could possibly postpone."

"That counts as letting me down in my book. It's not as if it's the first time. Are you inconveniencing all your customers, or have I been singled out for special treatment?"

"It's just an unfortunate coincidence. I'll make sure it won't happen again."

"Unfortunate is certainly the word. Unfortunate for you and your firm. Not just your firm, your family. What excuse have we this time?"

"I've had to deal with a problem with my car."

"And is it roadworthy now?"

"It will be when I pick it up. I'm using my father's at present." In the hope of having heard Fowler begin to relent Leo said "If it's convenient I could be with you in less than an hour."

"Please see to it you are. Any longer and I'll be giving your rivals my custom."

"I won't let you down," Leo said, only to hear himself confirm he already had. He was about to drive off when he realised he should have his old phone to hand if he was to carry out the only plan he had. He grabbed the bagged device from the boot and dropped it on the seat beside his, and did his best to ignore how close the dormant blank-faced object was as he drove out of Settlesham.

In less than twenty minutes he was at the motorway. The bag betrayed a restless rustle as he veered onto the ramp, but he needn't fancy the phone had sensed its fate and was poised to defeat him somehow. Just the same, he tried not to think of his plan as he sped off the ramp.

He had to keep glancing in the mirror – he was looking for a vehicle that would do the job he had in mind – while he did his best to pretend he was simply acting as a driver should. When he saw a lorry towering above the cars behind him he began to brake. Car after car overtook him, and then the lorry did. As its cab nosed alongside he lowered his window and gripped the wheel with his right hand while he groped for the bagged phone with the other.

Had it sidled out of reach? The roar of the lorry seemed to surge at him, threatening to blot out more than one sense, as he failed to lay his hand on the phone. He had to glance aside to find it exactly where he'd left it on the seat. Perhaps not just the uproar had interfered with his perceptions. He closed his hand around the bag and thought it put up a feeble struggle, as if its contents had – as if he'd picked up a dying bird or else a dead one rendered active by whatever was feasting within. The elongated lorry was halfway past him now. He glanced at the nearest massive wheel in a bid to gauge the distance as he made to pitch the phone onto the tarmac. His hand convulsed as its chill slippery burden seemed to, and he flung the phone away so hastily it robbed him of control.

The phone skittered across the road, well out of reach of the nearside wheels of the lorry. It had achieved another nightmare, then – the prospect of retrieving it from among the traffic or else suffering the hope that somebody would run it over. Then it came to rest, or at any rate Leo heard a wheel on the far side of the lorry catch it with a splintering crunch. As he reduced speed to let the lorry swerve into the lane he thought he saw a car scattering the fragments across the tarmac. He hoped nobody had seen him jettison the phone, but in any case what could they do? All the same, he was glad when the next junction let him leave the traffic behind.

A roundabout sent him back onto the motorway in the opposite direction. Not many more than twenty minutes later he was outside Fowler's house. Fowler was leaning on the cottage gate, ostentatiously baring his wristwatch, but took his time over strolling to the car. "Here as promised," Leo felt justified in declaring.

"That's why you're so jolly, is it? No need to make so much of turning up on time." Fowler inclined his head towards a medley of distant sirens as he clambered into the seat Leo had vacated. "I trust those aren't for you," he said. "You haven't broken any laws on my behalf."

"I wouldn't say so," Leo said but was relieved to hear the sirens growing more remote. "They can't have anything to do with me," he said and hoped he had no need to hope.

CHAPTER TWENTY-SIX

O nce Leo showed the attendant at the pound his driving licence and the insurance certificate with his registration number and thrust his credit card into a reader and signed a form, he felt he'd done enough. "May I have my car?"

The man clad in a jaundiced jerkin leaned across the counter a sliding window had exposed. "Where's the Parker, Rob?"

"They're all of them parked," his comparably burly colleague bellowed across several car roofs. "About time you done a few."

"The Parker car, mate. You remember. It give us a laugh."

"Yeah, well, I'm not having any now, And."

If they sounded like a double act, Leo wouldn't have paid to watch. "What's supposed to be funny?"

Truncated Andy's look suggested he'd seen a joke he didn't especially care for. "He just said it's not."

"You said my car was, and I wouldn't mind knowing why. Having to pay when you haven't done anything wrong is no joke."

"It's got your name on, hasn't it? Rob was parking a Parker." He plainly resented having to explain. "It made us giggle, any road. You need a bit of that round here."

"I'm glad if my car has stuck in your mind. Can someone show me where it is?"

"Still asking, Rob."

No doubt this meant Andy was, however unreasonably persistent it made Leo sound. "I've got a job to finish," Rob protested but stopped short of presenting any evidence. "Why don't you take him for a change."

"I assume it has to be here somewhere. Shall I look for it myself?"

"Rob won't have robbed it, if that's what you're wondering."

"I wasn't," Leo said, not least to placate Rob.

At least a hundred vehicles were parked in the roofless compound. Somebody appeared to have set out to line them up in several ranks before tiring of the task. Quite a few were hidden under hoods. Perhaps Leo's was, since he couldn't see it in any of the line-ups or among the scattered vehicles. When he tried enlivening it with the key fob he heard it respond, though not close enough to locate. Besides its plaintive call he heard a flapping of plastic and glimpsed a dark shape streaking across the compound. It dodged in a zigzag to avoid Rob and Leo before vanishing into a shadow that must be a gap in a wall. "Rat," Rob announced.

"We get a lot of those in here," Andy said.

Leo used the fob to rouse the car a second time, and again while making for the rank of vehicles the rodent had appeared from. Apparently the third shrill peep was as much as Rob could suffer. He stalked to the nearest draped car in the line Leo was heading for and hauled off the cover. It wasn't merely Leo's car; it was where the intruder had fled from. "What was a rat doing under there?" Leo protested.

"You'd want to know," Rob said.

"Why'd you cover that up, Rob?" Andy shouted. "Having another laugh?"

"Keeping the rain off. Like he said, they couldn't find nothing to prosecute."

"Don't go telling us that crap."

Leo felt as denounced as he assumed Rob was meant to feel. "Excuse me, which is that?"

"Him and his rain. We've had none for weeks."

"Watch out I don't piss on your head next time you have a nap," Rob said. "Maybe then you'll think there's some."

"Maybe I'll have a shit on yours when you're not looking."

"Guess what I'll be doing in your lunch box."

"Do you two often carry on like this?" Leo felt compelled to ask.

"You should hear us when there's nobody around," Rob said.

"Shrivel up your balls, it would."

"So long as it isn't my fault."

Both men stared at him. "How's it going to be that?" Andy demanded.

"I mean I'm glad if it's not." This felt too close to letting his fears linger. "I'll leave you to it," Leo said and shut himself in the car.

The attendants reverted to haranguing each other as he drove out of the pound. The mirror showed them beginning to gesture like antagonists in a silent film. He hadn't caused that, Leo told himself, unless his intervention had aggravated hostilities. If they routinely behaved like that, surely it could do no harm. The rat had been just a rat. However nightmarish the incident had threatened to become, he could leave it behind.

Five minutes took him to the motorway. He was halfway home when he saw traffic backed up for miles in the opposite direction. Two of the three lanes had been closed while a team attired like the attendants at the pound cleared away fragments of vehicles. All the way to Settlesham he saw cars and lorries racing to add to the jam.

He reached Settlesham with half an hour to spare before his next lesson – enough time for a coffee at home. Parking felt like a vindication, as if the car was advertising not just the firm but his innocence. He was letting himself into the house when he faltered on the doorstep while his hand jerked the key, gnashing its teeth against the lock. A voice had fallen silent at the far end of the hall.

In a moment it raised itself. "Is that Leo?"

Given its volume, he gathered it was asking him. "Just me, yes."

"Come and make it a foursome," his mother said.

Had they brought Kerr with them? What could the policeman want now? As Leo shut the front door the smell of coffee snagged in his nostrils and grew harsh. His parents still had the keys they'd used when they were looking after his grandfather, but the intrusion made Leo feel spied upon if not suspected. He tramped fast to the kitchen, increasingly ready to demand the keys, only to find his parents' companion was Ellen. "I should have known," he wasn't swift enough to prevent himself blurting.

All three looked taken at the very least aback. "What should you?" Ellen said.

"That you'd let everybody in. I'll have a coffee to wake me up."

"Why, have you been in a dream?" his mother said.

"If I have I'm not in any now." Less fiercely Leo said "Wake me up for going on the road."

"Maybe you can have a rest," his father said as Ellen disengaged the single remaining mug from a stack of stumpy hooks. "Who's your next lesson?"

"Lewis Chapman and his running commentary on everything he does even when you haven't asked him."

"One of mine, then. I'll take him. I'm here to tell you I can."

"That's great to hear. I couldn't be happier. When did it come back to you?"

"I woke up this morning feeling up to the job, and I was. We pretended Bev was my pupil."

"I do believe he's even better at it," Leo's mother said. "Maybe he needed the break."

As Ellen planted a mug of steaming Stygian coffee in front of Leo his father said "Thanks for looking after my pupils. I'll have them all back now."

"You won't be taking any on the motorway, will you?" Leo's mother said.

Leo wondered if his father hadn't regained all his skills, and then he saw the problem. "You mean because of the accident. They're tailing back for miles westbound."

"It must have been a bad one," his father said, "if they're still having to clear up."

Leo found it hard to say the word he had to utter. "Still."

"It happened yesterday, unless there's been another since."

The suggestion seemed pathetically welcome until Leo realised it changed nothing. "What did?"

"A lorry went out of control and half a dozen cars piled up."

With gathering reluctance Leo said "Do they know what caused it?"

"They were saying on the radio the lorry driver said some kind of big bird flew into his windscreen."

At least running over the mobile hadn't burst a tyre, and Leo tried to find this sufficiently comforting. "Don't look like that," his father said. "Tell him your news, Bev."

"I'm back to enjoying my food again. You're both invited round to help us celebrate."

"Well, that's—" A clutter of reactions, among them suppressed hysterical mirth, sent Leo stumbling over his response. "I'm glad for you," he said. "Glad for you both."

"That isn't all my news."

Leo hoped he had no reason to fear asking "What else?"

"I've been speaking to some of the neighbours who were at your talk."

Leo waited, only to wonder if her smile was supposed to complete her answer. "And?"

"They've had no problems since, and they were at the punch all evening. I'll let you know what Trevor Kerr has to say for himself when I tell him."

"Don't go losing a friend on my behalf."

"If he's a friend he'll want to hear. If he won't listen he isn't one."

"Seriously, no need to go confronting him. It's all over now, so let's forget about it. I mean to."

"That's very forgiving of you. I expect that's the best way to be."

As Leo fended off unwelcome thoughts of Alphafen his father stood up, draining his mug except for a trickle of coffee he wiped from his chin with the back of his hand. "I'll be off, then," he said. "Time we all got back to normal."

CHAPTER TWENTY-SEVEN

The parking spaces closest to the town hall were reserved for
councillors, however seldom they showed up. Plaques on the wall
boasted their names, and Leo saw he was invading Paddy Bloore's
paltry territory so as to back into an anonymous space. He was several
minutes early for collecting Ellen, though the clock on the tower above
the town hall insisted he was hours ahead, and he thought of a call he
could make. If he didn't risk it he would be left with doubts that were
bound to nag him if not grow worse. He searched online for the name –
he hadn't bothered to copy the details from the list on his old phone – and
touched the number as boldly as he could. It didn't bring him the voice
he would have liked to hear at once. "Anita Chattopadhyay's practice."

"She's still practising, then." This sounded too much like a joke Leo
hadn't meant to make. "I didn't mean she needs to," he said. "I was
saying she's still operating."

"Would you have the wrong number?"

"I don't see how when you said it's hers."

"It's just that she's not that kind of doctor."

"I know that. I meant operating as in, I don't know, functioning.
Doing her job."

"I can assure you we've had no complaints."

The reassurance Leo craved seemed intent on staying out of reach.
He was about to ask as direct a question as would stay polite when the
receptionist said "May I take your name?"

"Parker. Leo Parker. I was seeing the doctor."

"I remember you, Mr Parker." The comment was unreadably
professional. "Let me see when we can book you in."

"She's still seeing people, then."

"She is, yes. She can."

"That's all I've been trying to find out, that her ailment's gone away."

"You don't want me to book you an appointment."

"There's no need any more."

"Then it was kind of you to call. Would you like a word with Anita? She's free at the moment."

"You could pass on my wishes," Leo said, apparently to nobody. A silence that tempted him to end the call was broken by the doctor's voice. "Leo, how are you?"

"As well as I'm hearing you are."

"Not as well as you might be, then."

Leo felt as if dismay had clutched him by the guts. "Your receptionist said you'd got better."

"I have, but there's room for improvement. I think I mentioned I've always suffered from the condition. I'm back to how I was when we last met."

Leo barely swallowed an apology. "I'm glad of that at least," he said.

"Did you say you'd had no further problems?"

"I'm sure they're in the past. I'm cured," Leo said and felt consideration justified adding "Thanks to you."

"And thank you for calling to check up on me. Don't hesitate to contact me if there's ever any need."

There wouldn't be, Leo vowed without saying. He confined himself to a goodbye before laying the phone on the dashboard. So the nightmare he'd passed on to the doctor had faded like the rest. If the infected phone had caused the pileup on the motorway – if he had – at least that must surely have been its final act of mischief. He reached to open the passenger door and was raising a smile when he saw the approaching figure wasn't Ellen. "You're looking pleased with yourself," Bloore said.

Leo lowered the passenger window, but not much. "I'm hoping I've no reason not to."

Bloore gripped his newly wiry thighs and scowled through the gap. "Parking in my space made you feel big, did it? I saw you wonder if you could get away with it and decide you better hadn't. Lucky for you you did."

"I'm surprised you didn't call security."

"I wouldn't just for that. I might for you."

"I'd be interested to hear what you'd tell them. You didn't see what you say you did. I used your space to back in here, that's all."

"We know you're good at making people think they see things. Don't bother trying it on me any more."

"I wasn't and I haven't been."

"You've finished making everyone see insects, have you, Parker?"

"If you mean the photos I showed at the talk—"

"They were mixed up with it all right, but that wasn't all you did. Some of us have figured out there was something in the drinks."

"I don't believe there was, and I most certainly put nothing in."

"Try telling that to anyone who started seeing things."

Leo did his best not to let his question suggest any kind of admission. "Are you saying you did?"

"I'm seeing you and I wish I wasn't. What are you hanging round here for?"

"However much of your business it is, I'm waiting for my partner."

"Partner in what, I'd like to know. Better not be anything we don't want round here."

"It isn't." Leo felt goaded to add "She works for you and your colleagues. She puts up with your behaviour."

"What's the—" Leo's warning look cut off any epithet. "She'd better watch out what she's saying," Bloore said.

"You might consider doing that yourself instead of making allegations." As Bloore thrust out his bottom lip like a springboard for his response Leo said "Let me tell you the police have found no evidence against me."

"So they've been thinking it was you as well, have they? Hope they haven't finished."

Leo had begun to feel threatened by adolescence, as if the stopped clock on the tower were dragging them back into its paralysed past. "There's no evidence to find."

"That's what they all think till they're caught. Good at hiding stuff, are you?"

"I don't need to," Leo retorted, only to realise how much he still hid. The sight of Ellen crossing the car park came as a relief, but he didn't want to involve her in a confrontation. "Now you'll have to excuse me," he said, starting the car.

"Don't you want me seeing who you're waiting for?"

"Why wouldn't he?" Ellen said.

Bloore didn't merely look at her but pantomimed surprise. "Are we talking about you, Ellen?"

"I'd like to know who else you would be."

"So you're wondering as well."

"I'm not and I don't know why you are."

"Just seeing council property isn't being used for anything it shouldn't be. I didn't realise you'd got yourself involved with Parker."

"I think you mean Mr Parker, do you? He's Leo to his friends. I don't see why you should expect to know about us, Councillor Bloore."

"That's who I am and don't you forget it. I'm what the town wants me to be."

"You could say the same about Leo."

"You won't catch me saying that or a lot of people either." Before Ellen could utter the retort she visibly had in her Bloore said "I hear you've been telling tales about me."

"I'd like to know who says I have and which."

"It's one thing your Mr Partner didn't manage to keep to himself," Bloore said and grimaced at his notion of a pun. "He says you've been having to put up with me."

"I like to decide who touches me and how."

"Good God, I was only being friendly. You'd think I'd tried to rape you, the way you carried on." Apparently convinced that Leo had to sympathise with him, Bloore protested "None of the other girls seem to mind an arm round them."

Leo couldn't help wishing he were able to transmit a final nightmare. "Perhaps you ought to wonder if they do and haven't told anyone yet."

Bloore glared at him and Ellen. "So who are you going to tell?"

Since Ellen didn't answer, Leo felt he should. "Nobody as long as you behave yourself in future, shall we say, Ellen?"

"It sounds as if we have."

He wasn't sure how much she was reprimanding him as well. "Let's head off, then," he said, "or we'll miss the film."

As she ducked into the car Bloore said "I'll see you tomorrow at work."

Even if this didn't hide a warning Leo felt prompted to say "I do hope none of this will give Ellen any problems with her job."

"Not unless she makes them. Better see she doesn't." Bloore turned towards the town hall but swung around to add "Next time you won't have my space to poke into. We know how fond of invasions you are. And in case you were wondering, my car's being serviced."

Ellen didn't speak until they'd left the town hall and the dwindling sight of Bloore's back view well behind, and then she said "What on earth started all that?"

"Just stuff he's still trying to drag up. It's all past now. I wish he was."

"I expect he'll think twice before he bothers me in future. Don't feel put down, but I can look after myself."

"So long as you know you don't have to."

Ellen dealt his forearm just a token squeeze, presumably so as not to distract him from driving, and he strayed towards reminding her he no longer found it hard to drive. There was no sign of an accident on the motorway, unless the shard of glass that gleamed at him from the hard shoulder was a reminiscence of the pileup. Five minutes' drive from the end of the motorway took him to the nearest cinema complex in Liverpool.

He and Ellen were in time not just for the revival of *Casablanca* but for the onslaught of advertising that assailed them as they entered the small auditorium. Leo could have thought the sound was turned so high to lure the scattered spectators away from their small screens to the larger one. As he followed Ellen along a row in the middle of the cinema, the trailers began, consisting mostly of explosions that hurled noise and equally insubstantial debris at the audience. By the fourth trailer the assault resembled an unrelenting bombardment, and Leo sensed Ellen growing restless. "Shall I ask them to turn it down a bit?" he whispered.

"Don't make a fuss." Perhaps she was telling him not to draw attention, hers included, to her state. "Our film won't be like this," she said.

The final trailer made its point with the most comprehensive detonation of the entire raid. The screen implored patrons to switch off their mobile phones, most of which darkened as the auditorium did. The certificate for *Casablanca* appeared, promising mild violence and milder sex references and an undefined level of discrimination. "I can never watch this too often," Ellen murmured.

A fanfare announced the film and led into the title theme. The sound had dropped to a civilised level, and Leo settled into relishing the comforts of familiarity: the luminous images evoking nostalgia for an idealised past, the old tale enacted by performers who were all ghosts now, the dialogue so celebrated it felt as if the film were quoting itself. He'd never previously been aware how close the camera took you to the actors, though why should this be a problem? No doubt the smallness of the auditorium made it more apparent. He would have suggested moving further back if this wouldn't have interrupted Ellen's enjoyment of the film.

Here was Humphrey Bogart playing solitary chess. Successive shots of him advanced towards the audience while Peter Lorre discussed letters of transit that would see two people safely out of Casablanca. Dooley Wilson came closer too as he and his band played 'Knock on Wood'. Why should a song about luck bother Leo? Even if the performers declared themselves troubled and unhappy at the outset, their knocking earned them good luck, however much the hollow impacts sounded like summoning somebody to open a door if not a lid. Perhaps Leo's immersion in the film had faltered because he was trying to think what the close shots brought to mind. Why should he feel nervous of identifying the resemblance? Surely so long as his nerves didn't affect Ellen, there was no reason not to think.

As Bogart stood outside Rick's Bar a plane passed overhead, prompting a closeup of the actor. It seemed to tower over Leo, and the similarity he was trying to grasp lurched at him. Was it a memory buried so deep that he couldn't recall the actual experience? He knew only that the notion of giants thrusting their faces at him put him in mind of lying helpless in a pram. He hoped knowing that would let him engage with the film.

At first when Bogart joined policeman Claude Rains at a table they kept a reasonable distance from the audience, but as their conversation progressed the editing jerked them towards the brink of the screen, and Leo couldn't help recoiling. How could he rid himself of this ludicrous aversion? He simply had to stop imagining the colossal figures were capable of leaning down at him. They wouldn't be a threat even if they were looming over his pram. Had his inadvertent reaction nudged Ellen? He thought he'd felt her flinch. "Sorry," he murmured.

"I'm all right," she whispered so fiercely it suggested an accusation.

Rains ushered Bogart across the nightclub to introduce him to a pair of seated customers – officers, Leo saw. How could he have forgotten there were Nazis in the film? He needn't feel their presence could revive any element of Alphafen. Just because Conrad Veidt's officer behaved as amiably as anyone Leo had encountered there, that oughtn't to renew any of the threats it hid – and then the film cut to a shot of Veidt's sidekick. It wasn't just the largest closeup yet, it was darker than the rest of the shots in the scene, inexplicably dark. How long was it going to last? Had the projection frozen? Certainly there appeared to be a flaw in the image, a twitching silhouette like an unreasonably magnified insect fluttering its wings as it clung to the upper left-hand corner of the screen. Leo felt as if the face on the screen was solidifying the gloom of the auditorium, paralysing time while the enormous head prepared to swell towards him. Suppose it did when the frozen moment ended? He was unaware of digging his nails into the arms of the seat until his fingertips began to ache – no longer aware of Ellen until she spoke.

Her whisper had grown stiff, as though she couldn't risk relinquishing control. "Leo, if you don't mind, can we go?"

He found his voice had tightened too. "Why, what's the matter?"

"Can I tell you outside?"

He didn't want to think what she sounded desperate not to acknowledge, and he averted his eyes from the renewed activity on the screen. She grabbed the seat in front of her to shove herself to her feet and stumbled fast along the row. He thought she would end up trapped by the wall until he saw she'd reached an aisle so narrow it was virtually invisible, up which she dashed towards the screen. He could only follow her as glowing pallid faces reared above him, booming words that reminded him they were putting on a show. The notion didn't reassure him; it suggested the screen was concealing a secret it was about to reveal. At least Ellen was bound for an exit, a way back to daylight. He had almost caught up with her when he saw her mistake, but his warning cry lodged in his throat. She hadn't found a door beside the screen. It was a gaping mouth.

Had the image frozen again? Perhaps somebody had shifted the projector while trying to fix the problem. Surely some caprice of the projection had let the edge of the film stray off the screen. Though the immense mouth was maintaining its pretence of offering escape, the face to which it belonged had begun to nod towards Ellen, its eyes growing not merely wider but huger. The sight appeared to have arrested her, and came near to halting Leo helpless. A flood of panic overwhelmed him, and then it drove him forward "Not there," he managed to gasp, seizing Ellen's arm.

As he urged her past the front row he glimpsed a vast face composed of whitish light above them. It seemed not just to pace them, snagging their progress until he began to feel they would never escape, but to bulge down at them like a balloon that had learned to mouth language. He didn't feel they had succeeded in leaving it behind even once they reached the far aisle. As he hurried Ellen past the rows of seats he saw an immense shadow jerk across the length of the auditorium to head them off while its gigantic voice pursued them. No words were distinguishable, just a huge oppressive mumble that seemed bent on closing around them. All the eyes of the audience gleamed as if transfixed by whichever spectacle they were watching, and Leo could imagine he felt them help it grow more substantial at his back. He and Ellen were nearly at the solitary actual exit, and he only needed to ignore how the light from the screen appeared to be bloating the shadows that framed the door so that the outline suggested restless lips. At least the door didn't resemble a lolling tongue, or at any rate not enough to leave him loath to touch it, and he didn't flinch until he'd dealt it a furious shove, having planted just his knuckles on the padded fleshy surface. The door didn't budge. Of course it wouldn't, since it only opened inwards. He was reaching for the handle when the door poked out at him, licking the carpet as it came. He staggered backwards, clutching Ellen's hand, until he saw an usherette had opened it on his behalf. "Wasn't it what you expected?" she said not unlike a guard requiring a password.

"Not this time." Ellen was visibly ready to push her aside if the usherette hadn't moved out of their way. "Let's get right out," she said and didn't release Leo's hand until they were in the open. "I'm sorry for spoiling our film."

"So long as you're all right now, that's all that matters."

She appeared to be, which let Leo start to feel he could until she said "Don't you want to know what was wrong?"

"If you need to tell me."

"That's a strange way to put it. It makes me feel you'd rather not hear."

Though this was what Leo found he feared, he had to say "Go on if it helps."

"I hope talking to each other does. Isn't that how it's meant to work?" When Leo nodded, although mostly with the weight of her gaze, Ellen said "I thought I'd left all that behind."

"You have, haven't you? We're out of it now," Leo said, only to fear he'd seemed to know too much.

"I'm talking about a bit of my childhood. I must have been too young the first time I was taken to a film. I just saw all these monster faces coming for me. They were the people on the screen, obviously, but I thought they were giants going to do I don't know what to me. I didn't stop screaming till my parents got me home."

Leo had kept up his hope – that he didn't understand why she'd fled the cinema – for as long as he could, but now it deserted him. The only response he succeeded in finding was "Still, you did."

"That doesn't mean I didn't feel like it."

"When?" Leo said and immediately dreaded the answer.

"Just now." As if this might comfort at least one of them she said "It wasn't quite as bad as that. I'm not going to let it be."

"I won't either." This made him risk a last question, perhaps even a faltering hope. "What do you think brought it back?"

"It must have been some kind of stress. Maybe that business with Mr Bloore, but I won't be letting that affect me any more. I won't let him." As Leo did his best to share her optimism she said "Try not to mind if we don't go to films for a little while," and for a moment he was able to believe this would bring the nightmares to an end.

CHAPTER TWENTY-EIGHT

L eo had no idea how long the matrix sign persisted in declaring the airport car park full. At last a van dissuaded it by exiting in a cloud of exhaust thick enough for fog, and the barrier rose in a series of jerks reminiscent of stills from a film. Where was the space the van had vacated? Whenever Leo thought he'd found it, the apparent gap proved to be occupied by a car hidden by a larger vehicle. He drove around every floor, all the way up to the rooftop level, without finding anywhere to park. Had somebody managed to sneak ahead of him? How could the barrier have let them in unless a departure had left another space? Planes were rising in succession from the airfield, counting off the minutes to the flight he increasingly felt he was bound to miss. He drove down the ramps to ground level without glimpsing a single space and started upwards afresh at a speed that seemed close to lethal. It rushed him at a car that was backing out of a space on the fifth level. The brake lights branded his eyes, but had the driver and Leo reacted too belatedly? No, the vehicles were still inches apart, and Leo threw his car into reverse, only almost to collide with an approaching van. It and the other car began to flash their lights at him, so relentlessly it threatened to confuse him into striving to decipher their message. Then the car swerved away, a miniature gnomish mascot swinging from the mirror like a pendulum, and Leo swerved fast into the space. As the van lumbered past, wagging its own windscreen manikin, he struggled through the cramped gap the adjacent vehicle had left its neighbour. He hauled his suitcase out of the boot and trundled it across the gritty concrete as fast as its sluggish wheels would let him.

The windowless lift was the colour of fog. Wherever the dim light originated, its intermittence seemed to bring the walls billowing closer, rendering them less solid, treacherously infirm. Leo had to fend off an impression that he was inhaling some of their substance. As soon as the somnolent doors released him he bolted into the concourse, urging his luggage, which felt determined to loiter. He searched the nearest departure board for his flight and saw it was delayed by an hour. He wouldn't miss it after all, and didn't mind when a queue of travellers swung around to stare at his cry of relief.

As he plodded back and forth along a taped route towards the check-in desks the contents of the trolley that preceded him kept giving him a wide-eyed grin and swiping the tip of its limp pointed hat off its small smooth forehead – the toddler dangling his legs over the edge of the trolley did. Leo collected his boarding pass at last and hefted his suitcase all the way to the security gates, having despaired of the wheels. While the case staggered off for examination, a guard at the gate peered at the phone Leo had deposited in a plastic basket. "Will you activate your phone, please."

Leo retrieved it and showed it his face, only to be declared unrecognisable. He typed his passcode, which the phone rejected with a shudder and an emphatic clank. The screen felt as clammy as his fingertip, and he couldn't judge which of them was softer. How many digits had he mistyped? He was rummaging in his brain to convince himself he'd recalled the correct number when the guard said "What are you doing, sir?"

"What you told me to."

"I asked you to show me the phone is charged."

He refrained from protesting that she hadn't quite. He held up the phone for her to examine, but she took it from him so swiftly it felt like a confiscation. "I'm afraid this isn't charged," she said, "so we can't allow it through."

"Of course it is, or you couldn't see the screen."

"There is no screen. The phone is dead."

"What do you mean, there isn't a screen?" The unintended rhyme sounded like a childish sally at a joke. As Leo thrust out his hand for the phone he glimpsed activity at the far end of the conveyor belt.

A passenger had lifted down a suitcase and was wheeling it away, a claim with which it appeared eager to cooperate – Leo's case. "Hang on," he shouted. "That's mine."

"I'm afraid you'll have to surrender it."

"What are you talking about? He's stealing it or he thinks it's his." In a moment Leo realised the guard had the phone in mind. "Wait," he yelled, "that's my case," and sprinted through the security arch. The alarm began to shrill, and as several men in uniform converged on him the luggage thief sent him a mocking wave that descended to fling him a kiss. Leo fought to free himself from all the hands that grabbed him, but his struggles couldn't throw the seat belt off.

The high repeated note was telling passengers the seat belt sign had been switched on. As he subsided in his seat Leo remembered he was returning to Alphafen – returning what he'd brought home with him, whatever he might have to do. He hoped his wakeful spasm hadn't bothered his neighbours, a pair of men identically dressed to celebrate some occasion. Three more were seated across the aisle from Leo; in fact, he seemed to be surrounded by them. Weren't matching T-shirts usually the uniform for stag events? He couldn't imagine what kind of outing was denoted by the rakish pointed caps all the party wore, especially given the flesh-coloured material. Still, there was no need for the men to crouch in their seats as if they wanted to hide their appearance, and why were they doing so in unison? It gave him the uneasy notion that they were shrinking as he watched. Certainly they weren't as big as him, not nearly, indeed considerably less. Everybody in the rows ahead of him was hidden by the seats now, though this hadn't been the case. He couldn't see a single member of the cabin crew, even when he glanced back, trying not to notice how alike all the people he could see had become, in diminishing stature and facially too. Shouldn't their smallness leave them less threatening? He felt hemmed in by a crowd of malevolent infants eager to reveal how dangerous they could be. He jabbed the button to call a member of the cabin crew, preferably more than one, ideally all of them – jabbed until his finger began to ache, but only made the dwindling faces on both sides turn to him. He folded his hands to conceal how he was releasing the seat belt, and as it slithered into its slot he made a dash for the door at the front of the cabin, beyond which there had to be some of the crew – a pilot, at any rate. He wasn't even halfway there when a swarm of dwarfish shapes leapt into the aisle on every side of him. The shrill noise that filled his ears was no longer an alert but their vicious mirth as hands grabbed his legs and sent him sprawling. As his face thumped the thin carpet, which smelled like a mass of mud, a multitude of captors seized him. Some crawled onto his back to cling there as though demanding a ride, while others settled lower on him, pinning his legs to the floor. "Help," Leo yelled, but the final consonant was reluctant to take shape. "Help," he tried again, but the carpet gagged him as he struggled to raise himself even an inch.

"You must not fight, Leo."

The voice or the incessant beeping jerked him awake, or the hands that were holding him did. There weren't so many now, and they let go as he strove to focus his eyes. Hanna Weber had kept hold of his shoulders while she spoke, and her parents had been restraining his arms. As he realised the bleeps came from his phone alarm Gitte said "You are where you chose to be."

"Here is company," Emil told him, "for you in your bed."

For a moment Leo thought all three intended to join him, and then that Emil was offering his daughter or at least endorsing her unspoken proposal. When a weight landed on his legs he raised his head from the violently crumpled pillow. The bed already had another occupant, and as Leo flung the quilt back so that it wouldn't hinder his escape the creature scurried up his body to squat on his chest, clutching him with all its limbs like half a spider. Its elongated fleshy pointed cap drooped towards him, and so did its replication of the faces that had surrounded him on the plane. The virtually noseless nostrils snuffled doglike as if they were inhaling his panic, while the eyes enlarged by their lack of lids and the wide grin bereft of lips looked delighted to help comprise the face that had begun to dangle off the skull. Leo dug his nails into the edges of the mattress, not just in a bid to propel himself free of the intruder but for fear of touching the hunched grotesquely joyful shape, and the relentless note of the alarm seemed to drill deep into his brain.

He flung out a hand without knowing whether he meant to silence the phone or seize it as some kind of link to the world he used to believe was the whole of reality. His lurch knocked the phone off the bedside table and sent him over the edge of the bed, together with the quilt he was entangled in. At least this time his face didn't hit the floor, but most of the front of him did. Which floor had he fallen on? It looked confusingly familiar. As he shoved himself away from the bed before his unwanted companion could follow he saw he was no longer in Alphafen. He was home in Settlesham.

The phone was still trying to alert him, and he felt as if it had an unwelcome message for him: that the nightmares had been more than dreams – intimations of a future that was lying in wait for him. He was scrambling on all fours to silence the clamour when he realised he hadn't activated the alarm last night, however many hours ago that was, since it was daylight now. Who had interfered with his phone? It made him feel as though Hanna might still be able to reach him. He captured the phone and did away with the alarm as Ellen came into the bedroom. "Oh dear," she said, adding an apologetic grin. "I didn't mean to wake you quite like that."

Leo grabbed the bed and hauled himself to his feet. "It was you that put on the alarm."

"I don't know who else it could have been. You said you hadn't any lessons till later, and you were looking as though you could use some sleep."

"Not that kind."

She looked up from lifting the quilt off the floor. "What was wrong with it?"

"It was full of nightmares. Didn't you hear me calling out?"

"I didn't, Leo, or you ought to know I would have come to you. Maybe I was in the shower. Were they very bad?"

"No worse than I can cope with. I've kept them to myself, and that's all that matters."

"I don't want you to feel you can't tell me about them or anything else either."

"I won't be bothering you with them. Now it's my turn for the shower."

The onslaught of water helped to fix him in the moment and clear away patches of the night that were clinging to his mind, but he couldn't shake off the conviction that the nightmares had been warnings if not threats. A fierce coffee with his cereal and yoghurt finished waking him without relieving him of the impression. "Can I leave you to it?" Ellen said. "I ought to be getting to work. I can do without anyone saying I'm late."

"Don't give him any excuses for anything."

"I never do."

"I meant about being on time. The rest of it as well, of course." Leo felt as if his words were hindrances he'd begun to stumble over. "Have a good time with your friends tonight," he tried saying. "Have the best you can."

"I was going to. Nobody else is bringing a partner either, Leo."

Why was she reacting to notions he'd never meant to convey? It felt close to developing into a nightmare. "I wasn't talking about that," he said. "I can do with being alone."

"You can be whenever you want to be. Just let me know."

"For a while is all I'm saying. I was talking about tonight. Alone so I can think."

"Tell me any time I'm stopping you."

By now Leo feared anything he said would end up damaged in transit. He took her hand, which stayed as uncommunicative as he'd begun to think he should. "I just need to sort my thoughts out," he couldn't leave unsaid.

"Let's agree on that." She squeezed his hand, but not much. "Now I really have to go," she said.

He would have liked to start pondering at once, but he had pupils to teach. He couldn't risk any distraction from the task; he didn't care to think what might happen if his concentration faltered. By the time he finished the last lesson it was late afternoon. He parked outside his house and walked to the golf course, across which a path led to the Settlesham Countryside Experience. At least so long as he was by himself he couldn't harm anyone while he tried to think.

A row of fifties houses rendered tentatively hoary by oaken doors and carriage lamps faced the entrance to the path across the golf course. A stile acknowledged that the path used to cross a meadow, and a signboard grudgingly recognised the right of way, though the sign was largely concerned with warning anybody not a member of the club to keep between a line of marker posts and beware of golfers. Leo thought he had far more to beware of, if he could only identify how. Thorns of the unfriendly hedge that framed the stile scratched his hands as he gripped the posts to clamber down onto the path.

He hadn't foreseen how closely the golf course would resemble a model of a mountainous landscape, hummocks representing peaks, bunkers bringing dried-up lakes to mind. He was anxious not to be reminded of the Alps, but what should he focus on instead? How could he have infected Ellen in the cinema with his grotesque fears when he'd destroyed the contaminated phone? If the legacy from Alphafen was still lingering within him, how could he know when it would leave him, supposing it ever did? The possibility made him feel not just helpless but unforgivably dangerous. As he tramped across the golf course he felt he was striving to catch up with some realisation he might never even glimpse.

The click of clubs against golf balls halted him. Though the sounds came from both sides of him, he couldn't see a single golfer. Since this had to mean they couldn't see him either, mustn't it put him at risk? Perhaps this was about to be his latest living nightmare, a chase along the path while unseen assailants propelled lethal missiles at the target they didn't even know he was. No use seeking reassurance in how innocent the expanse of grass and sandy hollows looked beneath the enormous cloudless sky; anywhere he went could harbour nightmares, because they came from him. Frustration at his plight and at his utter lack of useful knowledge about his situation provoked him to raise his voice. "Come on then, play another trick. Can't you even show yourself, you cowardly bastard? Let's see what you can do here, then. I know you haven't gone away, so don't pretend you have."

Might the golfers think he was haranguing them? The idea didn't seem quite worthy of a laugh. In a moment he heard what might have been a response to his challenge – a club striking a ball somewhere out of sight to the left of him. He poised himself to dodge, but saw nothing hurtling towards him. He was holding his breath when somebody cheered, prompting an outburst of comments from her fellow golfers. Leo listened until he was certain the party was moving away from him.

There were still the golfers to his right, and he was afraid to shift before he knew which way they were going. He stared in the direction their sounds had come from and heard a player drive a ball with a click that seemed to borrow fierceness from the imprecation it provoked. Leo saw the ball fly over a hummock towards him, only to bury itself with a feeble eruption of sand in a bunker hundreds of yards from him. This didn't strike him as much of a nightmare, even for a golfer. "Is that the best you can do?" he demanded, though not of the player. "Go on, do your worst. Get it over with."

Nothing appeared to respond. He thought he was wholly alone, a state he was happy to start to embrace, until a stealthy movement made him look upwards. A hawk that appeared to be crucified by the sky was hovering above the golf course. "That's where you are, is it?" Leo muttered. "What are you going to do to me now?"

He'd hardly finished speaking when the hawk swooped, not at him but towards a field beyond the Countryside Experience. It disappeared behind a hedge and then rose with its prey writhing in its claws. So it had been just a hawk, and he was watching it sail across the fields when he heard voices heading for the bunker where the ball had lodged. By the time they arrived he could be at the far end of the path, out of reach of any peril. Might the incident at the cinema have been the final manifestation of his nightmare state?

A minute's energetic striding brought him to the Countryside Experience, which wasn't much more than a path along the outer edge of the golf course. At the time of its development several letters to the *Sentinel* had complained it was less than that – a joke. Some had protested that the council could have widened the mile-long track. Instead the project had constructed vantage points at some of the bends in the path, the only places you could pass another walker without having to avoid the thorny hawthorn hedges. The improvement hadn't enticed many visitors, and Leo hoped not to encounter anyone now that he felt able to enjoy the walk.

The route across the golf course had brought him to the midpoint of the Countryside Experience. He turned right, heading for the Settlesham Shoppery precinct and eventually home. Now he realised he hadn't visited the Countryside Experience since childhood – since he'd begun to correspond with Hanna Weber. Had he ever mentioned the place to her? He doubted he would have found it worth the ink.

A shriek greeted him at the first bend he came to – the cry of a fox. Each viewing alcove was guarded by a representation of a species likely or at any rate less than impossible to be spotted across the fields. The polystyrene fox was miming an escape it would never achieve. Despite its dogged vociferousness, it appeared to have been seized by lockjaw, paralysed with outrage at the cobweb that spanned its gaping jaws. As Leo passed the bend he revived the creature's screech, which sent a spider scuttling across the web in search of prey before retreating into its lair on the roof of the mouth. Leo might have fancied the cry was aimed at the only sign of life he could see, a rambler apparently seeking a gap in a hedgerow several fields away. The sight wasn't worth loitering to watch, and Leo carried on along the track.

At the next viewing point his approach roused a version of a skylark's song from a bird as tall as his waist. Its eyes were blind with blackened moss, while time or a vandal had dislocated the lower half of its beak, which jerked spasmodically up and down as it produced its automatic song. The trills and chirps were so harsh and blurred that Leo wondered if the mechanism had grown as fungoid as the eyes. Who were any visitors meant to imagine it was calling? Not the rambler across the fields, presumably a different fellow, since he couldn't have advanced so much closer in the time it had taken Leo to reach this section of the path.

Several narrow thorny zigzags took him to the next expanded bend, where a throaty croak or at least a bid to simulate the sound welcomed him. Age hadn't improved the call, which resembled a lengthy attempt to clear a gullet clogged with some intrusive substance. A child might have imagined the giant frog was growing desperate. Perhaps its throat was blocked by more of the greyish lichen that bulged from the sockets where eyes ought to be. How many people were at large in the fields beyond the outer hedge? While Leo couldn't locate the other two, surely the rambler ranging back and forth along the border of the next to nearest meadow had to be a newcomer, since neither of the others could have made such progress. There was no need to wonder how like a death rattle the distorted artificial croak might sound, let alone to fancy it was summoning the rambler. Rather than linger to distinguish the figure obscured by the less than distant hedge, Leo picked up as much speed as the hawthorn walls would let him.

He was making for a bend, though not a widened one, when he heard rapid regular footsteps ahead. As a minimally attired jogger panted into view, Leo glimpsed movement across the field. Had the rambler dropped into hiding or found a gap at the foot of the hedge to crawl through? Neither possibility seemed either appealing or natural, but Leo was distracted by recognising the jogger. "Arnold Hardy," he said.

"Leo Parker." Jogging on the spot shook Hardy's syllables apart as if he were separating them to educate a child. "Still learning?" he panted.

Leo found the question ominous, suggesting there was some insight he had yet to grasp. "What do you think I need to learn?"

"People," Hardy said and dislodged four more syllables. "Learning people."

"I'm very much still giving lessons, whatever you've heard."

"Nothing." By the sound of it Hardy resented the implied correction of his usage. "Just asked," he took breaths to add.

"I'm glad if everything's died down. Let me say you could be an advert for our firm. One of our star pupils, if you don't mind us telling people, or maybe you're just a natural driver."

"Don't mind." A pause for several breaths let Hardy say "Don't like bumping into anyone round here."

Leo couldn't see how this was connected. "There's someone else about," he said and peered through the hedge. "There was. I can't see them now."

"You." With an effort Leo was meant to hear Hardy said "You are."

Altogether too belatedly Leo realised Hardy was jogging up and down while he waited to be given space to pass. A desire for company had made Leo fail to understand, unless he'd ignored the situation. He felt oddly reluctant to retreat despite glancing back to see nobody behind him. "Sorry," he said and stood against the hedge – not the one bordering the field. "Go ahead."

As Hardy sidled past him, fingers clawed at Leo's back. Of course they were thorns, but he had to restrain himself from recoiling across the path. Why should he remind himself which hedge it was? Hardy's footfalls receded behind Leo as he made for the bend. He had just reached the next stretch of the path, and was finding its desertion as welcome as he thought Hardy would have, when he heard the jogger coming back.

Why had he turned around when he knew he would encounter Leo? Had something made him want company after all? It had encouraged him to put on speed as well and rendered his panting fiercer, but why had his footsteps grown so soft, as if he had decided to go barefoot? "Is that you, Arnold?" Leo called.

The question let doubts reach him. Perhaps he'd been fending them off. The panting didn't resemble a jogger's breaths as much as he'd tried to believe it did. It was more an eager snuffling, a quality he found harder to ignore now that it had descended closer to the path. Had the footfalls – the rapid padding that seemed to be growing softer and larger – multiplied as well? "Arnold," Leo shouted, twisting around to stare at the bend in the path.

How far away must Hardy be? Too far away to hear, perhaps, or even if he heard the plea, to help. Or was that a grudging monosyllabic response somewhere down the path? Leo was preparing to shout once more when he heard the snuffling turn away from him, and then the pursuit did. "Arnold, they're coming after you," he called at the top of his voice.

He heard no answer. In a few seconds the unappealingly infirm footsteps passed beyond audibility too. He held his breath while he listened for a sound, perhaps a cry. What would he do if one came? When none did, the silence seemed to solidify with ominousness. In a bid to outdistance his gathering panic Leo fled along the path.

A duck big enough to feed an extended family sent him a series of strangled squawks that could have signified it was being slaughtered on their behalf. A fieldmouse half his height squeaked like a rusty signboard in a wind. A butterfly with wings an arm's length wide stood on its cracked encrusted tail at a third vantage point, and Leo grew nervous of learning what its cry might be. When it stayed mute the silence felt like delayed menace. At least the viewing area showed him nobody beyond the hedge, and the path stayed deserted apart from him. All the same, he was glad when the Settlesham Shoppery came into view at the end.

The precinct had claimed the road beside the golf course for pedestrians. Just now Leo was the only one. The solitary sign of life was a fluster of sparrows busily competing for the last crumbs scattered around one of the skeletal metal benches that stood at intervals along the perimeter. Leo was halfway down the first wide stone-flagged street of dormant shops when he heard a cage clang shut around him.

It was the sound of shops donning their overnight shields. Shutters were clattering into their sockets throughout the precinct. The noise made him feel shut out, close to intrusive. Even the window displays that had been left exposed seemed unwelcomingly remote, but he shouldn't wish for company when he might like that even less. He didn't want to ponder what had happened on the path, he simply yearned to think he'd left the last of it behind. When he turned along the next street he was grateful to see someone working in a shop framed by the far end.

She had her back to him while she dressed a mannequin. As he made his way past crowds of faceless plastic figures she turned and noticed him. Her expression let him know the plate-glass window meant she felt safe from him. No doubt she had reason to react that way – more than one shop window was splintered and bandaged with tape – but she left Leo feeling like a dangerous trespasser. "I can't do anything to you," he muttered, urging it to be the truth.

He was still speaking when she returned to her task, and he hoped she hadn't seen him mouthing words at her. He had to pass her shop if he was to take the most direct route home, and why shouldn't he? She would be as safe as she believed she was. As he headed for the junction he glimpsed movements on both sides of him. They were his reflections in the display windows, however surreptitiously stealthy they felt, and he didn't need to look. He managed not to glance aside until he was almost at the junction.

Nothing stirred. Of course his reflections wouldn't, since he'd stopped to look, and he shouldn't feel that anything had frozen into immobility in order to pass for a mannequin. To do so it would need to have too little of a face. He was about to move on until he caught sight of a hint of activity that suggested something hadn't managed to stay entirely still – a trace of restlessness on the blank white egg a mannequin was using for a head. Surely this was his reflection, and he'd shifted without realising. There was certainly no need to imagine the rudiments of a face had made a feeble bid to emerge onto the surface of the egg. If they had, that could only be his reflection swelling up on the window as he peered uneasily closer. He could end the illusion by turning away, and he did.

He had to struggle not to glance around him. He mustn't fancy that followers were pacing him, ready to freeze the instant he looked, especially when yielding to the temptation seemed to show him embryonic faces struggling to take shape on the pallid featureless heads like insects determined to emerge from their cocoons. "Reflections," he told anyone who needed to hear, "just reflections," but the last word shattered into fragments as he broke into a run.

The sound of his sprint made the shopworker look around. She mustn't take him for a threat, especially when this might make him think he was. As he gestured to indicate he meant to turn aside opposite her shop he saw movement behind her. The contents of a faceless head were acquiring a kind of life. What could only be a tongue was writhing under the surface where a mouth should be. It poked at the apparently softened plastic, which parted just enough to let it loll forth, revealing it was plump and white. A pair of rounded lumps bulged beneath the smooth colourless forehead, and the left one split open to send Leo a wink, even if the blank white globe it exposed couldn't see him.

As one of the naked mannequin's handless arms jerked up to give Leo a complicit wave, his appalled stare made the shopworker glance over her shoulder. He didn't dare loiter to establish whether she would see what he was terrified to think he'd seen, but as he dashed along the cross street he thought he heard her cry out. He couldn't bear to look at his surroundings as he fled home; he'd retreated so deep inside himself that he wouldn't have been able to describe his flight through Settlesham. At last he reached the house and stabbed the lock and slammed the front door behind him.

What could he risk doing while he was on his own? It seemed that anything might mutate into a nightmare. He couldn't face eating, and made do with half a bottle of wine, followed by the other half. At least this slowed his thoughts down and went some way towards dousing his fears. It took him to bed in the hope of finding refuge in sleep, which took him unawares. Ellen wakened him with a lingering kiss. "Just to let you know I'm back," she said, and then he saw she'd touched his brow not with her lips but with the top of her head, which she'd lengthened towards him.

He couldn't be certain his effortful scream had wakened him, though he appeared to be alone in the unlit room. He fumbled at the dark until he found his phone and jabbed Ellen's number. "Just making sure you were there," he tried to say rather than gasp.

"I'm still with the girls. Is anything wrong? Do you want me to come home?"

"No," Leo said, though only to her second question, and did his best not to dread what might happen once she did.

CHAPTER TWENTY-NINE

They had nearly reached his parents' house when Leo saw an excuse to turn back, but it was too late: Trevor Kerr had seen him. "Leo Parker," the policeman said as if someone needed to be told, "and do I remember it's Ellen?"

"That's who it is," Ellen said, "and wasn't it Mr Kerr?"

"Inspector Kerr, that's correct. Still very much is. Are we out for our Sunday stroll?"

"I don't know if you are. We're here for Beverley's lunch."

"I believe it's a treat. I've heard as much from Brian."

"You won't hear any different from us."

"I'm not hearing anything from Mr Parker. He looks as if he's seen something he'd rather not have seen."

No doubt Kerr meant himself, but his observation made Leo glance about, afraid of seeing any sign of life that might portend worse. A plump bee was appraising flowers in garden after garden. Should he take this as an omen of the influence of Alphafen or even a transformed invader? As he stared at it, challenging the furry buzzing airborne lump to betray its nature, Kerr said "Not scared of bees at your age, surely? I suppose you never know when you might be stung."

"I was once when I was little, Mr Kerr," Ellen said. "It wasn't an experience I'd be anxious to repeat."

"Not too many stings are. I've dealt with some people who'd tell you. Do call me Trevor if we're likely to keep meeting. Just before I let you go, I've some news for Mr Parker."

Leo felt as if the conversation were a weight that had gathered in his skull, crushing his thoughts and hindering his ability to speak. Kerr's prolonged pause forced him to ask "What is it?"

"The official investigation has been closed."

"The one about Leo, you mean," Ellen said.

"I'd hardly be discussing anybody else with you."

"But you're saying they've finished with him."

"I said so, yes."

"Then I ought to tell you my parents have just come back from abroad. They left their car where Leo did. I told them how he thinks someone used his car, but they say there wasn't anything like that with theirs."

"I wonder what you think that shows."

"Maybe whoever's doing it has realised the police are on to them and now they're using somewhere else."

"You could think that, of course." Without conveying whether he did Kerr said "You'll be grateful your parents aren't involved."

"Them and Leo. I'm glad you've decided he wasn't either."

"It was no decision of mine."

"But you told us you'll be leaving him alone."

"No, I told you the investigation has been terminated due to lack of evidence. Mr Parker remains of great interest to me."

"What kind of interest would that be?" With audible deliberation Ellen added "Trevor."

"I don't know yet what he's been doing to people, but I'm sure he has."

"How can you say that when your people didn't find anything?"

At first Kerr's stare appeared to be his answer. "I'll tell you," he said. "You deserve to know the kind of thing you're dealing with."

"If you're talking about Leo, let me say right now I do."

"You'll forgive me if I wonder about that," Kerr said and turned on Leo. "You aggravate people's phobias somehow. It's some kind of mental trick."

This felt so close to a route to the truth that Leo was about to risk conveying some when Ellen demanded "What makes you think that?"

"Mr Parker knows perfectly well, but I see he's hoping you won't hear. When I interviewed him at the station he tried to make me feel the room was too small, and now the whole place feels that way to me."

"I really don't think that's a reason to accuse Leo of meaning to do any wrong."

"I'll be doing more than accusing before I've finished with him."

"If that's a threat you should remember I'm a witness."

"I'm referring to whatever action may prove to be appropriate." Kerr made his gaze into a forceful caution and then turned as he heard a front door open. "Now I think you've kept Beverley and Brian waiting long enough," he said for Leo's mother to hear.

Leo felt as if everybody was compelling him along the path while the buzz of the swollen bee drilled into his ears. As he and Ellen reached the house his mother said "What did Trevor Kerr want? That was quite a chat you were having."

"Just to let me know the police have given up investigating me," Leo said before Ellen could speak.

"I should think so, and about time too."

"Come and have a glass to celebrate," Leo's father called from the kitchen. "Make that a few."

This inspired Leo, or desperation did. "Why don't we all go out to celebrate," he said. "Treat's on me."

"I've already made lunch," his mother said. "The one we didn't have that time."

"Not the spread from then," his father seemed to think someone needed to be told. "The same as then but made today."

"I'd hardly be giving them stale food, would I? If I'd kept anything it would be crawling by now."

"Don't carry on like that or you'll be putting people off."

As Leo's mother headed for the kitchen Ellen caught his arm. "What were you trying to do?" she murmured past a hand beside her mouth. "Do you want to start things up again?"

"That's exactly what I'm trying not to do," Leo whispered so fiercely it twinged his teeth.

"Just let Beverley see we're enjoying her effort. There can't be anything to go wrong if it's like she said."

"What are you two muttering about?" Leo's mother called. "I hope it's a surprise we're all going to like."

Ellen's stare urged him to answer. When he found no words he could risk loosing she said "I think we've finished with surprises just now."

A balloon burst in the kitchen, jerking Leo's nerves, but it was the report of a withdrawn cork. His father had emptied a bottle of chardonnay into a quartet of glasses by the time the visitors joined him. "Here's to all the family," he said and raised his glass, inviting triple clinks. "Careful you don't crack it like that, Leo. Here's to all our troubles being over."

"Yours haven't started, have they, Ellen?" Leo's mother said and slapped her lip with her fingertips. "That's to say I hope they never do, and I can't see why they would."

She watched Leo take a gulp of wine followed by a second bid to douse his thoughts. What could come of reminding Ellen how she'd had to flee the cinema? She was never going to believe he was the cause. "That's going down well," his mother said. "Better get another opened while I see to the soup."

A vague watery aroma massed in Leo's nostrils as she ladled the steaming contents of a pan into a tureen. "Can you take it through, Leo?" she said. "I haven't made it wormy this time."

"I could think of better ways to put it," his father said.

"I was only telling him it's his kind of noodle soup. Don't you remember, Leo?"

A mouthful of wine barely helped him to brave asking "Remember what?"

"It was your favourite when you were little. Maybe tasting it will bring everything back."

She didn't mean this as the threat Leo was afraid to hear. As he bore the tureen to the dining-room, pale glistening rings bobbed up to cluster on the surface of the murky contents, and he did his best to avoid seeing a resemblance to eggs left empty by their occupants that had swarmed away to bide their time in the depths. He wasn't the child his mother had tried to bring to mind, unless he could revert to innocently relishing her cuisine. Might more wine help? More than Ellen and his parents would be able to overlook, perhaps. Surely if he managed to convince them he was celebrating, they wouldn't mind too much. Steam from the tureen drifted into his nostrils, and he strove not to turn his head aside; if he couldn't stomach the feeble insidious smell, how would he succeed in keeping any of its source down? He was trying to inhale a token greyish tendril without recoiling when the tureen jerked in his grasp, and the soup slopped upwards, nearly spilling on the carpet. A bell was shrilling in his ear – the phone beside him in the hall.

The interruption came as close as it could just now to a relief. He clutched the tureen tighter and hastened to plant it on the dining-table, only for the phone to fall silent before he could make for it. Not knowing who'd called or why felt dismayingly ominous – and then he heard his father say "Brian Parker. Pass With Parker."

Leo wasn't anxious to stay near the tureen. Surely just his haste had left its contents restless, noodles ranging about the surface as if disturbed by some activity the murk concealed. He was making for the kitchen when his father said "He's here with us. You can ask him yourself."

The words arrested Leo so abruptly he had to clutch at an upright of the banister. "Who is it?" he mouthed.

His father shaped the name with very little breath while his face turned the syllables into a question. "Hanna Weber."

For an instant Leo felt hunted down, unable to escape however desperately he tried, and then he saw the chance she'd given him. He pressed his finger to his lips and thrust out his other hand. Did the gesture look too rude? He was afraid his father would keep hold of the phone and speak as well until some sense of Leo's need appeared to reach him. His habitual slowness conveyed a reproof as he handed Leo the receiver. Leo closed his fist around the mouthpiece to deafen the phone all the way to the kitchen. "Don't anyone say anything," he urged. "Just listen."

The phone had begun to repeat if not to plead hello. "Who's that?" his mother insisted on being told.

"The girl from Alphafen. Listen and you'll hear." He laid the phone on the kitchen table while he stared everybody silent, and then he switched to speaker mode. "Hanna," he said. "What do you want? Why are you calling here?"

"I have not heard from you for too long a time. My phone says yours is incorrect, but I do not know how this could be."

"It was incorrect all right. It was infected."

"What will you have done with it?"

"Got rid."

"Will you have a new one now?"

"That's how it works."

"And you must have a new number."

"That's right, I must."

"You should give it to me now."

"So you can keep on hearing from me, yes? What are you so anxious to hear?"

"The news you would give me just the way I gave you mine."

"You gave me a lot more than news, didn't you? You sent it whenever I told you what I was planning to do."

"What does that mean? I do not understand."

"Who are you trying to kid? We both know the truth." Leo stared at Ellen and his parents to ensure none of them spoke. "Alps," he said.

He saw Ellen's lips part and gazed ferociously at them until she pressed them together. "What do you mean to say, Leo?" Hanna said.

"I more than mean. Your father tried to stop me finding out about them, but he should have realised it's online. All about the nightmares you made me bring home."

"You are mistaken, Leo. That could not be there."

"You mean you weren't. It all was. Only it didn't say how you had to learn what I was doing so you could turn it into a nightmare, and you managed to infect my phone as well."

"You must not think such things. It is not fair."

"Fair." Leo saw how close Ellen and his parents were to intervening, and raised his voice. "You tell me how what you've done to me is fair when all I wanted was to be friends with you and your people."

"He has found out so much, he should know the truth."

The interruption left Leo wordless until he saw it might prompt his companions to speak. "Emil," he said, not least to keep them quiet. "You've been monitoring what she tells me, have you?"

"I have heard part of what is said. I have seen you are upsetting her."

Leo saw his mother's mouth describe an outraged vowel and showed her his palm before she could add any sound. "So what do you think she's been doing to me?"

"She has been your friend. You should not hold her to blame."

"Who do you want me to blame instead?"

"Your Mr Churchill and the men who dropped his bombs on our town."

Leo's father made to object until Leo gestured fiercely at him. "What's happened to me is their fault, is it?"

"It is not ours. We were victims too. They let loose what Hitler meant to send to your country. You must see this is the truth."

"And then you people gave it to me. Tell me what I did to deserve that."

"You took what we could not control." Gitte had joined in. "You should know," she said, "Hanna did not want it for you. She sent you all her messages because she hoped you would tell her nothing was wrong for you. She would have stopped you ever coming to us."

"Then she didn't do much of a job."

"We made her bring you," Emil said. "The town did. We felt we had lived with enough when it had never been our fault. It was time the plague should leave us."

"I've had it now, and a lot of people who shouldn't have. It's well past time you had it back."

"There can be no returning," Emil said. "I tell you as a friend."

Leo's hasty gesture couldn't hush his mother. "What kind of a friend do you think you're being, Mr I don't even know what your name is?"

"We are Weber. We are being all we can."

"Which is no kind of a friend at all. It's worse than none, a lot worse. What did Leo do to any of you except try to make up? You pretended you wanted to as well, but you're more our enemies than ever."

"He was the only one of you who kept the contact with us. We should have liked an enemy to come instead."

"We were trying to protect our child," Gitte said, "just as now you are."

"Not the same at all. We've done none of you any harm. God forgive me, but right now I wish we could."

Leo's father barely waited for her to finish. "Leo, is there anything else you want to say to these people?"

"Not if you've heard what they said. I don't know what else I could say."

"Then don't ever try to reach us in any way again, Mr Weber and the rest of you. We've a friend in the police who'll make you wish you never had, and that goes for bothering our son in particular."

"Leo." Perhaps his omission of a farewell had distressed Hanna. "I am sorry that it had to be you," she said. "All my parents say is all the truth."

"Don't you people ever know when's enough?" Leo's father demanded. "Let me stop you right now and for good."

As his father seized the phone Leo heard Hanna start to speak. Did she begin with "If"? A solitary syllable was all she managed before she was cut off. "At least now we know exactly what they've been up to," his father said.

"I'm glad you've heard it from someone besides me at last."

"We should never have encouraged you to stay in touch," his mother said. "We thought we were doing it for everybody's best, but—"

"We didn't know what they were like then."

"We do now, and you mustn't let them work on your mind any more."

"It isn't just my mind. You heard what they said."

"I've never heard such superstitious nonsense in my life. I don't care whether they believe it, but you mustn't. I won't have them affecting you that way. You just put it right out of your head."

"We know you felt guilty about your friend who died while you were at school," Ellen said. "I think that must have got mixed up in your brain with your mission over there. That's what they played on even if you didn't know."

"Maybe they didn't either." The hint of insight only seemed to fuel his father's rage. "They knew they were having their revenge all right, whatever they tried to tell us," he said. "After all that time, and on someone who wasn't even born then. You wouldn't think anyone could hold on to so much hate."

"And now they'll have made my soup go cold, so I hope they're satisfied," Leo's mother complained. "Leo, bring it back for me and I'll heat it up."

He could only trudge to fetch it and plod with it along the hall. The tureen felt less burdensome than the coagulated lump that passed for his thoughts. How could he have imagined hearing the Webers confess would persuade Ellen and his parents of the truth? Even if they'd been convinced, how would that have helped? Perhaps at least they'd ensured that the Webers would no longer trouble him – that nothing from Alphafen would. "Here's the carrier," his father announced. "You look like a man who deserves another drink."

Leo downed the remains of his wine and a generous gulp of the replenishment. Everybody followed him when he bore the refilled tureen to the dining-room, and he did his utmost not to fancy they were compelling him to face the meal. "Don't you dare let those wretched people put you off your food," his mother said as she ladled soup nearly to the brim of his bowl. "We've had one of their lot do that to you already, and I won't have another."

Surely once the soup subsided in the bowl it would stop looking so inhabited. By the time everybody else was served, the swarm of tiny mouths in front of Leo had finished working their circular lips. He just had to hold the sight still with his mind, and when Ellen and his parents raised their spoons as if they were commencing a ritual to invoke domesticity, he managed to join in. He plunged his spoon into the greyish murk and swallowed the result as swiftly as his reluctant throat would let him. "Remember now?" his mother said.

Perhaps that could help. The timid flavour faintly reminiscent of chicken brought back a tentative sense of his childhood, of his life before he'd begun to correspond with Hanna Weber, before Billy had died in the derelict factory – before Leo knew there was such a place as Alphafen. This was the kind of summer meal he would have had then, and he tried to surround himself with the memory. "That's it, you eat up," he heard his mother say. "You make sure he has enough at home, Ellen. I've been worried he hasn't been feeding so well."

Leo succeeded in downing his bowlful, slippery occupants and all, aided by more than just another glass of wine, and eventually persuaded her he didn't need a second helping. Cold meats and salad were yet to come, and soon they came at him. Surely just his throat kept squirming, not the mouthfuls it had to keep down, since he couldn't see the activity he dreaded anywhere around him. He only had to trap the sensations and his thoughts inside him, held down by wine, more wine. "Drink up and forget all that rubbish we heard," his father said. "It's just a good job you won't be driving till tomorrow."

Dessert was trifle wobbling in a glass basin. Additional wine helped Leo ignore its resemblance to a stranded jellyfish reluctant to expire even once it had been chopped up and dumped into bowls. He would have preferred not to feel his portion of it slither down his gullet, nor to fancy fierce gulps of coffee were required to sear any remaining life out of it. "I think you enjoyed all that, didn't you?" his mother said.

All the wine he'd drunk sent him stumbling too close to the truth. "As much as," he said and managed to stagger back from toppling into it, "much as always."

"Then we'll all look forward to next time. Just be careful walking home when you've had so much to drink. Ellen, you see he does."

Steadying one foot in front of the other along the homeward route was indeed quite a task. Perhaps the errant antics it required were why he felt everyone he met was watching him, and people in the houses were as well. Ellen held his arm tight, and he tried not to throw his weight against her whenever he strayed from the trajectory he was intent on following. "I know you had to make an effort," she murmured. "Let's get you home and we'll see how I can help you relax."

At least she wasn't reminding him of the phone call, even by exhorting him to forget it. She let them into the house and guided him to the stairs, where he set about using the series of walking-sticks that was the banister. "Come and lie down," she said behind him.

It was more a matter of floundering onto the bed as the room tipped up, depositing him approximately on the quilt. As the lid of the walls came to rest above him Ellen said "Try and settle down now. I won't be long."

He heard her make for the bathroom, but dozed off before she returned. She roused him in more than one sense by running her hands over his thighs on the way to unzipping him. As his tentative response flopped forth she tugged his trousers and shorts down, taking his shoes with them. So this was the start of the aid to relaxation she'd had in mind. He closed his eyes as she reached up to stroke his face while she applied her mouth to him.

A noise distracted him – the buzzing of an insect. He found it dismayingly ominous until he identified the sound of an electric toothbrush. Had Ellen left it running in the bathroom? No, the noise had only just begun. The device must have fallen on the floor and been jolted into action. "Your toothbrush is on," he said as clearly as he could, and loudly too.

The voice that answered was so blurred he thought Ellen was making a joke about his, until not just her words reached him. "I'm nearly finished," she said around some obstruction.

For as long as it took him to lift his unsteady head Leo was able to hope she wasn't where it sounded like – in the bathroom – and then he froze as though he'd been seized by the neck. While the shape crouching between his legs was a blur, the spectacle in the dressing-table mirror beyond the bed was all too clear. It was naked, with glistening leathery skin reminiscent of a toad's. Now that its form was revealed it raised itself on its spidery limbs to show him its noseless face, the wide eyes and twitching nostrils as round as the lipless mouth. It was still caressing his cheek, not with a finger but with the tip of the fat conical tendril that extended from the crown of its head. When he grabbed the appendage to shove it away from him, it felt like a decaying yet lively snake. Before he could let go it came loose from the head, and he flung it, still writhing in the manner of a severed section of a worm, across the room.

Its owner scuttled after it into the darkest corner, where they seemed to seep into the shadow and the wall. There was no sign of them by the time Leo's gasps of disgust brought Ellen at a run. "A nightmare. A nightmare," he heard himself repeating, and thought he might never stop.

CHAPTER THIRTY

A lthough it was close to midnight, a few shoppers were at large in the retail park. Customers who looked not much more purposeful than sleepwalkers roamed the supermarket aisles, and Leo did his utmost to avoid them all. When a woman strayed into view at the far end of the wine section, preceded by a trolley piled with tins of cat food, he grabbed half a dozen bottles to plant in his trolley and sped it into the next aisle as fast as the enthusiastically contrary wheels would let him. At once he was surrounded by dolls whose presence seemed quite unrelated to the adjacent shelves of alcohol except perhaps in their tipsy floppiness. He was hastening past them and trying to ignore any memories they roused when a voice arrested him. "Everything all right there, sir?"

It was plain that the security guard, who had visibly built himself broad and solid, thought otherwise. "What wouldn't be?" Leo felt forced to ask.

"Just you've been acting a bit odd."

"Doing my shop for the week. Tell me what's odd about that."

"Honest answer, you've been looking like you don't want anyone seeing what you're up to."

"I've told you what that is, and that's all it is." Leo had to glance aside to reassure himself the dwarfish figures lolling around him were all dolls and keeping still. "If you must know, I'm trying to stay away from people," he said.

"Why's that, sir?"

"I think I may have an infection."

He more than thought, and the admission left him feeling too close to the guard. "Then you oughtn't to be out giving it to people," the guard said.

"That's exactly what I've been avoiding, but there's nobody else who can do my shopping."

"Maybe you should shop online till you've got rid of whatever you've got."

"There are reasons why I can't." Had a shape like an unnecessarily overgrown doll given in to flexing its elongated limbs as it sprawled on a shelf? Leo was unable to locate it among the toys it might be using for concealment. "I touched nothing I won't be buying," he protested in the hope of ending the confrontation.

"What else do you need, sir?" The guard had rediscovered professionalism, perhaps because a manager had glanced into the aisle. "I can fetch it for you," the guard said.

"No need. I'm done." Leo nearly had been, and there was nothing he couldn't forego under the circumstances. "I was on my way out," he said.

"The checkouts are the other way, sir."

"I must have got turned around. Past time for bed."

"Sweet dreams, then."

The unexpected inappropriateness seemed ominous if not ironic, or had he wished Leo sweat dreams? "You too," Leo said with a fervour that only earned a frown, and hauled the trolley away from the guard. Surely just the hour was making the man rub his eyes with a finger and thumb as if keeping watch had begun to trouble him.

At least the automatic checkout lanes were deserted, but Leo's nerves tugged at his guts every time an item proved recalcitrant to scan, in case a shopworker noticed his apparent plight and came to help. Eventually the payment slot finished gobbling his money and expressed its satisfaction by extruding an acknowledgment from another orifice. He wheeled the trolley as straight as he could to his car and heaved the Frugish bags into the boot, an action that reminded him how his previous vehicle had betrayed the smell of cannabis. As he and the trolley wandered back to the supermarket he saw the guard in the doorway, pinching his eyes harder than ever. Perhaps they were troubled by the floodlights that towered above the car park, consolidating a glare like insomnia made luminous. Surely Leo needn't fancy the man looked as though he wished he weren't seeing what he saw.

Leo was almost out of cash. Usually he wouldn't have replenished it anywhere nearby, but the encounter with the guard had left him wary of returning in case he drew attention to himself or even, worse yet, was identified. He drove around the retail park and found a bank on the far side from the supermarket. The cash machines on the front of the building were out of order, he suspected from tampering, but one was operational in an alley between a variously European restaurant and the bank. The screen roused its grudging illumination in the gloom as Leo located its slot with his card. He was typing his number when he glimpsed activity on both sides of him.

It wasn't in any of the bins belonging to the unlit restaurant. A man had stationed himself in the entrance to the alley while another silhouetted fellow made his way from the far end, calling "Got a light, chum?"

Leo didn't look away from the machine. "I could use some here," he said, jabbing one of the amounts the dim screen displayed.

"Funny feller." This came from the man outlined against the floodlights. "Stand us a meal then, lad," he said.

As the slot began to pulse with garish light Leo snatched out his card. Surely just his nerves made the slot seem to mouth against his fingertips as if it was sending him a wordless message. "I've only taken enough for myself," he said.

"So stick your card back in," the second man was close enough not to have to call.

His accomplice had moved closer too. As soon as the metal tray gaped Leo seized his cash and shoved the notes together with the card into his hip pocket. "No more money, sorry," he said. "Don't do this."

The man who'd blocked the way back to the retail park gave a laugh or else a grunt. "Who's gonna stop us?"

Before Leo could respond he heard movement in the gloom. He might have thought a cat or a large rodent was emerging from the bin behind the man, since the lid was rising. The occupant appeared to be wearing it as headgear until the dark hunched shape extended the crown of its skull to fling the lid all the way open. The clatter of plastic against the wall of the restaurant made the man twist around with a squeal of the soles of his trainers. "What the Christ?" he said, and Leo took the chance to dodge past him.

He wasn't swift or stealthy enough. As the man lurched to grab him, the watcher that was crouching on the garbage swarmed down the side of the bin and tripped him. He toppled against the bin, plunging one hand into the rubbish, where Leo heard glass splinter. "Never mind me," the man screamed at his companion. "Get your card in, quick."

Leo gathered this was a ruse to steal from his account somehow. He was hesitating outside the alley while he wondered how to prevent the theft when the man at the machine protested in disbelief "It's got my hand."

His crony was struggling to extract his arm from the bin without further injury. "What are you on about?"

"I'm telling you it's pinched my card and now it's got my fucking hand some way."

For a moment their plight left Leo feeling powerful, but it told him he was still a carrier. Whenever he came close to anyone he was putting them in danger of infection. Cries of pain and dread faded behind him as he drove out of the retail park. He wouldn't be returning, not least since the guard might have seen him buy his latest temporary phone and found the purchase suspicious. He had to take more care not to attract attention as well as keeping clear of people. He'd grown too conspicuous in the supermarket, and the incident at the cash machine only reminded him of the solution he'd had to embrace to his monstrous problem.

I can't risk harming anybody any longer, especially all of you I love. He'd left the note for Ellen and posted a copy through his parents' letterbox when he was sure they were both out at work. *I have to deal with whatever I've become however I can. Nobody can do it except me. Please don't try to find me, because I'll be making sure I can't be found. Maybe when it's all over I'll be able to come back.*

He'd seen no point in trying to be more explicit or attempting to explain further. He could only hope that just as the nightmares he'd inflicted on his victims had eventually dissipated, the infection he carried might too, but how would he ever know? The months since he'd fled Settlesham had suggested no solution other than to keep his problem to himself.

He encountered little traffic on the motorway, and none as he drove along an unlit country lane into the woods. Once he left the road for an obscurely winding track the car lurched from side to side while shadows crawled out from behind the trees to swarm into the depths of the forest. The autumnal pelt of the uneven earth slithered beneath the wheels as he peered at the secretive markers he'd taken weeks to dig out of tree-trunks. Nearly half an hour in first gear and very seldom second brought him to the glade where he'd hidden the caravan.

He'd taken a good deal of trouble to find a dealer sufficiently disreputable to ask no questions while accepting cash for it and the second-hand Land Rover. As the hummocked ground jerked the headlight beams across the glade he glimpsed a shape squatting outside the door of the caravan. A woodland walker who stumbled on the stranded vehicle – not that anybody had, so far as Leo knew or hoped – might have assumed the owner had tried to domesticate the forest by posing a garden gnome, if an unusually grotesque specimen, outside his residence. "Welcoming me home, are you?" Leo muttered, but the glade appeared to be deserted when he left the car.

He didn't switch off the headlamps until he'd carried the supermarket bags to the caravan and turned on the lights inside. The combined illumination barely touched the enormous dark around him. The lightless woods stepped forward on their multitude of legs as he doused the headlamps, and he searched for words to reassure him as he made for the caravan at speed. "I'm alone" was all he found to whisper. "I'm alone," he said louder to remind himself he had to be, and nothing answered as the night consumed his voice.

AFTERWORD

You might reasonably assume this book began with nightmares. Certainly I have them, and value them as free horror films, but they're almost never developed into fiction. *The Incubations* started life elsewhere, as a note I made in 1988 towards a novel that eventually appeared as *Midnight Sun*. My original idea was that a town had been twinned with one inhabited by magicians, presumably a settlement like the locale of Algernon Blackwood's 'Ancient Sorceries'. My protagonist would visit it and return transformed in some occult fashion. Subsequent notions for *Midnight Sun* led me away from the initial concept, and the novel left it so far behind that the two might as well have been unrelated. The twin town idea remained available for development, and incubated until I was casting about for a novel to follow *The Lonely Lands*. Until then I hadn't considered why towns should be twinned, but once I did, developments began to gather.

The Second World War had already haunted my tales – I present 'Second Sight' as evidence – but what it released in Alphafen came as a real surprise. My creative method is instinctive, not mechanical; I vow never to rely on artificial intelligence, or artificial stupidity as I'd have it known, and I'm a great believer in happy accidents in the writing process. I didn't encounter the notion of the alp until I was researching the locale, and it came as a crucial revelation. It released me from the limbo where many works in progress languish until some notion gives them shape.

Like all my recent first drafts, this novel was ruthlessly rewritten (I wish some of my earlier stuff had been, but it's too late now.) I deleted the start of chapter sixteen, where Leo begins to affect those around him; I felt the reader might simply find the scene unmotivated to the point of gratuitousness. Was I wrong? It is here. You must judge.

"Hey, mate, stay off my wife."

"Never touched her."

"I'm telling you stay off."

"And I'm telling you I never. Didn't touch you, did I, love?"

"Don't you fucking talk to her. It's you and me."

"He wasn't touching me, Den, so just—"

"You can shut your fucking trap as well. Stay right off, mate, or I'll land you one."

"Pardon me, but your wife is correct, you know. The gentleman was simply resting his hand on top of the seat. Shall we calm ourselves down?"

"I'll fucking calm you down in a minute, pal. What's it fucking got to do with you?"

"I did give the lady my seat, so you might say I have a stake in the proceedings."

"You can keep your fucking hands off there as well. And you, mate, I'm watching you. Try it again, I'll break your fucking hand."

"Where else is the gentleman expected to steady himself? Would you rather he fell on your wife?"

"He's right, Den, so why don't you list—"

"Hey, I'm having to stand as well. I haven't fucking fell on anyone. Not going to neither, but I will if you don't keep off her, mate."

"Perhaps we should all rearrange ourselves so that you are by your wife."

"I'm going nowhere because of him. I never touched her and she knows it, and you do, so if he's saying different he can stick it up his arse."

"I'll stick something up your arse in a second, mate. Do like he says. Get right away from her."

"I'm fine where I am."

"Move or I'll fucking move you."

"Let's see you try. Bring it on. I'll put you in the hospital."

"Gentlemen, I didn't mean to exacerbate the situation. Kindly stop before anyone gets injured."

"Den, you heard him. Stop it now, and you as well."

"Will you stop that. Excuse me, that hurt me. Stop at once."

As the brawl began to escalate, Leo was afraid it might spread all the way down the carriage to him. It looked as though the passengers standing closest to the combatants had joined in the fight, and then he saw they were battling to fend the struggle off. Several of the commuters who'd found seats on the oppressively crowded train were phoning the railway police, and when the train slowed down for the next station, four officers were waiting on the platform. They had to clear passengers off the train in order to reach the belligerents, who had quieted at the sight of them, only to be identified by everyone their fight had touched. The police manhandled them off the train, followed by the wife protesting on her husband's behalf in between condemning him aloud. The displaced passengers crowded back into the aisle, and eventually the train lumbered out of the station....

Ramsey Campbell
Wallasey, Merseyside
3 May 2024

SECOND SIGHT

A Short Story

Key was waiting for Hester when his new flat first began to sound like home. The couple upstairs had gone out for a while, and they'd remembered to turn their television off. He paced through his rooms in the welcome silence, floorboards creaking faintly underfoot, and as the kitchen door swung shut behind him, he recognised the sound. For the first time the flat seemed genuinely warm, not just with central heating. But he was in the midst of making coffee when he wondered which home the flat sounded like.

The doorbell rang, softly since he'd muffled the sounding bowl. He went back through the living-room, past the bookcases and shelves of records, and down the short hall to admit Hester. Her full lips brushed his cheek, her long eyelashes touched his eyelid like the promise of another kiss. "Sorry I'm late. Had to record the mayor," she murmured. "Are you about ready to roll?"

"I've just made coffee," he said, meaning yes.

"I'll get the tray."

"I can do it," he protested, immediately regretting his petulance. So this peevishness was what growing old was like. He felt both dismayed and amused by himself for snapping at Hester after she'd taken the trouble to come to his home to record him. "Take no notice of the old grouch," he muttered, and was rewarded with a touch of her long cool fingers on his lips.

He sat in the March sunlight that welled and clouded and welled again through the window, and reviewed the records he'd listened to this month, deplored the acoustic of the Brahms recordings, praised the clarity of the Tallis. Back at the radio station, Hester would illustrate his reviews with extracts from the records. "Another impeccable unscripted monologue," she said. "Are we going to the film theatre this week?"

"If you like. Yes, of course. Forgive me for not being more sociable," he said, reaching for an excuse. "Must be my second childhood creeping up on me."

"So long as it keeps you young."

He laughed at that and patted her hand, yet suddenly he was anxious for her to leave, so that he could think. Had he told himself the truth without meaning to? Surely that should gladden him: he'd had a happy childhood, he didn't need to think of the aftermath in that house. As soon as Hester drove away he hurried to the kitchen, closed the door again and again, listening intently. The more he listened, the less sure he was how much it sounded like a door in the house where he'd spent his childhood.

He crossed the kitchen, which he'd scrubbed and polished that morning, to the back door. As he unlocked it he thought he heard a dog scratching at it, but there was no dog outside. Wind swept across the muddy fields and through the creaking trees at the end of the short garden, bringing him scents of early spring and a faceful of rain. From the back door of his childhood home he'd been able to see the graveyard, but it hadn't bothered him then; he'd made up stories to scare his friends. Now the open fields were reassuring. The smell of damp wood that seeped into the kitchen must have to do with the weather. He locked the door and read Sherlock Holmes for a while, until his hands began to shake. Just tired, he told himself.

Soon the couple upstairs came home. Key heard them dump their purchases in their kitchen, and then footsteps hurried to the television. In a minute they were chattering above the sounds of a gunfight in Abilene or Dodge City or at some corral, as if they weren't aware that spectators were expected to stay off the street or at least keep their voices down. At dinnertime they sat down overhead to eat almost when Key did, and the double image of the sounds of cutlery made him feel as if he were in their kitchen as well as in his own. Perhaps theirs wouldn't smell furtively of damp wood under the linoleum.

After dinner he donned headphones and put a Bruckner symphony on the compact disc player. Mountainous shapes of music rose out of the dark. At the end he was ready for bed, and yet once there he couldn't sleep. The bedroom door had sounded suddenly very much more familiar. If it reminded him of the door of his old bedroom, what was wrong with that? The revival of memories was part of growing old. But his eyes opened reluctantly and stared at the murk, for he'd realised that the layout of his rooms was the same as the ground floor of his childhood home.

It might have been odder if they were laid out differently. No wonder he'd felt vulnerable for years as a young man after he'd been so close to death. All the same, he found he was listening for sounds he would rather not hear, and so when he slept at last he dreamed of the day the war had come to him.

It had been early in the blitz, which had almost passed the town by. He'd been growing impatient with hiding under the stairs whenever the siren howled, with waiting for his call-up papers so that he could help fight the Nazis. That day he'd emerged from shelter as soon as the All Clear had begun to sound. He'd gone out of the back of the house and gazed at the clear blue sky, and he'd been engrossed in that peaceful clarity when the stray bomber had droned overhead and dropped a bomb that must have been meant for the shipyard up the river.

He'd seemed unable to move until the siren had shrieked belatedly. At the last moment he'd thrown himself flat, crushing his father's flowerbed, regretting that even in the midst of his panic. The bomb had struck the graveyard. Key saw the graves heave up, heard the kitchen window shatter behind him. A tidal wave composed of earth and headstones and fragments of a coffin and whatever else had been upheaved rushed at him, blotting out the sky, the searing light. It took him a long time to struggle awake in his flat, longer to persuade himself that he wasn't still buried in the dream.

He spent the day in appraising records and waiting for Hester. He kept thinking he heard scratching at the back door, but perhaps that was static from the television upstairs, which sounded more distant today. Hester said she'd seen no animals near the flats, but she sniffed sharply as Key put on his coat. "I should tackle your landlord about the damp."

The film theatre, a converted warehouse near the shipyard, was showing *Citizen Kane*. The film had been made the year the bomb had fallen, and he'd been looking forward to seeing it then. Now, for the first time in his life, he felt that a film contained too much talk. He kept remembering the upheaval of the graveyard, eager to engulf him.

Then there was the aftermath. While his parents had been taking him to the hospital, a neighbour had boarded up the smashed window. Home again, Key had overheard his parents arguing about the window. Lying there almost helplessly in bed, he'd realised they weren't sure where the wood that was nailed across the frame had come from.

Their neighbour had sworn it was left over from work he'd been doing in his house. The wood seemed new enough; the faint smell might be trickling in from the graveyard. All the same, Key had given a piano recital as soon as he could, so as to have money to buy a new pane. But even after the glass had been replaced the kitchen had persisted in smelling slyly of rotten wood.

Perhaps that had had to do with the upheaval of the graveyard, though that had been tidied up by then, but weren't there too many perhapses? The loquacity of *Citizen Kane* gave way at last to music. Key drank with Hester in the bar until closing time, and then he realised that he didn't want to be alone with his gathering memories. Inviting Hester into his flat for coffee only postponed them, but he couldn't expect more of her, not at his age.

"Look after yourself," she said at the door, holding his face in her cool hands and gazing at him. He could still taste her lips as she drove away. He didn't feel like going to bed until he was calmer. He poured himself a large Scotch.

The Debussy preludes might have calmed him, except that the headphones couldn't keep out the noise from upstairs. Planes zoomed, guns chattered, and then someone dropped a bomb. The explosion made Key shudder. He pulled off the headphones and threw away their tiny piano, and was about to storm upstairs to complain when he heard another sound. The kitchen door was opening.

Perhaps the impact of the bomb had jarred it, he thought distractedly. He went quickly to the door. He was reaching for the doorknob when the stench of rotten wood welled out at him, and he glimpsed the kitchen – his parents' kitchen, the replaced pane above the old stone sink, the cracked back door at which he thought he heard a scratching. He slammed the kitchen door, whose sound was inescapably familiar, and stumbled to his bed, the only refuge he could think of.

He lay trying to stop himself and his sense of reality from trembling. Now, when the television might have helped convince him where he was, someone upstairs had switched it off. He couldn't have seen what he'd thought he'd seen, he told himself. The smell and the scratching might be there, but what of it? Was he going to let himself slip back into the way he'd felt after his return from hospital, terrified of venturing into a room in his own home, terrified of what might be waiting there for him? He needn't get up to prove that he wasn't, so long as he felt that he could. Nothing would happen while he lay there. That growing conviction allowed him eventually to fall asleep.

The sound of scratching woke him. He hadn't closed his bedroom door, he realised blurrily, and the kitchen door must have opened again, otherwise he wouldn't be able to hear the impatient clawing. He shoved himself angrily into a sitting position, as if his anger might send him to slam the doors before he had time to feel uneasy. Then his eyes opened gummily, and he froze, his breath sticking in his throat. He was in his bedroom – the one he hadn't seen for almost fifty years.

He gazed at it – at the low slanted ceiling, the unequal lengths of flowered curtain, the corner where the new wallpaper didn't quite cover the old – with a kind of paralysed awe, as if to breathe would make it vanish. The breathless silence was broken by the scratching, growing louder, more urgent. The thought of seeing whatever was making the sound terrified him, and he grabbed for the phone next to his bed. If he had company – Hester – surely the sight of the wrong room would go away. But there had been no phone in his old room, and there wasn't one now.

He shrank against the pillow, smothering with panic, then threw himself forward. He'd refused to let himself be cowed all those years ago and by God, he wouldn't let himself be now. He strode across the bedroom, into the main room.

It was still his parents' house. Sagging chairs huddled around the fireplace. The crinkling ashes flared, and he glimpsed his face in the mirror above the mantel. He'd never seen himself so old. "Life in the old dog yet," he snarled, and flung open the kitchen door, stalked past the blackened range and the stone sink to confront the scratching.

The key that had always been in the back door seared his palm with its chill. He twisted it, and then his fingers stiffened, grew clumsy with fear. His awe had blotted out his memory, but now he remembered what he'd had to ignore until he and his parents had moved away after the war. The scratching wasn't at the door at all. It was behind him, under the floor.

He twisted the key so violently that the shaft snapped in half. He was trapped. He'd only heard the scratching all those years ago, but now he would see what it was. The urgent clawing gave way to the sound of splintering wood. He made himself turn on his shivering legs, so that at least he wouldn't be seized from behind.

The worn linoleum had split like rotten fruit, a split as long as he was tall, from which broken planks bulged jaggedly. The stench of earth and rot rose towards him, and so did a dim shape – a hand, or just enough of one to hold together and beckon jerkily. "Come to us," whispered a voice from a mouth that sounded clogged with mud. "We've been waiting for you."

Key staggered forward, in the grip of the trance that had held him ever since he'd wakened. Then he flung himself aside, away from the yawning pit. If he had to die, it wouldn't be like this. He fled through the main room, almost tripping over a Braille novel, and dragged at the front door, lurched into the open. The night air seemed to shatter like ice into his face. A high sound filled his ears, speeding closer. He thought it was the siren, the All Clear. He was blind again, as he had been ever since the bomb had fallen. He didn't know it was a lorry until he stumbled into its path. In the moment before it struck him he was wishing that just once, while his sight was restored, he had seen Hester's face.

ACKNOWLEDGEMENTS

As always, Jenny read the chapters of the first draft as they were completed. Once again Imogen Howson trained her skilful scrutiny on the final version. My editor Don D'Auria is a writer's boon, as are Nick Wells and the rest of the Flame Tree team – Maria Tissot, Gillian Whitaker, Jamie-Lee Nardone, Sarah Miniaci, Josie Karani, Jordi Nolla, Yana Koleva, Olivia Jackson….

The book was worked on at the delightful Deep Blue Sea apartments in Georgioupolis on Crete and at the Festival of Fantastic Films in Manchester.

At 10.43 on 24 October 2022, I was in the midst of the paragraph about the cat on the Alphafen balcony when a moth or small butterfly – I believe the latter – appeared on the outside of my workroom window.

At a World Fantasy Convention – either Tucson in 1985 or Providence in 1986 – the author and anthologist J.N. Williamson accosted me in the hotel corridor to commission a new tale for a book he was editing – nothing too obscure, about two thousand words with a twist. I'm generally up for literary challenges, and so 'Second Sight' was born.

ABOUT THE AUTHOR

RAMSEY CAMPBELL has been given more awards than any other writer in the field, including the **Grand Master Award of the World Horror Convention**, the **Lifetime Achievement Award of the Horror Writers Association**, the **Living Legend Award of the International Horror Guild**, and the **World Fantasy Lifetime Achievement Award**.

Among his many novels are *The Hungry Moon*, *The Influence*, *The Wise Friend*, *Thirteen Days by Sunset Beach*, *Think Yourself Lucky*, *Somebody's Voice*, *Fellstones* and *The Lonely Lands*. His trilogy *The Three Births of Daoloth* further develops the cosmic horrors he invented in his first published book, *The Inhabitant of the Lake*. The Spanish film *La influencia* was based on his novel *The Influence*.

FLAME TREE FICTION

A wide range of new and classic fiction, from myth to modern stories, with tales from the distant past to the far future. Flame Tree Fiction includes the trade fiction imprint, **Flame Tree Press**, featuring tales from both award-winning authors and original voices, along with short story anthologies, mythology and folklore collections and classic works in the **Beyond & Within, Collector's Editions, Collectable Classics, Gothic Fantasy** and **Epic Tales** series.

OTHER TITLES

SPECIAL RAMSEY CAMPBELL EDITIONS
The Invocations: H.P. Lovecraft Short Stories
The Damnations: M.R. James Short Stories

GOTHIC FANTASY COLLECTIONS
Lovecraft Short Stories • *Lovecraft Mythos New & Classic Collection*
M.R. James Ghost Stories • *Algernon Blackwood Horror Stories*

OTHER TITLES BY RAMSEY CAMPBELL

Ancient Images • *Fellstones* • *Somebody's Voice* • *The Hungry Moon*
The Influence • *The Lonely Lands* • *The Nameless* • *The Wise Friend*
Think Yourself Lucky • *Thirteen Days by Sunset Beach*

***The Three Births of Daoloth* trilogy**
The Searching Dead • *Born to the Dark* • *The Way of the Worm*

Available at all good bookstores, and online
at **flametreepublishing.com**